GREY FALL AND OTHER STORIES

JEAN KNIGHT PACE

JACOB KENNEDY

To all those who have loved Grey Stone and Grey Lore

GREY BROTHERS
A NOVELLA

PROLOGUE

Two sons born to a Lord of Grey
Two sons tasked to find their way.
But ways lead long on paths not straight
And the Grey pulls hard for love and hate.

A BROTHER CAN NEVER HATE his brother, no matter what the epic poems say. But they can come close. And quite often do.

THESE TWO BROTHERS waited at the top of the falls. The watercraft would likely be here in minutes—the craft carrying the body of their father, dressed and perfumed by the women of the family, then sent down the river. Their job, before it crested the falls into the crashing rocks of the ocean, would be to weight it so that when it fell it would sink.

And they were already fighting.

"We need to drag it to the East," Brayton said, standing knee deep in the rapidly flowing waters.

"The current will push it closer to the western bank. It will be easier from there," Rohan replied, wading to the center and staring upstream.

"And harder to return to the water."

They could see it now, a speck in the distance—the wooden box that held all that remained of their father glinting in the light of the high white sun.

Sweat beaded along their foreheads. "You know, if we could shift, it would be easy any direction," Brayton said.

"It will be easy regardless," Rohan answered. "If we take it from the West."

"Easy for you," Brayton grumbled. He was the smaller of the brothers by nearly a head, and did not make up for this height difference in breadth as some males of their kind did. If they went west, he would have to cross the stream.

As the watercraft got closer, they could see the flow of ribbons and flowers, petals blowing off of them due to the speed at which it was approaching. Brayton gritted his teeth. "West it is." At that speed they would never be able to hook and drag it from the East, and there were just the two of them left of the males in the family.

Their mother's sisters and their daughters had dressed the body. But the sisters of Sadora had borne no sons. When their sister had died, and years later, their mother, their father had stood by their sides—still broad-backed and thick-armed. Now, they alone remained to perform the final task of the dead.

Rohan held the hook, eyes set on the metallic loop at the forefront of the casket. Brayton watched as well, holding his own hook, but only as backup if his brother missed. He did not.

Rohan caught the hook, and together the brothers hauled the water vessel to shore. It was true that, with the current on their side, the task had felt light.

Light.

It would not be for long.

The upper portion of the casket remained open, showing their father's still face. White as the lower sands, his hair now gray. The colors of the dead. He had lived long for their kind, though not nearly as long as his father before him—the once-king—he who now haunted the woods, whether in flesh or spirit, no one was sure.

They covered Wittendon's face, first with the black cloak, embroidered with the roses they were told their grandmother had loved.

"Are you ready?" Rohan asked his brother.

They both glanced down at their father.

Brayton placed a flower in a crown around his head—tiny white lilies—the same they'd used for their sister and mother. Along with a small splay of pink roses over his throat. And then the most important part of the ritual—two heavy metal rods. Attached to either side of the casket.

"Ready," Brayton replied, his voice thick.

Rohan slid the wooden covering over their father's face.

They both breathed deeply, pausing. The casket was already sinking in the shallows. They would have to catch the current and shove it hard enough that it would crest the falls. Each took a side, veins bulging as they thrust it toward the center of the stream. The water caught. For an instant the watercraft bobbed, then sank, tipping over the edge, the metal catching the sun, shooting it back in the spray of water.

And then their father was gone.

Brayton sat on the shore, his head in his hands. His brother crouched beside him, sweat still beading over his lips, eyes glassy.

And from the woods, the wind howled, sounds very much like an old man gone wild.

"He should have lived longer," Brayton said, swiping at his face and standing.

"He lived a good life," Rohan replied, not moving.

"All the more reason to wish he had been with us longer."

Rohan did not reply except to say, "We must hurry to the bottom shore. They'll be waiting to begin the wailing song."

"I hate the wailing song," Brayton replied, dragging to the path.

"And yet it must be sung," Rohan murmured, following behind him, casting a quick glance toward the howl that still seemed to take up from the woods though the wind had stilled.

Everyone had left the wailing grounds except their two ancient aunts and the councilman appointed to read the will of the departed.

The will reading began at sunset, the councilman's voice a dull drone as though he had long since grown tired of reading the lives of the dead to those who still lived.

Nothing within was of great surprise to the brothers. The property would be sold, the profits divided evenly between the brothers. Which was just as well. They already owned their own quarters in the ruling sector where their father and mother had both worked to build up a new world from the ashes of the old.

Their father had included a letter for each of the brothers, along with one of their mother's rings—to be given to the woman of their choice, should they be lucky enough to find one so profound and beautiful as their mother. That was how their father had phrased it.

Their aunts would receive all of their mother's remaining gowns, cloaks, jewelry, and personal effects, at least any that they wished. Most of it had been sold or given away when she had died, but a few family pieces remained. Wittendon had also allotted Sadora's sisters a small sum of money. They seemed quite content with that, and after giving each brother a kiss, had departed arm in arm.

"And that is all?" Brayton asked the councilman when he had concluded.

"Did you expect more?" Rohan asked him.

Brayton glanced down at the letter in his hand, then stuffed it in his cloak. "I had hoped."

The councilman looked from brother to brother.

"You are welcome to go, Councilman," Rohan said gracefully. Brayton grunted in agreement.

Casting one more glance at the brothers, the councilman walked back toward the woods.

"Even our father did not know the final whereabouts of the stone," Rohan hissed when the councilman was gone.

"He knew," Brayton replied. "He just didn't care to tell anyone. Not me, not even you." Brayton looked at him suspiciously. "Right?"

"Of course," Rohan sputtered. "And you know Pietre died nearly two decades ago. After that, Father lost track."

"Father was not one to lose track," Brayton replied.

"You mistake him now for Mother," Rohan said, trying a joke.

It didn't work.

"I had just hoped it was information he would entrust to us, after he was gone."

"It's not information we need," Rohan said.

"It's information we deserve," Brayton spat back.

"Is it?"

"If Father so desperately wanted to protect the stone, then yes, it would have been nice information to have."

"And that's your goal? Protecting it?" Rohan asked.

Brayton didn't answer at first. "My goal, as opposed to our father's, would have been to use it for good. Rose—" His voice broke on the word. Neither brother spoke for several minutes, the name of their sister hanging in the air.

"Rose did not ask for a change," Rohan finally said.

"With the stone, with a change of suns, Rose could have lived in a different era, in a different world," Brayton murmured.

Rohan did not disagree, but said, "Even then some died. Like Grandmother."

"Not from the wasting sickness," Brayton said.

And now there was no room for disagreement, for it was true.

Humanlike ailments had never before taken their kind. Now they did.

In silence the brothers turned toward the path in the wood, their backs to the ocean, though the sounds of the waves breaking in sprays against the jagged rocks still pounded in their ears.

"Just let it be, Brayton," Rohan said as their paths were about to part. "It's over."

"You're wrong," Brayton said. "It is only just beginning."

ONE

10 years later

Rohan

The cloaks of the Council were red and gold, the same colors of his people's once-kingdom.

The Council wore these colors for ten consecutive years —for the duration of the time a human was in the top position of the Council—and then when the Council leader switched, so did the colors. When a shifter held the top position, the colors of the Council changed to green, the color the humans had chosen, though they hadn't had a once-kingdom to go off of.

"Nervous?" his wife, Cerilla, asked.

"Oh, just following in the footsteps of both my parents," he said casually. "What's to be nervous about?"

"So, yes," she replied.

"Utterly," he said, bending down to steal a kiss.

She didn't make him steal it.

"And how are you feeling today?"

"Still a bit sick." She paused, looking long out the window. "You'll remember the meat pies, won't you? They're the only thing that make the nausea a little bit better. Strange how the humans have been dealing with this child-sickness for generations. How do they do it?"

"You know, many would complain that the changed worlds have put shifters in a situation where they have to deal with it too," Rohan replied.

"That would be an understandable complaint," she said, a slight scold in her voice that reminded him he still didn't have to deal with it at all. "But I understand your meaning. Why should we wish for an ease that the humans have never had?" She sighed, holding her growing belly. "If only the new world could have shifted us to the shifter way of living—long life, few diseases, nothing like this."

"It shifted us both toward the center," Rohan replied. "Better for humans."

"And worse for us," she finished.

"Is it worse?" he asked. "After all, we've grown in compassion, in education, even in certain types of strength as we've been forced to work to find it in ourselves."

"All good points," she said. "And one reason you'll be amazing on the council. But you have to admit that it's easy to see how some of the shifters would want to go back."

"I admit that it's easy to see. Especially if one of them is your brother."

"Still a loud voice at court?" she asked.

"The loudest," he answered, looking at himself in the cloak. "And gaining an equally loud following."

∿

Brayton

It was the first time money had exchanged hands. At least under the table. Brayton promised himself it would be the last, but right now he needed information about the stone. And a man in this sector claimed to have some.

Brayton couldn't tell if the man was actually old, or just looked it from years spent in hard living. His face was rough as bear leather, except for the large gash that ran along his cheekbone, seemingly from a recent brawl. Judging from the mess of scars as well as the three empty ale mugs that sat in front of him, brawls were a fairly normal part of this man's routine.

Upon payment, the man immediately used several of the coins Brayton had given him to order more ale. Which seemed a bad start to the conversation.

It wasn't.

The ale loosened his lips more than Brayton could have wished, and by the end he had the last location of an underground group, as well as several names of people still purebred from Pietre's line.

"The Wardens, they call themselves," the old man slurred. "They move. So don't plan on them being there. But maybe it'll give you some hints about where they are now."

"And why do you tell me this?" Brayton asked.

"Because I need more coin," the man replied, banging his mug on the table.

"*Need?*" Brayton asked.

"Want," the man replied.

"And?" Brayton asked. "They cast you out? A woman wronged you?"

"They took my grandchild," the man replied, striking his mug more persistently. "Cursed cult, and they took her from me."

Brayton nodded as the barmaid shuffled over, sloshing half the drink on the table, tipsy herself. "Did she go of her own will, or did they take her?"

"Does it matter when she's a child?"

Brayton cleared his throat. He wasn't entirely sure he would have wanted this man as a grandfather either. "How old?" he asked.

"Thirteen."

"Just like Pietre of old."

Their eyes met over the mug.

"What good does it do to have a new world if the humans are going to take your children just like the shifters used to? Use them to get what they want. You need a drink?"

"No," Brayton said. "Thank you." He dropped a few more coins on the table, nodding to the innkeeper.

BRAYTON LEFT THE INN, wandering to the old castle district. Normally, he spent his mornings in court, but it was Rohan's first day on the Council. It only seemed fair to give him *one* day without the Originists making it too hard. One day. He hoped Rohan used it well. Brayton planned to.

He fingered the map in his pocket. The old man had circled the hideout—as he'd called it—an old armory in the southernmost sector of the Head City, now called by many Freeland. The humans met in the cellar. Of an armory. Was the human group now acquiring weapons?

He paused on the name the old man had given him. *Wardens.* A name implying they'd been tasked with the supervision of a thing. A self-given name. Just like the task itself. No one had asked or assigned them to the job of guarding the stone. They'd taken it on themselves.

His group, the Originists, had a different mission. Restoring the stone so that all would have access to it. His parents' mission, as he saw it, had been to bring equality to the people. How was that possible if the stone stayed with only one race? If, however, they held it in common, they could all study it, perhaps even learn to use it to grant more power to their citizenry as a whole.

Imagine the common evolution that would take place if their wolken kind could be rid of sickness, of early death. Imagine if they could use that to help the humans as well.

Instead, the stone stayed hidden. And everyone remained stuck in this middle place—too small and weak to cause real changes that could benefit everyone.

His band of Originists didn't need to hide in an abandoned armory, acquiring weapons illegally. They'd been accruing weapons, quite aboveboard, for the last five years. All of it legal. Each member purchasing the allowable amount of blade and mace.

He pushed away the empty feeling in his pocket from the coins he'd given the man. It was, after all, barely a breach. The man had clearly wanted to talk. He had merely paid for some drinks.

And now this other resistance group—literally underground if the cellar was any indication—this group of Wardens was getting their weaponry in secret. And forcing children into their ranks—the children of Pietre, or at least his great-grandchildren.

What exactly they were resisting was unclear. It wasn't the government, which he was disappointed to say, was much more on the side of this human resistance group than on the side of the shifters' rights that had been ripped from them only a generation ago.

Why the humans should have every advantage of the world shift, as well as sole access to the stone—a stone they kept hidden—he could not understand.

Especially when this group of humans—practically rebels— existed on the fringes of government. Whereas his group of Originists were simply a dissenting group in council (*not* a resistance)— one that believed the whereabouts of the stone should be known, and that it should be placed in a common location—either accessible to all, or to none.

Rohan argued that no such thing was possible. If it was accessible to all, it would be stolen by one. And if accessible to none, well, that opened the door for bribery and corruption—'a different type of theft' Rohan called it.

Tomorrow they would meet with the Council again. A variety of dissenting groups were allowed to gather and speak, so that their voices might be heard. That was how the head Councilwoman—currently a human—put it.

But Brayton didn't trust a human councilwoman.

He pulled the map out of his pocket, committing the lines and curves to memory.

Tonight, before the sun sank into darkness, he might have time to visit the armory, to explore the cellar and see if anything had been left behind.

~

Something had.

Rohan

Rohan noticed the absence of his brother that first day in the Council. But only just barely. After all, matters of court and council moved swiftly. Before noon break, they'd already seen everything from stolen cattle to unclaimed babies left on orphanage doorsteps to unrest in the northern sector over certain actions of the dogs to an inventor who came to them asking for a patent for a certain explosive he believed could be added to a slingshot-like mechanism and used in the armory as a weapon.

By the end of the day, he'd forgotten about his brother completely, and barely had the energy to remember his pregnant wife and the meat pies he'd promised to bring home for dinner, her most recent craving. He hoped that when he arrived with every variety the bakery had to offer, Cerilla wouldn't vomit at the sight of the pies, as she'd occasionally done when her cravings and repulsions had switched suddenly.

He needn't have worried, for when he arrived home he found her too ill to eat anything—craving or otherwise.

He went to the street and paid a messenger boy to locate his wife's mother and bring her to them. She would understand, somewhat, the pains and dangers of pregnancy. Though he realized that Cerilla's mother had never born or birthed a child in this manner, for she had been the last of a generation that did not suffer through birth.

Cerilla had been just one month old when the sun had changed.

Rohan brought his wife a glass of water, which she sipped. He noticed that so much sweat was dripping down her face that the tiny sip of water would never combat it. "Won't you have a bit more?" he asked.

"I'm fine," she said. "Just a fever."

Fever. The first part of the sickness that had taken his sister.

"They happen, you know," Cerilla said, sensing his thoughts. "In this new world. And usually they are nothing."

Rohan had yet to have a significant fever. But his sister—hers had gone from small heat and tossing dreams to the type of sweat he now observed on his wife's face, to no sweat at all, because no water had remained. She'd died soon after from the wasting sickness—aptly named.

His wife closed her eyes, and he set the glass on a table by their bedside. "Perhaps," she murmured through her near sleep. "Perhaps in addition to my mother, you might call on a human healer. Or midwife. They have been doing this for longer, you know. Much longer."

For forever, Rohan realized. And, yes, he would send a messenger immediately to the nearest healer. He thought briefly of his aunt Zinnegael, a mysterious woman he'd met only once in his life—when he was a child and his sister had been sick.

Zinnegael would be old now, and would hardly be able to make the journey from her wood to the gates. Even if she could make the journey, it would not be swift, and he needed someone swift.

Because after Cerilla's mother arrived, no one else would be allowed to minister to his Cerilla's needs. No matter how competent or experienced or wise the other party might be.

~

THE BENT OLD woman arrived two hours ahead of Cerilla's mother.

She did not look like much.

She also did not bustle or wring her hands with worry over the fever, which was what Rohan had spent the last hour doing.

She laid a hand with webs of prominent, protruding veins upon Cerilla's head. "Bring a cloth," she said curtly, not using his title or bothering with any niceties at all. "As cold as you can get it."

While he rushed around getting cloth and water, she stooped over an old bag, pieced together with bits of thin fabric, digging through jars and satchels. She resurfaced with a bundle of leaves as well as a few round, black seeds.

"And put the kettle on, child," she said, as he swabbed the wet cloth over his wife's face.

The old woman took it from him, settling it along her forehead. "And another cool cloth for her neck."

He nodded, performing each function as quickly as he could.

"She is with child," he said, as the kettle heated. "Will the concoction harm the baby?"

"A baby is hardly going to come to you without a mother to bear her," the woman said, not answering his question.

Rohan bit back an argument. Not an argument against the truth of her statement because no argument could be had there, but an argument about the use of dangerous herbs when his wife had been sick for only a day.

The healer pulled more dark herbs from a blackened satchel.

"Do you think the, uh, medicines are safe?" he asked, trying the question in another way.

"She is hot with fever," the woman responded. "Very hot. And that is *more* dangerous for the coming child than these herbs will be."

An unsatisfactory answer, but one that—also—resisted any type of argument.

"There is nothing else?" he asked feebly.

"There is cool; there is mint," she answered. "But your wife is very hot. The unborn too. The mother can endure many hours of recovery; the child cannot."

No further questions came from Rohan as he shuffled through the house performing each task she required of him. More cool cloths, a pitcher of water from the small creek behind their house. Steam the mint. Add it to the cloth. Three round seeds, two flat nuts, eight gray leaves. In her tea, every hour. "See that she drinks it, boy."

"With food?" he asked.

"The old witch Zinnegael would encourage a little honey, I expect," she asked. "But most of my clients cannot afford such things."

"I will get it," he answered. "And pay you with some as well."

For the first time, the old woman smiled. He was surprised to see that all her teeth were not only in the correct places, but white and clean as well.

"That, dear, would be quite nice. On top of my regular fee, of course."

"Of course," he answered. Her regular fee, he was sure, could barely be more than a pittance. But when she left, it was with three gold coins, a bushel of bitter mint, and two jars of honey.

In exchange, she patted him on the cheek and said, "When the child comes, call me again. These herbs, they will stay, unless you move them through the girl child as quickly as possible. I will help you."

He nodded. "Thank you." And then, as the door shut behind the woman, he murmured, "Girl child?"

His wife reached up for his hand, her eyes still closed, her cheeks still flushed. He took it, sitting by the stool at her bedside.

By the time his mother-in-law arrived at the setting of the sun, the bright red of Cerilla's face was returning to a rosy hue. She sweated still, but the old woman had assured him that this, too, had a function. Remembering his sister, Rose, and the way the waters of her body ceased just before her death, he did not question.

When his mother-in-law tried to stop the sweat, he held her hand. "Let the air cool her."

There must have been something in his voice, because his mother-in-law stopped.

He rose from the stool. "Please sit, Mother," he said, using the term of respect. "More than anything, she desires your company."

Smiling, she sat, cooing over her grown child, patting Cerilla's face, her hand, her growing belly.

One room away, Rohan prepared the final tea. And, pushing away thoughts of his child—for the healer woman would deal with any of those troubles later—he brought it in so that his mother-in-law could tip it into her own daughter's lips.

CHAPTER
THREE

Brayton

A few drops of human blood. That was all Brayton could see from the surface—a stain that almost matched the rusty latch on which it had been left. Which is why those who called themselves Wardens had missed it.

Missed it when most of the room had been meticulously cleaned —of blood or other evidence. Meticulously cleaned, and then meticulously re-cluttered, so as not to arouse suspicion through a too tidy cellar.

Brayton wandered the room. The armory had been abandoned years ago, maybe even decades. Yet, the floor was now swept and scrubbed, even as old swords, rusting in their hilts, had been tipped crookedly against the wall, bits of leather lain on the table in a haphazard sort of way, a dusty mug or two stacked in the corners.

Brayton recognized this method from his own youth, when he'd had a friend or female over and had not wanted his mother to know. He wondered now, looking at the clean but messy room, if his mother had actually known everything. And for a beat, he missed her —the keen eyes, the soft face. "Brady," she had called him, the only person ever to give him a nickname.

He shook off the sadness, moving along the edges of each corner. Although cobwebs could be found in the upper edges of the room, the floor was clean, not even a drop of candle wax remaining.

And why would someone clean the floor that should have borne the filth of several decades? Why, unless something had gotten on it, something someone didn't want seen?

Which is why it was not on the floor that he found the blood, nor on the walls or even ceiling, but on that small, rusty latch, so easy to miss in the cleaning process. He made his way back to it.

The latch was attached to a solid wooden door bearing multiple chains. The money room, to be sure, where a safe had once been kept. Though most of the chains were broken or rusted, the room was still locked.

Brayton removed his handkerchief and pulled from it a thin metal spike. The man from the market—grimy with oil from head to foot—had told him it might take a few tries, but that this device could open nearly any lock.

The man had been right. On both counts.

Unfortunately, by the time Brayton had gotten the hang of it, and then made his way into the cramped room, by the time he'd heard the groans from the locked safe, by the time he'd picked this second lock, and opened the safe door, the man locked inside was nearly dead. Whether from wounds or suffocation, Brayton couldn't be sure. Either way, in the man's lucid and desperate state, the newly-freed captive opened his mouth wide, more than ready to talk to his savior.

Until he died only moments into their conversation.

This was not ideal.

Nor was their conversation, which had consisted mainly of several screams, which Brayton had unsuccessfully tried to muffle, and the phrase, "You cannot..." repeated over and over.

Brayton had seen several dead humans throughout his years, as well as the shifters of his family who had passed to what some called a 'beyond.' But he had never seen one taken by violence. He found the sight easier to stomach than the scent, which prickled through his skin, making him nauseous and dizzy.

He was about to lay the man on the too-clean floor when he noticed—or rather felt—a wound at the base of the man's head. He jerked his hand back, wiping it on his handkerchief before tentatively turning the man over to examine him. Perhaps if he'd taken a little more care to tend to the captive's wounds earlier, he might have had a bit more time with the man. Although, frankly, neither of them had been in an ideal state for an examination.

Absentmindedly, Brayton brought his handkerchief up to his forehead to wipe the sweat from his face, and then thought better of it. He took a deep breath, letting it out slowly.

The wound appeared to be the result of a violent injury. Brute force more likely than sword or dagger. But from whom?

Had the human rebelled against the other Wardens? That seemed the obvious choice with the cleaned room. But if so, why?

Of course, the man could have been an outsider who came unwittingly into this location and found them. Perhaps threatened to tell? After all, the armory had been long abandoned. An old shack more than a functioning business. Any beggar or vagabond could have stumbled into the hideout unwittingly. Then, wishing for a bit of coin, threatened to tell the authorities unless paid off. The Wardens might have destroyed him due to a threat. But then why not thoroughly kill him? Why leave him hidden and half dead?

Brayton looked into the graying face of a man younger than he was, looked at the room that hadn't been used for longer than his lifetime, looked at the green tunic the man wore, and noticed a small insignia along his shoulder.

It was then that another thought came to him. Perhaps, the man had been left up above as a lookout. The lookout had succeeded—the rest of the Wardens leaving in time—but this service had cost the man his life.

But if the Wardens had left in a hurry, they wouldn't have cleaned the room. And if not them, then who?

Someone who didn't want anyone to notice if another person came along. Didn't want anyone to notice the room. Or the man bound up and hidden.

Someone who had left a man, but was hoping to come back, ask for more information.

Brayton stood, about to spread his coat over the human's face. And then thought better of it. What would he say if someone asked why *he* had been in an abandoned armory with a dead human?

Even if he could come up with some plausible reason, the excuse could cost him his reputation—a thing that was already slipping as the humans continued to grow in power and influence.

He cast a glance at the man, then stuffed the bloody handkerchief deep into the pocket of his cloak. "From dust to dust is usually what the humans say," he said to the corpse. "In your case, I'm afraid it's going to be a bit more of metal to metal." With a heave, he thrust the man back into the safe, although he did not shut or lock it thoroughly. The next morning, he would report a smell coming from the armory—something he had noticed on his evening walk through the sector.

The body would be found.

Unless...

He paused, gazing at the safe that now concealed the dead man's face. He fingered the lock, clicked it tightly shut. Thinking.

Someone had left the man here. Someone who would likely return. And soon—if he expected the prisoner to be alive for questioning.

Brayton wrapped his cloak tightly around his body, then stumbled his way through the dark cellar, crouching into a black corner.

He would wait till morning. Wait and watch and listen.

Who had been looking for the Wardens? And who had not wanted anyone to know?

~

Rohan

ROHAN WATCHED HIS WIFE SLEEP, peaceful as a child. Her small mound of a belly rose and fell throughout the night.

He placed a hand on it, just to feel the rhythm of it.

His sister had died at a young age, almost senselessly, a victim to the wasting sickness. His father had been stubborn about the sickness—insisting that the humans had dealt with sickness for eons, forgetting that the humans had dealt with child death for eons as well.

By the time his father had worried enough to bring his sister into the woods and all the way to Zinnegael's house, young Rose had been too far gone, the waters of her body dried up.

Rohan hoped that this memory, the trauma of watching his sister wither and die, had not caused him to overreact with his wife. But the healer had said that the fever must come down, and that she would return when the child was born.

Even so, Rohan rose from his bed, digging as quietly as he could in a drawer with pencil and paper.

At the least he could send a small missive to his aunt. If she was no longer alive, well, that would be good to know as well. And its own odd loss to have not have said goodbye or seen her off in the ritual way of their people. Not that she was of their people, not exactly.

Perhaps it was for this reason that his father had told him of a way to get hold of her, but only to use it if needed, so as not to abuse her kindness. Was he this desperate—his wife peacefully asleep, the healer promising to return?

Was it worth begging the services of a very old dog, a great-grandchild of the once-great Humphrey—a dog who would know the way, who would carry a message.

Rohan held the pencil above the paper, the bright light of the nearly-full moon carrying through the window. And then scratched a few simple lines.

～

Brayton

BRAYTON HAD BEEN PREPARED to wait.

He had not been prepared to hear sounds almost as soon as he'd settled into the corner. The slip of a door, light footsteps down the old stairs, the soft swish of trousers rubbing in a rhythm of quiet haste.

The door to the money room opened, and the figure paused in the darkness, breathing in the scent. Stale blood, old sweat, and something newer. Death. Brayton smelled it too, though he had grown accustomed to the scent. The newcomer had not.

More speed now, as the newcomer fumbled quickly for the key, flinging the door open.

That smell—death and blood and the stale beginnings of decay —it had been faint up until that point. But with the door flung open, it burst into the room as the body tumbled to the ground.

A curse from the shadowy figure.

Brayton tipped his head to the side. The voice was different than what he had expected—higher, lighter.

Slowly, the figure turned a tight circle in the room, the bright eyes scanning each inch of the darkness, finally settling on the corner where Brayton sat.

"Have your eyes then adjusted, Mid-councilwoman Shanna," Brayton said, rising to his full height.

"Pardon, Brayton Wittendonzon. I had assumed the breathing to be coming from inside. It appears that I was quite wrong."

"Quite," he answered.

"I hope you will pardon my language," she continued.

"Your language is perhaps not the biggest issue at hand," Brayton responded.

"I received word about a scent," she said. "And came to inspect."

"A scent?" he replied. "So soon smelled. Did you also receive word about where the key to the safe was hidden, as you found it quite promptly?"

"I am nothing if not zealous in my duties," she replied.

"Yes, zealous would definitely be the term for what you have done," Brayton answered, wrapping his cloak tightly around his body and feeling the bloodied handkerchief in his pocket.

"He was not dead when last I saw him," she said, her neck still high even in her confession.

"Well, he is quite gone now," Brayton said.

Striking a match and lighting a short torch that she pulled from her cloak, she bent over the dark figure. "Quite," she replied. "But not for so very long." She looked up at Brayton, squinting her eyes, trying to see from her light to his corner of shadow.

"Mid-councilwoman Shanna, I appreciate the work you have done to allow the voices of the Originists to be heard in court," Brayton said. "Do you now wish to see it all undone?" He gestured to the body, his eyebrows a sharp line of concern.

Brayton wiped the sweat from his forehead with the back of his hand. "This has gone too far. We're a group committed to protecting the rights and talents of the shifters, not a band of murderous rogues."

"With a cause committed to finding the stone, committed to sharing it with the humans—an event the Wardens seem determined to prevent," She said. "I had only wished to ask him a few questions. And I had said as much. *He* began the aggression. *He* continued it until nearly incapacitated."

"Nearly?" Brayton asked.

"This was an unhappy side effect of my search, but not an intentional crime."

"A crime does not have to be intended to be a crime," Brayton said.

"Is that what you think?" Shanna replied.

"What I think hardly matters," Brayton said carefully. "But the Council will not regard it as a *side effect.*"

"The Council will regard it as nothing since the Council will not know."

"So now you intend to hide it?" Brayton asked.

"*I?*" Shanna asked, moving closer to him with the torch. "That man reeks of death, but that is not all I smell on his person. He carries your scent just as much as mine. And with the coming Moonface, all of our kind will know this."

"I committed no crime," Brayton replied.

"You found a man dead," Shanna replied.

Brayton pinched his lips together, not mentioning that the man had not exactly been in the fully dead state when he'd found him.

"Look at yourself, Wittendonzon. You've got his blood on your shoes, the pocket of your cloak. This is no longer a crime that just *I* have committed."

"By the moon," Brayton murmured. "What have you done?"

"I just wanted to ask him some questions."

"Your method is ill-suited for that activity," Brayton replied. "At this point someone from his family has surely reported him as missing to the guards. If it goes long enough, that news will make its way to the Council."

"Accidents happen in the new world."

"Accidents happened in the old world too, especially to the humans," Brayton grumbled, feeling like his brother.

Mid-councilwoman Shanna must have felt that way too. She gave him a harsh look. "We have the same goals, you and I. Or at least I think we do. They have the stone, which they keep hidden from all of our kind, presumably so they can one day use it against us, to keep us weak enough that we do not rise up against them."

"Even as they continue to grow stronger," Brayton murmured, looking to the dead man, and thinking of the statute to come up soon before the Council—one proposing a human *queen* to lead the council.

"Ideas, good man?" Shanna asked. "To hide this?"

"We tell those of my party to come," Brayton said slowly, staring into the darkness, away from the dead man and Mid-councilwoman Shanna. "And perhaps some of the Council."

"It seems you misunderstand the word 'hide,'" Shanna replied.

Brayton shook his head, holding up a hand so she would let him finish. "This was my plan originally when I had thought this site would be full of Wardens hiding the stone, coercing citizens, working against the law. I had a plan to bring everyone here, to witness it." He sighed at the larger loss, at the fact that the Wardens had somehow managed to move on too quickly and efficiently for them to keep up. "What better idea than to proceed as though I think I've gotten an amazing bit of insider information? For what guilty parties would intentionally draw people to the scene of a crime?"

"You'll tell them to come here?" she asked.

"Well, not exactly me, but a messenger," he said. "And yes. My party will get news of a tip that I had gotten—information about some unsavory activities. Unfortunately, when they arrive, they'll find an empty armory—swept clean and then re-cluttered in a hasty effort to hide the fact that they had been here."

"I'm listening," she said.

"It will be an unfortunate loss to have missed them. And with no clues as to their current whereabouts."

"In this way your presence will not be missed in Council," she said. "Because, of course, you will be here, investigating the scene with the rest of your party."

"Correct," he said. "And though I might look a tiny bit the fool for having missed them..."

"A fool is not a killer," she finished for him.

"Not at all," he replied. "As for you. You will have arrived at Council. Quite early, actually."

"To deliver the message?" she asked.

"Of course. You are swift. And convincing."

"I am," she responded. "But what do you intend to say about the body that they find here? A body that reeks of us both?" She raised an eyebrow as though suspicious that this was simply a ruse to implicate her and her alone in the crime.

"I do not intend for them to find a body at all," he answered. "Or anything that reeks of one."

He looked up the stairs, imagining the darkness outside. One more night and the moon would be completely full. At exactly the moment when search parties would be organized to locate the missing man. At such a time the senses of the shifter guard would be heightened, their scents easy to recognize on the body.

Brayton pinched his lips together, feeling already the sharpening of his teeth. One more day to the full moon.

"So we lead our group here," Shanna was saying, chewing gently on the words.

"But not to the body," he continued for her. "You will clean this room as you did the others—this time remembering the latch," he said, pointing to the blood. "And I will take the body...somewhere else."

"Yes," she said.

"Now to figure out where," Brayton said, wiping the sweat from his face.

"To a place that ruins scent," Shanna replied. "And eventually bodies."

∼

Rohan

ROHAN FOUND the dog just before dawn, in an unsavory part of the city, sleeping soundly near the dumpster of a tavern that still stank of bodies, libation, and old fish. The animal woke from a sound sleep as Rohan slipped the missive into a thick collar he wore.

"I am sorry, friend," Rohan murmured to the scruffy animal—so different than his ancestor, Humphrey.

The dog only offered a low growl in reply, irate to have been awakened. He shook one paw of dust that had accumulated and then the other. Rohan felt as though if the animal could still speak, he would say something along the lines of, "Well, I guess a guy's got to earn a living." In fact, the dog waited quite patiently for the cold coin to be deposited in another slot of the collar.

It was only when the animal staggered away that Rohan wondered if perhaps the whole thing might be a bit of a scam, for it didn't seem the animal had any idea of where his own tail might be found, much less the hidden home of a once-witch.

Rohan sighed, his shoulders drooping. There was not much to do about it now. The gold coin had wandered away, along with his missive.

And the mysterious Zinnegael—she was likely long dead anyway.

∼

Brayton

BRAYTON ARRIVED at the grieving path with ease—the place shifters went to send their dead to their rest beyond. Or at least to the salty waters downstream where their bodies would return more quickly to the earth.

The place he sought was several lengths beyond the grieving path. A beautiful spot—beautiful and treacherous, with only one narrow trail to the lookout. Many a hiker had slipped on his journey to the top.

Looking at the sharp tip of a peak, a place often lost in a ring of cloud, Brayton wondered briefly if this was not just a convenient way for Shanna to lose two bodies instead of one.

She had assured him that with the coming Moonface, he'd be able to travel the path with ease. And indeed his journey so far had been uncommonly swift—his legs strong even in the deep night hours, his sight keen, his arms and back barely feeling the weight of one simple man. He'd draped the body over his shoulders and carried him under his cloak. This way, if someone happened to spot him, he'd look like a stooped man, not someone carrying the dead.

He pulled on the arms of the dead, taking a breath, bringing his gaze away from the peak and back to the path at hand. He didn't need to go far. Just to the first dangerous drop, where he could let the body fall, tumbling down the rocks and to its final rest. Perhaps someone would find the body among the rocks or washed up from the waters. Perhaps not. Either way, salt, sand, and sun would do their work to remove Brayton from this business.

As long as he could find a good place to dispose of his own clothes as well.

He knew that since he was already soiled with the man's blood, he was the most logical choice to dispose of the body. Still, Brayton couldn't help but feel that, if things got messy, this fact would also make it quite convenient for Shanna to frame him for a murder that she, herself, had committed.

She had tried to soothe those concerns by pointing out that since she was the one who would send the missive to the Originists, she would be the one who would be more likely to take heat if any blood was discovered uncleaned.

Brayton sucked in a deep breath, trying to concentrate on the task at hand. When he was done, he would clean his shoes and cloak in the salty waters of the ocean. After that, he would burn them. Simple enough.

Light deepened with the morning and he hastened his step, practically running. He didn't want to be seen in this place, and he *did* want to be seen back at the armory as soon as possible.

THE FIRST DROP-OFF came about 300 feet up, and Brayton was relieved. Not only was the path steep, narrow, and flanked on either side by sharp cliffs, but the rock leading to it was loose. He'd lost his footing several times, scraping his shins on the final stumble. Panting, he laid the dead man on the path, looking both below and above him. The place was quite deserted. Thank the moon. At the edge beneath him, he could hear the solid crash of water, could taste the salt as it settled onto his lips.

He looked at the man's face—young with sharp features—and shook his head. "I wish we could have spoken in a more effective manner before you slipped into the beyond," he said. "And I hope what you find there is to your liking."

He wasn't sure what he believed about the beyond, but surely the man deserved some type of goodbye. With a bow of his head, Brayton tipped the corpse over the edge.

He looked away then, reminding himself that he had neither killed nor trapped this man who now bore his scent.

And then, moving quickly but carefully, he hurried to the base of the path, and then broke into a run.

By the time he reached the armory, he wore his best red cloak, along with a pair of felt shoes—nothing a man would wear while climbing a deadly path. He was *not* early. But he was there. Clean-handed.

FOUR

Rohan

Rohan could not help but notice the absence of his brother for the *second* day in a row. Not just his brother, but all the Originists. Well, nearly all.

One old, blind man did show up, holding his sign as usual, and looking as though he believed his brothers and sisters in protest were with him as usual. The appearance of that one lonely man sat unsettled in Rohan's stomach. If none had arrived, he would have assumed that Brayton had given him two days to get settled instead of just one. But with the arrival of the hunched, elderly member, Rohan couldn't help but wonder where everyone else had gone. And why?

Rohan asked for a brief pause. "Good sir," he said, stepping down from his place on the stand and addressing the blind man who still held the same sign from the day before. "Where might the rest of your party be? It is soon their turn to stand at court, to state their grievance before the Council."

"Their grievance is the same as always," the man practically spat, not bothering to turn toward the sound of Rohan's voice. "A stone shared by man and shifter should not be controlled by only one of those parties."

"I would ask you to hold your grievance until the appointed time," Rohan said in an official voice, glancing toward the stand, where the other junior councilpersons waited. "I only wondered where the rest of your party is today. Normally, they stand quite together."

"They have been called away on urgent business," he replied.

"I see," Rohan said. "And when did you learn of this?"

The old man took several long seconds to clear his throat most thoroughly. "Quite early, Councilman—the time urgent business most often happens."

"I see," Rohan replied. "And who was it that gave you directive to stay?" He was about to ask if it was his brother when the old man answered.

"One of your own," he said through the spittle that flew from his toothless mouth. "And a lovely thing too."

Rohan bowed his eyebrows together. It did not sound quite like his brother.

"Voice like silk, and skin like satin."

"I see," Rohan said, looking to the stand and noticing the empty seat among the mid-councilmembers. "And are you aware of the business to which the others are attending?"

"Business that is none of yours, with all due respect, Councilman."

"Of course," Rohan said.

"Now, if you'll just allow me to speak when it is my turn."

"Yes," Rohan responded. "I will."

∿

Brayton

"THEY'RE LONG GONE," Brayton's friend Iorn said, as he ducked down the stairs to the cellar of the armory.

Brayton fell into step with Iorn, looking around the room as he had that first night. Looking at the clean floor, walls, ceiling, and taking note of the sloppy weapons.

"They definitely *were* here," Iorn said, noticing the clean chaos. "Though not, it seems, to gather weapons."

"Or perhaps not those left behind," Brayton said.

Iorn shrugged. "Probably just a meeting."

Brayton heard what Iorn left unspoken. *And meetings are things people are allowed to have.*

"I guess we'll never know," Brayton said. "Unless we get stabbed in the back by an illegal sword."

"Unless that," Iorn replied.

Brayton glanced at the locked door of the money room. With any luck no one would even want to go in, which meant it didn't matter how well Shanna had gotten it cleaned. But Iorn had noticed the glance. Brayton gritted his teeth at his stupidity.

"Or maybe they weren't here for weapons," Iorn said. "But something more valuable. What do you think? Money chamber?"

"Likely," Brayton answered, his voice smooth and clear.

"Shall we?" Iorn asked, moving to the thick door.

Brayton managed a smile. "Of course."

Since no one had a tool for lock picking this time, or at least no one willing to volunteer that information, and since Moonface was coming that night, three of the shifters lined up near the door. "On my count," Iorn said as they prepared to heave their bodies against the locked door.

It worked in two tries. By the skies, they were strong before Moonface. Brayton tried to imagine that power all month, all year, all of a lifetime. It seemed impossible. Why his parents had worked to give such a thing up, he could not fathom.

"Empty," Iorn said, wandering through the dark room. "Safe's open though. Maybe they did take the money."

"Freshly cleaned," another shifter added, sniffing. "This place reeks of vinegar and lemon. My own mother couldn't have gotten it cleaner."

Brayton let out a slow, quiet breath of relief. And then, in the light of a torch someone had brought in, he noticed a bit of paper peeking out from under the safe. Just the smallest triangle of a corner.

Unfortunately, Iorn noticed it at exactly that moment too. He reached for it, but Brayton beat him to it, swooping down and looking quickly for blood. None, thankfully.

"Shifters," he said. "Use just a bit of that brawn to lift this edge off of this paper. It's probably nothing, but..."

The shifters had lifted it before he could even finish his sentence and he swept the bit of paper into his hand. "Probably nothing," he murmured again, then pressed his lips together.

"Anything useful?" Iorn asked.

"A love letter," Brayton said, raising his eyebrows.

"You're kidding," Iorn hooted.

A love letter scrawled with the nub of pencil, likely by a man who, hours later, would be dying. *I'll meet you, my love*, the missive read, *at the cusp of Moonsilence*. The time when the moon went blank, vanishing into the dark night sky. The weakest time for his people, and the safest time for humans to meet in the woods. A crude map was drawn.

"Not much of a penman, was he?" Iorn said, reading over his shoulder. "Now, which of us lot is going to show up and terrify the unlucky lad at Moonsilence when he's expecting a lady friend who never got his letter?"

Brayton laughed. "No one. This letter is probably ancient. The unlucky girl who missed this invitation is surely a grandmother by now."

"You suppose they were meeting up in this room?" Iorn asked, to the hoots and crude gestures of the men.

Shanna had come into the room and rolled her eyes.

Brayton looked into her face before tucking the missive into his cloak. "Well, gentle shifters, I believe our work here is done."

Mid-councilwoman Shanna chimed in. "I'm sorry for wasting your time. Perhaps the next lead will prove to be more fruitful."

"Ah, well, more fun than another day in Council," Iorn said, and several of the shifters grunted their agreement. Brayton shared a look with Shanna.

They were losing steam, the group of them—tiring of protesting a thing that seemed too solidly within the bounds of the law. These were shifters who wanted adventure, who longed for strength. They weren't men of court.

And that thought worried Brayton.

Rohan

Rohan sighed as they dragged the body from the waters.

The man had been reported missing nearly a week ago. He'd been declared lost until a thrill-seeker had spotted him from the peak of Grief Mountain. Grief Mountain. Named thus for many reasons—a place people came to watch the waves that had swallowed their loved ones. To remember.

Or a place people came to forget—choosing to make a quick end to their own sorrows when life seemed too long, too hard.

Rohan gazed at the sharp rocks that jutted from the salty waters below for several seconds before turning back to the shore.

The man who found him had seen a body floating on the waves —gray and shimmering as a whale. At least from a distance. Up close, he wasn't nearly as beautiful.

The hiker had seen him over a day earlier, but the rocks near the grieving path were too treacherous for swimmers or sea craft. This had forced the rescue party to create a rope and hook, which had been ineffective to say the least. Finally—after hours of trying—a seasoned, infuriatingly patient fisherman had snagged the body. Which now lay on the beach, bloated and practically featureless.

The old hag who had reported the man missing claimed he never would have walked the path, but Rohan knew plenty of men to do things their grannies never suspected.

The old granny mourned now in the stomping, shrieking way of certain human sectors. Rohan definitely preferred the more solemn, low-toned send-off of his people, but then he supposed that was a bit of the race-judgment his mother had often spoken of. Different kinds weren't better or worse, just different.

The hag rolled now on the ground, her screams making his ears ring slightly. He supposed that *occasionally* different kinds might be better or worse, or maybe just different enough for him to need to step away and take several deep breaths.

"Who did this to you?" the woman shrieked in the distance.

Rohan couldn't help but roll his eyes. It wasn't the first body they'd found that had tumbled from these cliffs—either accidentally, or intentionally when a life hadn't gone the way they'd planned. Though it was true that a man this young was unlikely to take his own life, it was hardly impossible, especially with the hardships of some lives.

In his mind, Rohan composed a little speech: *My dear woman, it is difficult at times to lose a loved one, especially in such a cruel way as this...*

And then, mid-thought, he noticed a bit of fabric caught on a rock. Not the greens and browns and linens that the humans preferred, but a bit of black cloak made of satin with delicate lines of thread woven throughout in a pattern much like the waves below. A wealthy shifter's cloak. But why would anyone—wealthy or not, shifter or human—wear a cloak up such a treacherous path?

Rohan took the cloth, turning it over in his hands, slipping his fingers over the soft thread. It was likely just a bit of cloth from a careless wanderer—someone who may have begun the path on a whim and then thought better of it, or even someone who had just been passing by on the way to the grieving path. Perhaps even a bit of cloth found by a bird and then abandoned in a distant location.

Still, it bothered him, fluttering in the breeze, like a death flag left and forgotten to the winds of the sea.

He took the cloth and tucked it into his pocket.

FIVE

Brayton

Brayton followed the crude map, making his way to the appointed spot during Moonsilence.

It felt futile. After all, the man was dead and his lady friend would never have received the missive. But Brayton wanted to be sure there was nothing special about this spot, about this time. Wanted to ensure it wasn't a common meeting spot for the Wardens.

Judging from some of the crude sounds he heard from the bushes, it wasn't. Although it was a common meeting spot for another purpose—human lovers. The darkness of Moonsilence hid them perfectly under the already dense forest canopy.

He turned to leave. But as he did, he spotted a small trail into the woods. That seemed strange since most of the humans would take the larger path back to the head city.

He approached two thick trees that stood as sentinels and noticed that one had a small bit of cloth hung intentionally on it.

Green like the leaves. Something that would blend in, unless you were looking.

Brayton stepped through the trees onto the path. It didn't take long to realize that there were several narrow paths going several directions—perhaps paths the wolves walked in search of their dinners. Or perhaps paths deer walked in order to avoid becoming dinner. Either way, every time Brayton had a choice of direction, he looked for the small swath of green fabric. And every time he found it, as he made his way deeper into the darkness.

The final swatch of fabric hung from a sapling that grew at the top of a cliff. Not the best hiding place as during the day or even on a bright night anyone standing atop this stone could probably be seen for miles. And see, he thought. A nice lookout, but where would they hide if they spotted something?

Brayton tapped his foot impatiently on the rock beneath him. And it tapped back—a hollow echo.

He bent to the ground, putting his ear to the stone. No voices, or any other sounds either. But. Hadn't his mother told stories of clandestine meetings beneath the earth? The perfect hideout.

He knocked on the stone. Again, it knocked back in an echo.

In the darkness, he worked his way over the surface on hands and knees, looking for—he wasn't quite sure what. Until he found it—the small slit in the earth, barely wide enough for his shoulders to fit through. He had no idea how narrow it became after that.

He slipped his feet and legs through the opening. Then wiggled his hips and waist into it. At this point, he could still lift himself out easily with the strength of his upper body, but if he went farther, he would be committed to the climb or the fall, for his feet still felt nothing beneath them.

Taking in a breath, he eased farther into the hole, narrowing his shoulders and then allowing his body to drop.

Less than a foot. His feet hit the bottom with an echo that let him know which direction lay open ahead. The sound was the only thing that let him know, for except for the slim line of starry sky above him, this was the darkest place he'd seen in his life.

Using his hands he followed the line of the wall that led into a thin crevice, which soon widened. "Just like Mother's stories," he murmured, wondering if this was in fact one of the old tunnels used by the rebels. The thought was interrupted, however, when his shin hit a sharp edge with such force that he hissed out a curse.

The curse hissed back to him. When it did, he found that he stood within four walls, shaped from the stone. What he'd hit appeared to be a stone table at its center. If he didn't know better, he would have thought it was an altar for some ancient cult to make sacrifices.

But he knew it from his mother's stories. A meeting room. Which was completely empty.

Of course if any of the Wardens had been here, they would have heard him in his clumsy efforts to find them. But if anyone had been here, the logical choice would have been to meet him, armed, and take care of things.

He felt the hairs rise along his spine at the thought. And wondered—was it now really the Wardens he was looking for? Or some kind of reason to have disposed of the body of a dead man? Because if the Wardens were really rebels arming themselves and seeking to do evil to the shifters, then his actions would have been justified. But if not...he was party to a crime with no justification whatsoever.

Behind him, he heard a scratching sound—like a stone drawing along the wall.

He whirled around, drawing his sword. With the complete darkness, he could thrust a person through with ease if they didn't know he was there.

Another thought that made his spine tingle.

When a voice came to him through the darkness. "It's me. Lower your weapon."

A familiar voice. Feminine, tight.

"How did you know I was here, Mid-councilwoman?"

"How could I not?" she replied. "With all the ruckus you made."

"And how did you know I was holding a weapon, Mid-councilwoman?" he asked into the darkness.

"Because I would have been doing the same," she replied, coming closer to the sound of his voice.

He lowered his weapon, but did not sheath it.

"Anyone else here?" she asked.

"Not a soul," he replied. "Except you. If I didn't know better, I might think you have a crush on me, Mid-councilwoman Shanna."

"But you do know better," she said. "Instead of love, we have a vested interest in protecting our own backs."

"That we do. How did you find it?" he asked. "The opening."

"I watched you."

He nodded, though he realized she likely couldn't see it.

He heard her pull something from her pocket, and raised his sword again, but all she had was the light of a match, which she had struck along the walls. One tiny light in a sea of blackness.

"I don't suppose you brought a lantern," he asked, trying to keep his voice light.

"Not exactly," she responded, fishing in the pockets of the trousers she always wore. "But my mother did teach me a trick of two." She struck another match, this time holding it to a piece of fabric, which lit.

"How long will it last?" Brayton asked.

"I've soaked the tip in a bit of wax," she answered, "so it should give us a few minutes."

"Were you expecting a cave?" Brayton asked.

"Only dark woods," she replied, making her way meticulously through the room, which looked very recently abandoned—dirt disturbed, markings on the table as though people had recently been working or writing there, even crumbs of food.

"Not the tidiest, are they?" he asked, trying to fight away the panic he found growing in the confines of the walls. A panic that only increased when he actually saw how tight the quarters were.

"Just in a hurry," she replied.

"But they couldn't have known we were coming. Even *we* didn't know we were coming."

"True," she said. "But they knew their human friend *didn't* come. And that's enough reason to move."

"I only wish we knew who the note was for," Brayton said.

"Whoever it was, the dead man expected her to come back to the armory in search of him," Brayton said.

"A thought we could have put to better use a week ago."

Brayton *had* put the thought to good use, though he hadn't told Shanna this. He had walked past the armory every day since, and had seen no one. Not only that, but he'd left a small line of chalk near the opening—a line that would likely have been disturbed if someone walked down the stairs. No one had come. At least no one unsuspecting.

Shanna's face flickered in the light of the makeshift torch as they both looked around. All they found was a bit of string on the floor, connected to a hold that led back to the opening.

Once there, with the help of Shanna's light, they found a thin rope ladder you could hook to a bit of metal for climbing.

"Ladies first," he said.

"Take this," she said, handing him the torch, then hoisting herself up without the help of the ladder.

He handed her the remaining flicker of flame through the opening and wiggled his way up the ladder.

By the time he'd wormed his way through the opening, Shanna had extinguished the light and sat underneath the sapling waiting.

"The humans are supple," she said, noticing the sheen of sweat along his face and arms.

"The humans are small," he replied, glancing at her, then narrowing his eyes.

The ragged piece of green fabric that had hung from the sapling. It was gone.

~

SOMEONE HAD COME to remove the markers, which meant the Wardens were either very recently departed, or that they had sent a runner to retrieve the trail markers.

It also meant, perhaps, that the Wardens were moving quickly, getting sloppier. And if that was the case, perhaps they had more to hide than a stone.

Or perhaps it meant that he was not the one doing the hunting, but the one being hunted? And if so, by whom?

Brayton ran from point to point, hurrying back the way he'd come—or the way he thought they'd come—Shanna trotting behind him asking questions, which he didn't bother to answer.

Each marker at each trailhead missing. Without them, it was dangerously easy to become lost on the path. And they soon were.

"Do you have that cursed torch?" he asked, after wandering for over half an hour.

"How did you make your way there?" she asked.

"There were markers," he said shortly. "And they're gone."

She lit the bit of torch, which did almost nothing in the darkness of the trees. He missed the moon. Missed the world of his forefathers where two moons had hung, bright and strong. Like his kind.

"Do you think this is going too far?" Shanna asked.

"Asks the woman who killed a man."

"He died," she said. "I did not kill him. I don't even remember dealing that final blow to his head," she said with more than a little accusation in her voice.

It was not an argument Brayton intended to continue while lost in the woods.

"Shhh," she said suddenly, cocking her ear to their left. "Do you hear that? Moaning."

"Someone hurt?"

"Oh, I don't think so," she said, following the sound, slowly at first, then more quickly. Abandoning the deer paths, they stumbled through weeds and briars toward the faint rocking moans that turned soon to whispers.

"Oh no," Brayton murmured, shifting his path so he would be able to avoid the couple hidden in the thicket.

Shanna was well ahead of him now, her light flickering against the leaves above them.

And then they were there, in the clearing. At Moonsilence. Just another couple. Though very different from the sort who usually came here.

"Shall I meet you tomorrow to discuss our next adventure?" Shanna asked, extinguishing her light.

"I'd rather you didn't," Brayton said, following the wide path back to the city.

"We'll be stronger working as two."

"We work with a group," he said. "A legal group in court."

"Is that so?" she asked, looking back over her shoulder into the darkness, then pulling out one of the green swaths of fabric. "Found this, just at trail's end."

Brayton narrowed his eyes. Had the Wardens missed it, or been too slow to get it? Or had she been the one to remove them all, following after him as she'd done so? And if she had, was it to throw the Wardens off? Or him?

"You look perplexed, Wittendonzon."

"As I am," he replied.

"Well," she said, stepping closer in the darkness. "A place like this will do that to you."

As she said it, one of the human couples emerged from the bushes, looking disheveled and holding hands.

Shanna pulled Brayton's head to hers, her cheeks hot against his face. For a moment, he thought that she would actually kiss him in this ruse to go unnoticed. As it was, she only held him there, breath to breath, until the other couple giggled their way far enough along the path.

"And now I think it's time to go," she said, her voice flat and businesslike.

"Long past," he replied. "The whole thing is starting to feel ridiculous anyway." As he said it, the shadows in the trees seemed to lift, everything feeling lighter.

Except perhaps for the distance he continued to put between them.

CHAPTER

SIX

Five months later

Rohan

The babe came with a silence that stunned all in the room.

Birth in the new world was never a silent event. Rohan sent for the old woman, clinging to the promise she had made, as the baby clung to life, the small breaths from a miniature chest.

"Breathe for her, Rohan," Cerilla said. "As you've seen the humans do."

He *had* seen the humans do it—a futile practice for most of the dying—one mouth placed over that of another, two breaths moving together as one.

"I do not know how." But he placed his mouth over the child, feeling only a whiff of air as the baby's lips grew blue. He breathed, not as mightily as he could have.

47

The baby responded, sucking it in. He tried again. And again. Until the chest moved more solidly, until the little lips began to root for her mother's milk.

Rohan stood, wiping sweat from his face. "Where is the old woman? She said she would come."

A boy stood in the corner, his hands clasped in front of his body as though to protect himself. "She is not here, Councilman."

"Then where?" Rohan asked angrily.

"She is dead," Cerilla said bluntly.

The boy nodded.

"Dead?" Rohan asked, as though unfamiliar with the word. "But then who will pull the poison from the child?"

"You have breathed it out of her," Cerilla said. "Perhaps that was all that was needed—after all, it was the type of thing the human healers would do. And I will feed the goodness into her. It will be enough."

Rohan thought of the old woman's insistence on sending for her, and did not feel sure. "Is there another apothecary in this sector? Or even this city?"

"There are many healers," the boy responded. "Shall I fetch another?"

"Yes, do," Rohan roared and the boy scampered off.

The baby did not even fidget at her mother's breast, tucked close and warm as any healthy child would be.

By the time another healer arrived, the baby was pink and thriving. Eating, fussing, making good use of her diaper.

"She is perfectly well," the other healer said. "Do you know what the old woman gave your wife?"

"Something for a fever," Rohan said, leading the much younger healer into another room to discuss it. "What might that have been?"

"Peppermint," the other woman piped up. "That is the herb we most always use."

Rohan frowned. "No," he said. "That was not it."

"There isn't much other," the younger woman replied.

Rohan nodded, his lips tight. Where had the messenger boy found this woman? Nursery school?

But even after he sent for another, and another, none of them could tell him what the old woman might have used to drive down a fever. Peppermint was indeed the most common. Other herbs included hibiscus, lemon leaf, and even thyme, but none could drive a fever down as fast as he'd described, and none would put an infant at risk.

"No one responsible would use anything to endanger the babe," the final woman said. She was an old wrinkled fruit of a soul, who held her lips in a constant, tight pucker.

"What about one who was irresponsible?" Rohan asked.

"Some know more of mushrooms than I," she answered cautiously, as though Rohan was going to rush out to the gardens and pluck them from a dung heap. "Though I can think of none for fever. And are you sure the woman was a healer?" the woman asked with a quick glance to the side.

He knew that there were some humans who dealt in other arts, things with candles and potions and chants they claimed reached through the beyond. This woman had done none of that. "She was brought to me as one who heals and I did not ask further questions. She created a tonic of leaves and seeds."

The wrinkled woman nodded. "Sounds standard enough."

"Some of the seeds were round and black. Others flat," Rohan added.

"And the leaves?"

"Dark and gray. The smell unfamiliar, but not unpleasant."

"You're sure they were not hairs."

Rohan wrinkled his nose. "Quite," he answered.

"Well, then I suppose the baby should be fine," the woman said, as cheerfully as her sour mouth seemed able to manage. "And the healer is dead?"

"So I am told."

"Then I cannot help you more."

Rohan had to bite back a comment about how painfully clear that was. "Thank you, good woman," he said instead.

~

Brayton

BRAYTON WALKED HOME at the edge of the woods, after a night at the taverns. The day before, his group of Originists had been disbanded by the Council. The only consolation was the fact that his brother had not cast a vote against him. Of course, that consolation had come only because his brother had been on leave with his new baby —a pretty pink thing they were calling Nadi.

He hadn't really imbibed much with the few men and women who had been left of the Originists, partly on account of his smaller size, and partly because he'd wanted to keep his senses about him. He needed to think.

A few months ago, in his ambition to stop a group that he believed was holding and hoarding a precious and powerful relic, he had accidentally stumbled onto a murder—a murder which had also been an accident. At least that's what Shanna had said. And he believed her. After all, she had come back for answers, and dead men provide precious few.

Both had been complicit in hiding the crime.

And then both had been determined to track down the remaining members of the Wardens—to find that thing that would make their own indiscretions feel justified. Something terrible or illegal that the human group must have been doing.

The tip of the sun peeked above the horizon, casting the outskirts of the city in gray.

They hadn't found the group. And, truly, even if they had, there was no guarantee they would have found them to be at fault for anything—whether that was coercing children to their cause, or gathering illegal weapons, or anything else.

These things were rumors at best—rumors cast from the lips of old, drunken men. Rumors that often did not hold the weight of much truth. As far as he knew, everything the Wardens were doing was within the bounds of the law. The fact that they were so careful in hiding seemed odd, but then there were plenty of shifters more disgruntled and less tame than he—shifters who were seeking them out, some might even say hunting them down. So even aggressive hiding couldn't necessarily be counted against The Wardens.

He turned onto a wide street that led to his quarters. Perhaps it was time to stop chasing a white goose, and start to go after a position where he could make an actual difference. The Originists had been a start, but perhaps there were higher places he could climb to have a wider influence.

He walked the neat path to his house tucked into a wooded corner as a pink sky broke the morning. Yes, he realized. It was time to be done with nonsense, to leave the past in the past, and to move forward. And upward.

He wandered through his dim kitchen, hanging his cloak, rolling his shoulders and wishing for a long morning sleep. He washed his hands, then face, before reaching for a mug to fill with water. But in place of a mug, on the otherwise empty table, he noticed a small brown envelope, sealed in wax.

It had not been there before.

A slim line of sunlight slanted through the window and he picked the letter up, turning it over in his hands.

No name, no address, no place of return.

He broke through the wax, and a bit of torn paper fell out.

I know what you did.

The letters were ragged—intentionally drawn to be nondescript and unnatural.

Brayton plunked onto his stool, blowing out a hot breath. "I did nothing," he muttered, though he knew that perhaps it no longer looked that way.

He turned the paper over again and again, as though some new information would appear on it—perhaps payment information, which he would fully expect on a blackmail letter. But he found nothing.

The sun rose higher, the birds' morning song changing into the business chirrups of mid-day.

Only one other person knew of his actions. Mid-councilwoman Shanna. He rose from the table, the stool crashing down, and flung open the door. Only to see Shanna standing there, fist in the air, as though she was about to knock.

One look at his face and she said, "I've received one too."

"Well, that's just what you'd say if you had sent it, isn't it?" Brayton asked, his face hot with anger. "The perfect thing to make you look innocent. I wish I'd never waited to see who did it. I wish I'd never found you."

"The feeling is mutual," Shanna said, letting herself into the quarters and noting the fallen stool. "But it wasn't me." She walked to the stool and righted it.

"And why am I to believe that?" Brayton asked.

As he said it, a large tree outside the house fell to the earth, rumbling the ground.

"Because they're trying to get me too," Shanna finished as they both hurried to the door. "Or at least let us know that they could. When I got home, I walked into my locked apartments to find a set of knives laid out on the floor, making an arrow. To my dead canary." Her eyes filled with tears. She was either a very good actor, or truly frightened and sad.

He shook it off. She was a good actor, calm, collected—he'd seen it himself.

Outside, the tree had clearly been cut—a wedge sawn out of it, so that it would fall in a specific way, perhaps even at a specific time. He looked to Shanna. Her face had gone white. If the tree was her work, then she was really quite talented—able to send a letter, feign fear and sadness, and sabotage his yard.

All the while, looking like death. He noted her appearance, which was usually so careful, meticulous even. Now, several locks of hair had tumbled from her tight plait into messy knots at her ears and neck, and her face was flushed at the cheeks, but pale everywhere else. Eyes puffy, lips white.

He stepped over several branches toward the trunk, looking for signs of footprints or anything else.

Shanna followed, glancing down at the wood chips left from cutting out the wedge. She picked one up. "You know, I might have suspected you as well, except I knew you wouldn't have time to do it if you were in your quarters. And you are."

Another tree crashed on the opposite side of his house, this time taking with it a piece of the roof.

Brayton leapt over the trunk, running as fast as he could.

To find only the downed tree, cut in just the same way, and a broken fence. No other evidence that anyone had come.

Or gone.

CHAPTER
SEVEN

Three Months Later

Rohan

S tanding out in the cool night, glancing to the stars, Rohan pulled in a long breath. His daughter, Nadi, was now nearly three months old. She appeared healthy enough. As he exhaled slowly, a melody flitted through the air.

"Hello?" he said into the darkness.

The night hung still and dry. He breathed again, let it out slowly, and heard the hum in tune with his own breath.

"When dead things leave their mark, it lasts.
Whether woman, herb, or fruit long past.
Perhaps not spirit, ghost, or witch,
But the oldest healers use a bit of pith
Of ancient fruit, left itself to die.
For fever's removal, cyst, or sty."

"Zinnegael?" Rohan said. He had met her only once when he himself was a child—in a deep wood that felt so much like a dream, he was almost convinced that it was. When his sister had been sick. And that sickness, even Zinnegael could not fix.

"In this world," his aunt had said, "shifters die too."

He hadn't listened, nor had his father. They should have, for his sister *did* die.

Now the ghostly voice responded, barely audible in the wind,

"Not my mistress, but a messenger sent your way,

And better than one like sour whey."

Rohan couldn't help but smile. That part did sound like what his aunt would have said about the last healer.

The voice continued.

"But some old medicines a residue leave

From ancient fruits rotted to seed.

Already months have come and gone,

The toxin through small body drawn."

"And how do I get rid of the residue?" Rohan whispered into the wind.

Through the darkness, he caught a glimpse of two yellow eyes, like candles flickering. And then they were gone.

At his feet, he saw a small satchel, similar to one used for storing tea leaves. Inside was a bit of powder that looked like milk that had dried.

With one last whisper in the wind,

"On her tongue, like cat to dish.

A bit of herb to push out the pith.

But warnings come and warnings go,

This final thing you too must know.

With this aid the child's time will go longer

Though with the time, she'll end weak, not stronger."

Rohan bent over to retrieve the satchel and he noticed his wife standing in the doorway, looking white.

"Did your aunt mean to help?" she asked, a tight pinch to her voice.

"We must choose," he said, turning the satchel in his hands. "We can have her strong for a short period of time, or weak for a longer time."

"I have no intention of choosing between those options."

"That, my dear," Rohan said, rubbing his head with his hands, "is not the part that is your choice."

Brayton

THE BLACKMAILER, whoever he or she was, never asked for money, never made demands of any kind. But, on a regular basis, things would be harmed or ruined. A chicken with a slit throat, a basin of water filled with floating, dead beetles. Flowers cut from their stems. Crops dug before their time. A slim crack through a window pane, a spoke driven into the floor and left protruding. And sometimes a note. A map of their path through the woods, a stone from the grieving path where he had dumped the body, a bit of ash from the clothes he'd burned with a thread from the fabric still inside, or a weapon from the closed armory.

The torture continued for months. It would go for days in a row. And then there would be a pause. Long enough to believe that perhaps their blackmailer had tired of the game. Long enough to believe the torture had ended.

Until it would begin again.

Brayton started losing sleep. He developed rituals, checking every lock, noting the placement of each item in his house, following patterns he knew he could remember, so that if they broke, he could be sure it hadn't been by him. He stayed in as much as he could, waiting, watching.

Shanna fared even worse. Where Brayton tried to control the madness, she did her best to numb it. She began with tonics first, moving on to teas and elixirs from healers. And when those no longer soothed, she moved to powders and other concoctions received from women who lived at the fringes of the wood, dealing in dark herbs and darker arts.

Her appearance suffered. She chopped her hair into a crop so she needn't clean it. Her body billowed and then thinned at intervals too rapid to explain. And her position with the Council—Brayton knew from his brother—was at risk. One more indiscretion on her part and she would be removed.

AND THEN, just as suddenly as it began, it stopped. Weeks, then months, into a year.

Brayton began to venture on walks. He visited his brother and new niece. Shanna began meeting with a healer trained in such matters. She cleared the tonics and toxins from her shelves and began growing her own herbs and vegetables. Her face cleared, her eyes no longer dim and lost.

She arrived at his house one beautiful morning, in black trousers and a blue cloak.

"You're looking well," Brayton said, preparing her a flowered tea.

"We've gotten a second chance," she whispered, not bothering with small talk.

Brayton nodded, removing the satchel from the hot water.

"He must be dead," she said.

"I can only hope it," Brayton replied.

CHAPTER
EIGHT

Eight Years Later

Rohan

Rohan thought on the rhyme often as his daughter grew. *Though the time might go longer*, his daughter would be left *weak, not stronger*. Yet, it seemed to be, well, wrong. The child was as strong as any other. Maybe stronger. She ran with the wind, played as a butterfly, laughed like a song.

Years ago on the night a cat had tasked them with a choice, his wife had refused, leaving it solely in his hands.

He had picked up the medicine, medicine sent from his aunt—his father's half-sister, and a powerful woman to be trusted, or at least his father had trusted her. He'd turned the packet over in his hands, the medicine light as dust. And he'd decided. If he'd had a choice to have his sister longer, he would have chosen it. Was it a selfish choice? He didn't know, couldn't tell. But it was his choice.

He'd placed the medicine in a bowl, and let the infant lick and play with it until it was gone.

His wife had never asked which choice he'd made, and he had never told her.

He had not been sure what to expect, but some indication by this point, these eight years later—a tendency toward illness perhaps, a weak body, a dim mind—*something*. Whatever he had expected, the strapping eight-year-old in front of him was not it

In fact, at this very moment their child, Nadi, raced through the house, half dressed, trying to escape the attentions of her mother, now pregnant with their second child.

"Catch her," his wife shouted, laughing.

He reached out, but Nadi dodged, a little dance on her tiny feet. She was wearing only a white slip, her hair flying in wild tangles as Cerilla chased her with a pink dress, its ribbons fluttering in the pursuit.

"Gotcha," Rohan said, reaching from around the stool and sweeping her into his arms.

She giggled and squirmed as Cerilla took her, wiggling the dress over her head.

"I hate pink," Nadi said.

"Well, it's not your choice," Cerilla replied. "Auntie Lili has chosen it, and truly you'll look a peach in it."

"She's not my auntie yet," Nadi said. "And I don't want to look a peach. I want to look a bear."

"I've no doubt that you'll somehow accomplish both," Cerilla said, sitting down and resting, one hand on her growing belly.

"I thought you liked Auntie Lili," Rohan said.

"I do," Nadi replied. "But she has to get married to be my auntie."

"Well, with any luck, that will be accomplished by evening fall," Rohan said. "Now, come here, so I can brush your hair."

"You'll do it too hard," Nadi whined.

"Then you'd best let your mother help you."

"Do we have to add the ribbons?" Nadi asked.

"Don't you want to be pretty for Uncle's wedding?" her mother asked.

"No," she said simply.

"Ah, child," her mother said with a smile. "When you get married, you can look however you wish. How's that for a deal?"

Rohan pinched his lips together at the thought, hoping, though he was afraid to, that one day she would grow to that age, grow and be well enough.

"What if I don't want to get married?" she asked.

"Well, then, you can look however you wish when you don't," her mother answered.

~

Brayton

BRAYTON KNEW that news of the wedding had surprised his brother. In some ways, it had surprised him as well. But in the second chance he'd been granted, he was ready now for something new. And what better way to begin than with a beautiful bride—Lili—a young shifter—nearly ten years his junior. He'd wanted that, a piece of innocence, the idea that he could find in her a fresh start as a new man.

And a new man he felt.

A small group of friends circled them, holding hands as was traditional. Shanna attended. Not as guest. Rather, as a full-level councilwoman, she officiated.

On the final line of the final vow, she winked.

They were free.

His niece dropped petals of white, creating a path to the new marital house. A larger quarters, set just outside the ruling sector. A place much like the one Rohan owned.

Brayton was, in fact, considering a position as junior councilman himself. He'd spent the last several years in the business sector, doing quite well buying, investing, and selling things for much higher prices. It was lucrative work, but not as satisfying as he had hoped. If he really wanted to make a difference in this world, it seemed that the best way to do it was not through petitions or political groups or even donating money. No, the best way to do it was by becoming part of the council itself. Since his group of Originists had long since disbanded, some of its members still hunted the stone, though most simply hunted women at taverns late into the night. And he wanted more than that.

He whisked his new wife over his new threshold and was greeted by a small white cake and an enormous pile of gifts.

His wife laughed, popping open a bottle of wine from the stack of wedding presents left in their new home. "Time to celebrate, my love."

"I had other ideas of where to start," he said, wrapping her up in his arms and sliding a hand under the sash that tied the back of her gown.

"You know it's traditional to open the presents first," she said, giggling.

"But who will know which we did first?" he asked.

"My mother is probably peeking through the windows right now," Lili said.

Brayton jumped back and she giggled again.

He shut the curtains, but his bride had already begun unwrapping gifts. "It'll give you time for the excitement to build," she said with a wave of her hand.

"Not sure how much more excitement I can handle building," he said, watching her dark hair fall over a bare shoulder.

"Well, then get to opening," she laughed.

He did. Dinnerware and bed sheets. Decorations for things he didn't understand the need for. Small boxes designed to hold coins of gold for the happy couple.

He slipped a knife through a piece of tape, expecting a coin to drop into his palm from the miniature box. Instead, a white slip of ragged paper fell from it, much like the note he'd found in an envelope on his table all those forgotten years ago.

"Meet me at the Lion's Tavern to discuss...options."

It had been eight years, two months.

"And what is that, my love?" Lili asked, leaning close.

He shifted slightly. "Nothing to worry about, my dear," he said, his voice as light as he could make it. "Just a bit of an inside joke. From a very old...friend."

SHANNA ARRIVED LESS than an hour later, as he'd known she would.

"Ah, Councilwoman," he said, his voice lifting as high as he could manage.

"I've brought the new couple a gift," she said, her face nearly as white as the petals that still lined the path to the house. "A bit belated I'm afraid, though once you taste it, I expect I'll be forgiven."

Brayton felt every line of his face hardening. *Trust me,* Shanna mouthed, pouring a tall glass for Lili.

And, just as Brayton had suspected, his new bride was asleep in moments.

"When will she wake?" he asked.

"An hour or so. Brutal headache as well." She slipped a small pill to him. "Give her this for that. I'm so sorry."

"Another canary dead?" Brayton asked.

She simply held the slip of white paper in her hand—identical to his own. "Do we meet him?" she asked.

"He is dead," Brayton asked. "This must be another."

"It *must* be nothing. We're caught in a game we're not going to win."

Brayton looked at his sleeping wife, wondering for a moment if it was time to turn himself in, to treat himself to an actual fresh start.

Just as Rohan rushed to his door, Nadi in his arms. "She collapsed," he said, his voice breaking. "Along the path on the way home."

~

BRAYTON STUFFED the note into his pocket.

Shanna scowled, but he ignored her. Some things were more important, even, than blackmail.

"It took hours to find her," Rohan said, his voice a panic. "She was near your house."

"Put her in the bed," Brayton said, nodding to the unused marital bed.

"Haven't you another?" Rohan asked, glancing at Brayton's sleeping bride.

Brayton rubbed his head. "Not yet. Just...it's fine. You need to find Zinnegael."

Rohan pinched his mouth shut.

"Or perhaps you've already found her," Brayton said, seeing his face.

"She sent a message when Nadi was still a baby. With a medicine."

"And?" Brayton asked.

Rohan paused, looking at Shanna.

Shanna opened the door. "I'll be outside."

"I had to make a choice," Rohan said, then repeated the rhyme.

"A short, strong life, or a longer, sicker one," Brayton murmured. "Though you have really no idea what short means, or long either."

"Correct," Rohan said, miserably.

"Well, what did you choose?" Brayton asked.

Rohan lifted his eyebrows.

"Long," Brayton said, answering his own question. He put a hand on his brother's shoulder. "I would have chosen the same."

"Moonface is tonight," Rohan said. "I'm hoping it revives her well enough."

"It will," Brayton said. "But…"

"I don't know," Rohan said before his brother finished. "I don't know what to do after that."

"You know what's better than Moonface?" Brayton asked, his voice thick, his hand clamped around the note in his pocket.

Rohan looked at him. "Stealing the stone and using it to turn the world back is hardly an option at this point."

"Isn't it?" Brayton asked. "It's always an option—that's sort of the point, and the reason the humans are determined to hide the stone from us."

"Brayton," Rohan said, like he was too tired for this old conversation.

"The stone could help her."

"The stone could kill her."

"The stone could turn the worlds," Brayton said. "What if we had it, if we studied it? What if we could figure a way to use it—even temporarily—in a way that could help us, while still sparing the humans?"

"That sounds complicated," Rohan asked. "One might even say impossible."

"We don't really know what's possible or not," Brayton answered. "We haven't had a chance to study the stone."

"You know exposure to the stone kills most shifters, right?" Rohan asked.

"Well, then we work with the humans—progressive thinking ones," Brayton said.

"The stone is hidden," Rohan replied.

At that moment, Shanna tapped on the door, Cerilla by her side.

"My dear," Rohan said.

"Let's go home," Cerilla said. "The sun is setting and the full moon will revive her as we walk."

Indeed, a dull darkness was settling into the corners of the house. Brayton felt it pushing against him as his brother gathered

Nadi into his arms, her little head stirring as the sun sank, granting power for this one night, to the moon. And to his race.

Brayton felt it in his blood, in the sharpening of his teeth, the prickling of his skin.

"We have only minutes," Shanna said, when the door closed. "Lili will wake with ease when the moon rises."

"Excellent," Brayton said. "I've got a wedding night to commence."

Shanna shoved her note in front of him. "What are we to do?"

Brayton crushed the note in his thickening paw. "If he—or she —" he said with a nod to Shanna. "—wants to meet so badly, then perhaps it's time."

Shanna squinted in the darkness, her wolken eyes taking on an orange tint.

"If we can't run away," Brayton said. "Then perhaps it's time to run towards."

ONE WEEK LATER, Brayton waited at the tavern, just as he had years before when he first got a tip on the whereabouts of the Wardens. It'd been so long since he thought—really thought—about them and the stone.

He thought now, about what it would cost to chase the stone again, and what it would cost not to.

A man staggered to his table, plunking down in front of him. He wore a dark cloak, the color of the midnight sky, his face still shadowed by the hood. But even with the hood, Brayton recognized the chin—the line of scars that ran up to the mouth.

"We meet again."

"Ah, so you remember," the gruff voice said, waving the barmaid over and ordering what was surely not his first drink of the day.

"As I recall, your precious child had been taken by the humans. A granddaughter whom I expect does not actually exist."

"Ah now, we all make compromises to the truth, don't we?" the man said, looking pointedly at Brayton before lowering his hood.

Brayton examined his face more closely. "You look older than I remember," he said. "Much."

The barmaid plunked two drinks down on the table, and the man raised his glass in answer. Brayton pushed his drink to the old man's side of the table.

"Trying to kill me with drink, are you?" the man said. "I've already tried. It doesn't work."

"Clearly." Brayton saw now that the man was older than his own father, much older. "You remember the changing quite well, I take it."

"A day I'll never forget," the old man replied.

"The changing was a day that was supposed to help the humans," Brayton said.

"Indeed it did," the old man answered.

"But it didn't help you."

"It did not." The man polished off his first glass, and pulled Brayton's close to him, cradling it in both hands as though it was a cup of hot cider, not a hard brew.

"I guess I should have guessed when I first met you. You're shifter, not human."

"You were not in the market then for knowing things you didn't want to believe."

Brayton nodded. "Shall we get on with business?" The barmaid shuffled past, and he raised his hand to indicate two more drinks.

"I want the stone and am too old to get close to it," the man said.

"Interesting," Brayton said. "And here I was worried you'd be asking for money."

"I've no use for money," the old shifter said, slurping his drink.

"Well, you have some uses for it," Brayton said with a raised eyebrow at the now-empty mugs.

"I want the stone," the shifter said. "And need one to get close to it."

"I don't know," Brayton said. "You're good at disguises. Pretend to be human, tell them you want to join their ranks."

"Unfortunately," the old shifter said. "I have a face that is difficult to trust."

Brayton squinted into the man's eyes—also scarred, he noticed, at the edges. "You do," he said.

"And a body too ancient to be near such a powerful stone for long."

"Then what do you plan to do with it?" Brayton asked. The stone weakened all shifters, and could eventually kill them, but those born before the changing of the suns were especially prone to weakness.

"You'll need a band," the old shifter replied, without answering his question. "Similar to the one you once led."

"Impossible," Brayton said. "That's a group I could never re-form."

"Oh, I don't want *you* to re-form anything," the shifter said. "I already have the men. They just need someone to lead them."

"And how did you find them?"

"Much like I found you."

"So men with crimes to their names, men whom you blackmailed?"

"Or bribed," the old shifter said with an ugly smile, his scars stretching.

"Men who commit crimes are not usually men who want another to *lead* them," Brayton said.

"'Lead' is perhaps not quite the right word," the old shifter replied. "But they need some brains, and perhaps a bit of a mascot— a person with some sway in court, some power in our culture."

"And if I refuse?"

The shifter produced a bit of fabric—deep black with fine threads woven through.

Brayton narrowed his eyes, remembering that horrible morning when he carried a dead man on his back. "Where did you find that?"

"Oh, I didn't," he said. "I stole it—or part of it. I wanted the original owner to keep a bit of it too. So we could make a match. If necessary."

The shifter ran a rough finger along a line of thread, fraying where the cloak had torn. "Do you remember the dead man's name?"

"I never knew it," Brayton answered defensively. "Nor do I wish to."

"Oh, wishing things now, are we?" the shifter said.

"I got tangled up in the nasty business quite by accident."

"Accidents happen in the new world," the old shifter said, finishing his fourth and final drink. "Jamus—that was the name of the human."

Brayton cursed, and the shifter seemed to sway in mirth.

Brayton wished he would keel over. And, truly, Brayton wasn't sure how the old man could even speak when he'd had so much to drink. "And what might your name be?" Brayton asked.

"I've been a creature of many names," the shifter replied.

"Care to give me one of them?" Brayton said.

"I do not," the shifter said. "But speaking of names, you might also be interested to know that I've been in communication with the dead human's family. They know who you are too." He pushed two empty mugs back in Brayton's direction, then waved at the barmaid for two more.

"And what do they know of me?"

"Oh, they don't know *you* by name," the ancient shifter continued. "Not yet. But they know of one who carried their dead on his back, all the way to the first peak. They know the way the body tumbled to the rocks below. They know he was already dead."

"And how do they know this?"

"Because people know what they wish to believe. And I told them."

The barmaid plunked two more mugs down. This time Brayton took a sip.

"Don't worry too much," the old shifter said. "Finding the stone will help you too. That little niece of yours—doomed to die before she even hits adulthood. Your closest friend, nearer to madness than you know. And your precious young wife—ready to bear your first child, isn't she; a boy I'd say?"

"I don't see how you could know any of that, especially with my wife. We've only just married."

"Well," the shifter answered. "It's like I say. People know what they wish to believe. They also tell what they think to be harmless."

"But you find the harm."

"My boy," the old shifter said. "I always find the harm."

～

Rohan

THE FULL MOON had helped Nadi. But now it waned, and with its light, Rohan saw his child weakening. As Moonsilence approached, Nadi lay in bed, taking broth from her mother, tossing about as though she had a fever, though she had none.

"Is this how she is to live the next years of her life?" Rohan asked, pacing back and forth.

His wife did not answer. She prepared a mint tea, cracked more bones for another broth, shredded chicken into a stew for the two of them to eat after Nadi had fallen into another night of troubled sleep.

He tapped the table until she handed him the eggs for cleaning.

His wife twisted a cheesecloth into a tight ball around the sweet cheese, let the whey drip into a bowl to feed to the animals. "Chop," she said, handing him several carrots and a sharp knife.

He obeyed, accepting each task his wife gave him from washing a bowl to picking slugs off the greens before boiling. He wondered at the fact that her mind could move to other things when his was stuck on the one singular problem of his daughter's health.

"And it came on so suddenly," he muttered, dropping the slugs into the small dish of vinegar.

"Did it?" she asked.

He looked up from the dish. "Of course," he answered.

She sat at the table across from him, and now it was her fingers that tapped against the wood as he peeled a large pile of potatoes.

"I know of one thing that might heal her. Your brother's been speaking of it for years."

He scraped three more peels off the potato before looking at her. "You can't possibly mean…"

"I can," she said.

"It would mean changing the suns, the world as we know it, as my parents fought to make it."

"It would not necessarily mean that," she replied. "The stone has other uses, though only for a precious few."

Rohan narrowed his eyes. "The Grey?" he asked. "But how would you even—" He stopped. "Supposing that what you're implying is true—that our daughter was…resistant to the Grey, perhaps even strengthened by it, there's no way for you to know. Because there isn't a drop of Grey available in this land."

"Oh, Rohan, sometimes Brayton is right—you *are* a little naïve."

"What do you mean?" he asked, the vegetables abandoned in a pile on the table.

"There is plenty of Grey to be found. Just not in the usual places."

"You have some Grey," he said, his mouth almost numb around the words.

"I do not," she replied, scooping up the peeled vegetables. "But I did for many years. And every month, I would put a little in her tea for her. Your father was a Greylord, and the first time she got sick you were in Council. I figured it was worth the risk."

Understanding dawned, along with fury. "You can't be serious. You used an illegal substance in our child's tea."

"I told you I refused to make the choice all those years ago," she said. "You made it, but I didn't. I swore I'd find a way. And I did."

"Cerilla, possession of the Grey is…"

"…punishable, I know," she said. "But you needn't worry about the illegal substance *that was keeping your daughter well.* Because I can't find any more. Not in the underground markets, not anywhere."

"I didn't mean," he said. "That our child wasn't worth—"

"I know," she replied, touching his face, her look both hard and soft at once. "But you do put quite a bit of trust in a government that can barely be trusted."

"My mother and father founded it."

"And they did a wonderful job," she said. "But government is still an imperfect art form. Or perhaps we are just imperfect beings in our execution of it. Either way—" She stopped abruptly.

"You cannot find more," he answered. "And now Nadi declines."

Cerilla pressed both palms against her eyes, as though to hold in the ache. "But there is one thing, one thing that could strengthen her. It's not even illegal, just hidden."

"The stone," he said.

"Does Brayton have any information?" she asked, dabbing at her eyes with her sleeve, like a bit of onion had gotten in them and nothing more. "Any at all about its whereabouts?"

"I'll ask him," Rohan said. "I'll find out. Don't cry, darling. We'll figure something out."

"And if the humans don't want to share?" his wife asked.

"My father did a lot for this land," Rohan said. "They will remember. They must."

"Humans have short memories," she said.

"Let's not dream of bridges to cross until we've come to those waters."

"Ah, but you *are* trusting."

"I consider it one of my greatest assets," he answered, not entirely joking.

"As do I," she said. "Usually."

"If we find waters, we'll build boats."

"You are good at that," she said.

"And Nadi too."

"Yes, and Nadi too." She set the mint and a small bowl of broth onto a tray, and made her way to their daughter's room with a vase that held a singular rose—her dead auntie's namesake.

Three months later

Brayton

This new group was *not* a government-sanctioned resistance group.

It was—Brayton paused on the thought—a group of ruffians at best, something closer to a gang than a collective group of lobbyists.

One shifter, who continuously snorted a substance Brayton did not ask about, offered a map with their latest movements. "Patterns?" he asked. "Isn't that what the old man said you're good at?"

Brayton wanted to say that he wasn't much good at anything except getting in too deep. Instead, he simply nodded.

"Then find one," the shifter said, taking a snort. "When the time comes, I'm going to be ready." He pointed to his nose. "I'm building up my resistance to the stuff."

Brayton looked at the powder the man snorted—an iron color that probably *was* iron, as he doubted it had much Grey in it, especially if the man could snort it like that. "Are you a Greylord?" Brayton asked casually.

"Self-made," the man replied.

Okay, definitely just iron. Probably poisoning his skin, but that wasn't what today was about. Brayton laid the map down, following their path. He immediately found the armory, as well as the cave in the woods, though he was careful not to draw attention to his notice of them. "I see no pattern," he murmured.

The man moved to snatch the map back, but Brayton slapped his hand down, keeping it. "Which doesn't mean I won't. Patterns run in more than just lines. What else do you know about this map? Topography, etc."

"Topo-what?" one of the men said.

"How high or low the areas are. Or, for that matter, have the areas they've hidden been densely wooded or rock or populous cities?"

Most of the shifters shrugged, but one slender man came over. "Some are cities; some not. More than that, I can't tell you."

"Never mind," Brayton said. "I know one who can."

Shanna found the pattern almost immediately. "City, wood, stone, wood, city. Every time," she said, pointing to the locations. "Usually abandoned buildings when it's city."

"Join us," he said.

"You know I cannot," she answered.

"And I can?" he asked.

"You have no title to lose, and no infractions to help you lose it," she answered. "But come to me. When you have questions." They paused, looking at each other.

"How is Lili?" Shanna asked.

"Troubled by her growing belly, though I find it quite lovely," Brayton answered.

"She could not be anything but lovely."

Rohan

R OHAN TAPPED on his brother's door twice before it got an answer.

Lili appeared, looking slightly bigger around the middle, and a little ruffled as though she'd been napping.

"Oh, my dear," Rohan said. "I'm so sorry to have woken you."

"Nothing to be sorry about. I need to get moving today anyway."

"I was hoping to find Brayton. Is he in?"

"He's been gone for two days now," she answered. "Some special project that keeps taking him out on business."

"And how are you?"

"A little lonely, but otherwise well. Every time he returns, he dotes on me hand and foot. Until the next travel."

"And what is the business?"

"Something lucrative, he claims," Lili answered.

"And of what nature?" Rohan pressed without trying to press.

"I'm afraid I'm no use with business. Every time he's home we talk about the baby, the house, those things. Oh!" she said suddenly, patting her belly. "Do you need money? For Nadi. Let me get you some."

"No, no," Rohan said quickly. "I was only hoping to talk to Brayton. My own little business proposal I'm working on. He does have a good head for business, doesn't he?"

"He does," she answered.

Rohan fingered a bit of rock placed on the mantle. "From one of his trips?"

"He thought it pretty," she replied.

"May I?" he asked, picking it up. "Ah, but Nadi would love to see this," he said casually.

"Well, then, take it for her," Lili answered.

"I'll bring it back next time I come."

"Oh, darling, keep it if it'll bring Nadi joy. Brayton would say the same."

Rohan smiled, making his way through the door. As soon as he was out of sight, he veered from his usual path to one he could see got frequent use.

"Councilwoman," Rohan said when he arrived at Shanna's door. She had cages full of birds he could hear singing."

"Rohan!" she said. "What a surprise!"

"Not unpleasant, I hope," he said.

"Of course not," she answered, perhaps a little too quickly.

"I found this delightful little piece," he said, holding up the stone. "And wanted to gift it to Nadi. But first I wondered what region it might be from. And I know you're a whiz at that with your many travels."

She took the stone from his hand, casually turning it over, examining the lines of blue that ran through the stone. "Some call it peacock ore," she said. "For obvious reasons."

"Of course," he said.

"It would have to come from a region with a lot of iron, because that's what creates the unique coloring. Iron and exposure to the air in a particular way. I'd say this one would have to come from Renai."

"Newly mined?"

"I have no idea," she said, glancing down at it. "Value is the same regardless. You could get a pretty sum for a piece like this."

"Well, that's not what I'll be needing it for. Nadi will love the colors. From iron."

"And air," she added. "It's a beautiful type of tarnish, really."

"Tarnish," he murmured, holding it to the light. "Yes."

Brayton

BRAYTON WAS LOSING CONTROL, if ever he actually had any.

The iron-snorting man—called Rjen—dropped the body at his feet. "Found this one," he said, "hiding something."

"And you killed him?" Brayton said, stepping back from the body, more careful this time not to leave a trace of himself on the man.

"Nah, just fought him, real fair and stuff. At the square, so there were witnesses."

"Wonderful," Brayton grumbled. It wasn't technically illegal, this sort of brawling. At least in a few of the sectors. Though it was rare for the blows to actually come to death.

"You shouldn't have killed him," Brayton said.

"Ah, now, at that point with him being so stubborn and what not, it woulda attracted more attention if I'd let him live. They usually plead mercy."

The fact that he hadn't did seem to indicate he had something bigger than the usual thing to hide. Still, no matter what the iron-snorter—Rjen—said, it *could* attract attention. Though it was also true that the type of person involved in these brawls was rarely the type to attract attention from anyone except the rabble he occasionally angered.

"What city were you in?" Brayton asked with some resignation. If it was really a pattern that the humans were following, their next stop would be in a city. An abandoned building of some sort.

"Renai."

"And what sector?"

"The type wheres you can kill a man and not get noticed."

"And what was he hiding?" Brayton asked.

"Couldn't figure that part out."

"Which is exactly why it would be slightly nice to have a man with a mouth that still moved."

"Ah, he wasn't moving it anyhow."

"Did you check his pockets?"

"For cash, yeah."

Brayton used all his willpower not to roll his eyes. "Anything else?"

"Oh, he didn't have no cash, just some of them green bits of cloth."

Brayton closed his eyes, trying to be patient. "You did keep them, I hope."

Rjen dug around in his trousers—not in a pocket, but in the actual trousers, which Rjen had been using as a pocket. He produced several scraps.

Brayton put on his gloves. "Wonderful," he said with a tight smile as Rjen pulled the final piece from a particularly sweaty location in his trousers.

But then he saw them—the tiny marks in the corner of each scrap—lines that looked like small topographical measurements.

"Wonderful," he murmured again, holding them up. Tiny maps leading the holder to the places he was to mark. Only now it was Brayton who held the markers, Brayton who could find the trail. If he was fast enough.

"I trust that this," Brayton said, indicating the body, "will be gone when I return."

"Where you headed?" Rjen asked.

"To the woods outside of Renai," he answered, waving to the slender one—a man named Titri.

Rohan

ROHAN TRAVELED to the mines just outside Renai—the place Shanna had said the peacock ore could be found.

He was not entirely sure anymore what he was looking for—the stone or his brother. He had a feeling that when he found one, he might find the other. What he would do or ask at that point, he was also not sure.

Why was his brother seeking the stone again after all these years? What did Brayton hope to get out of it?

Brayton could not use the stone like Rohan might be able to, at least if what Cerilla believed was true. If Nadi was a Greylord—or was it Greylady?—she might be able to draw quite a bit of strength from such a stone, maybe even a full healing. His father had told the story of the final Motteral Mal, of the changing, of the time when he put the Sourcestone in his mouth—his entire body firing with its power. "A terrible power," his father had said. "Too strong for one man to hold."

Perhaps it was true, but with Nadi's affliction, Rohan hoped it was just the right amount for a sick child to hold.

The mine shaft was abandoned, much as Rohan had expected, but traces remained. Scuffs from boots, freshly used tables and tunnels. But nothing at all to indicate where they might be next. Well, nothing except the path through one of the underground passages—a place where carts used to rumble, but where he now found fresh prints in the dust. A tunnel that led, if he was not mistaken, under the woods to the next city. Which was not Renai.

No. These people are heading back.

Back to his own woods, his own city.

It made perfect sense when he thought about it. That they would run in circles. Leading away then back again. After all, many of them likely had ties, families. They might want to protect the stone, but they wouldn't want to go too far. Not unless they had to. And at this point, why would they? The stone was perfectly safe. This movement was all just...precaution.

Except that somehow with his brother's mysterious business he wasn't so sure.

∾

Brayton

"It's not here," Titri said, before they'd even reached the center of the town.

"What do you mean?" Brayton asked.

"Look at the scraps," Titri answered. "They look human to you?"

Brayton ran his finger over the coarse fabric, which was much like the humans would use. "It could be," he said.

"But is it? You know the best, I'm just taking a guess," Titri said. "I don't know fabric, but I know Rjen."

Brayton held the pieces up to the light, then pulled out the scrap of fabric from years before. And it was true. These new ones looked hastily dyed. In fact, the one that had been in his palm the longest had begun leaking dye into the sweaty creases of his hand. But they didn't have to match to be real. Surely the humans could buy cheap fabric just as well as expensive. And yet. If he was going to hang a fabric on a tree, would he want it to fade at the first dewdrop into a white or yellowed cloth? Would he want it to bleach in the light of the sun?

No, because that would give them away to any who were looking. And he would never want that.

Brayton cursed, stuffing the cloth into his cloak.

"You ain't after money like the most of us," Titri said. "But I ain't invested in going on some wild goose chase with you."

"Why would Rjen have wanted to send me on a goose chase?"

"If I had a guess, I'd say it was to keep you a few steps behind."

"And why would he want me behind?"

"Your guess is as good as mine, but I'm not interested in staying behind."

"Then why did you agree to come with me?"

"Maybe I wanted to see it a little from a distance, to see how it would play out."

"He's going to kill them," Brayton said. "The humans."

"If he has to," Titri said. "Most of them would. The old man offered a thousand pieces of gold to the man who brought it to him."

"Gold you'll never see," Brayton said.

"And why is that?" Titri asked.

"Because that stone would kill you before you could get a chance."

"We would take turns carrying it," he replied. "We already planned it out."

"Oh, I've no doubt of that," Brayton said.

Titri narrowed his eyes. "And what do you mean? Your voice? You're saying something without saying it."

"You'd take turns carrying it alright. You'd steal it and then carry it till you collapsed, too spellbound by the idea of that much gold. And then another would definitely take it off your hands, this time with gloves, but eventually he would die too. And then another would do the same thing. Carrying it till the stone killed him—or his companion did. And on and on. The stone would still, eventually, make its way to the old man, leaving a trail of bodies in its wake."

"Well, if we can't carry it, can the old man?"

"No," Brayton said, his mind spinning.

"Well, if he can't, then what good's a powerful stone to him anyway?"

"None," Brayton said, looking through the woods to a different path, a path back home. "Not without one to carry it."

TEN

Rohan

Rohan stepped through his own door just before dusk.

"Did you find it?" Cerilla asked, placing a hand on her burgeoning belly. She was due within the next moon cycle.

"Find what?" Nadi asked, cradling a doll in her arms.

"Oh, just a bit of medicine for your tea," Cerilla replied.

"I did not, but I believe it's getting closer."

"Closer?" Cerilla asked.

He moved near to his wife and whispered. "Is there an old building, or something near here? Somewhere a group of people could hide?"

"Let me think," she said in a hush.

But Nadi piped in, "There's the old farm."

Rohan cleared his throat. "What did you say, my pumpkin?"

"You wanted to know about abandoned places," Nadi said, wrapping her doll in a bit of green cloth. "You could go to the old farm."

"You could hear me?"

Nadi nodded. "'Course, Papa."

Rohan nodded. "And how do you know of this old farm?"

"Oh, Tessa and I used to play there, when I was well."

"Your friend?" Rohan asked, not saying the part he was thinking. *Your human friend.*

"Yes," Nadi answered. "A rich shifter used to own it before the changing. After that, his servants took it over. One of them was Tessa's Papi."

"Her grandfather?" Rohan asked.

"Yes," she said.

"And where is he now? Why is it abandoned?"

"He died," Nadi said, making a sad face. "When Tessa was young."

"So just a few years ago?" Rohan asked his daughter, with a smile.

She shrugged, the concept of years and time still too long for her young mind to hold well.

Rohan looked at his wife, who nodded, then mouthed *Killed by thieves.*

"But what of his sons and daughters?" he asked.

"Oh, Tessa just has her mama, and her mama didn't want to stay. Not all the time anyway. She usually just stays in their little house."

"But Tessa comes back sometimes," Rohan said, putting the pieces together, and suddenly understanding why his daughter could hear him so well.

"Yes," Nadi said. "And when she does, we play there. It always makes me feel better."

"And have you seen her lately? Tessa?" Rohan asked, though he knew the answer. He and Cerilla both looked at Nadi's dirty shins, her scuffed elbows.

"We climbed trees at the farm," Nadi said. "So many trees."

∿

Rohan could barely eat through dinner. The thought of the stone, right under their noses, all these years, as the Wardens came and went.

But supposing it was right there. He could not exactly march in and demand it. Even if he could, he could never just take it. But perhaps, perhaps if they understood what it would mean to Nadi, perhaps they could help. How they would help, he was not sure, but he could ask. Beg if he must. It was a thing that could not even be called a plan, but it was all he had.

"You're nothing if not an optimist," his wife said as they cleaned up after dinner.

"But I haven't said anything," he replied.

"You didn't marry me because I was stupid," she answered. "I know what you know. It explains other things too, like how sometimes she was so strong after returning from play—being so close to the stone. But how are you going to get it?"

"I'm not," he replied, thinking, realizing finally what he must do. "I'm not going to get it. But you've given me the final piece."

"What do you mean?" she asked.

"I'm going to ask them to stay, stay right where they are, in that farmhouse, near to Nadi."

His wife nodded. "It might," she said slowly, "it might be enough. But they move for a reason."

"Yes," he said. "Which means if they are to stay, they'll need..."

"Security?" she said.

"Invisibility," he said. "There's nothing on earth that could protect them well enough if certain shifters find out. No, they'll need to remain unseen."

Brayton

WHEN HE AND Titri returned from the wood, the shelter was empty. Save for a young boy, waiting at the threshold with a note in his hand.

"Are either of you called Brayton?" he asked.

"I am, child," Brayton replied. Titri moved through the chambers, seemingly looking for someone who had been left to tell them where to go, though Brayton wondered if he was really looking for bodies of those not wanted on the expedition.

Brayton held out a hand to take the letter.

"With your due respect, sir," the boy replied. "I am to check first. I was directed to find a scar."

Brayton eyed him for a moment, then turned his wrist over. When playing tag as children, Rohan had chased him straight through a long window, which neither of them had seen. Brayton's arms had been outstretched and he'd taken the brunt of the sharp glass as it broke.

The boy glanced at Brayton's wrist, then cleared his throat. "Thank you, sir. Will there be a return letter?"

Brayton only motioned for him to wait outside the door before slitting the letter open with a long nail.

We've found a way to keep Nadi well, but I need your help. There is a substance not far from here, on an old farm. The farm is not abandoned, but must appear to be so. For the foreseeable future. Can you help?

Brayton turned the missive over in his hands, time and time again. His brother's name on the front of it, the sector from which it came.

"Boy," he said, calling the child back in. "Did you bring this directly to me?"

"As directly as I could," the boy answered.

Brayton nodded. "And how direct was that?"

"I was told you had business dealings in Renai, and once in the city I met your friend—Rjen—and he told me where I could find you."

Brayton closed his eyes in a long blink. "And whereabouts did you see the one called Rjen?"

"Just past the square?"

"Travelling in which direction?"

The boy started to fidget as though he thought he might be in trouble. Brayton pulled a thick coin from his pocket and tossed it into the air.

"Out of town, sir," the boy replied, his eyes watching the coin. "To the west."

"I've a response for you to return to my brother," Brayton said, pulling a second gold coin from his cloak along with a piece of paper. "You know where he lives, I trust, since he was the one who sent you here."

"Yes, sir."

"Very good. Take this to him. No stopping. No dawdling. And no matter what, don't allow another to read what I have read. It's a secret, you see. A surprise. For my niece."

"I understand, sir."

"As a bit of insurance, if you deliver it successfully, I've instructed my brother to give you two *more* gold coins, just as fat as these are." He printed those instructions neatly on the letter. "Oh, and one more thing, boy."

"Yes sir?"

"I need you to run."

He scrawled a note on the paper, then stuffed it in the envelope.

"Must be quite the surprise, sir," the boy said as Brayton resealed the envelope and handed him the coins.

"Oh, it is," Brayton replied. "It most certainly is."

THE BODIES LAY in broken heaps at various points throughout the wood, as though they themselves were the markers. Some were still warm, though most had cooled. Not human, but shifter.

About half of his own "band." They had killed their own. Brayton muttered a curse as Titri turned the most recent body over.

"You're too late, it seems," Titri said.

"And you're lucky you came with me," Brayton snapped, stepping around the carnage. "You think they have the stone?"

"I think they're on their way to it."

"Why kill their own?"

"A thousand reasons," Titri answered. "These ones were slow; or they doubted the cause; or maybe someone with a sharp dagger was having a bad day and felt like it."

Brayton turned to him. "Charming. I expect that once they've found the stone, we'll find the trail of the remaining men dying in the woods and tunnels. Should lead us right to them."

Titri stepped back at his words. "The moon is coming tomorrow night."

"Oh, I know," Brayton said. "I feel it in my bones, same as you. Same as they. Same as our friend, the old man. It will make them confident, that feeling."

Titri nodded, then asked, "Do you know his name? The old man?"

"I'm beginning to think I have an idea," Brayton said, remembering his mother's stories, remembering his father's tale of the Motteral Mal. Remembering many things as they made their way along the path that would bring Brayton home.

Rohan

THE BOY ARRIVED at Rohan's door, his forehead glistening with sweat just before evening meal. He bent over, panting, as he handed Rohan the envelope.

Rohan slit the paper of the envelope and pulled two coins from his cloak, surprised to have gotten a response so soon.

The place is not safe. Get away from it as quickly as you can.

"Will you be needing a response delivered?" the boy asked, his eyes light and eager.

"No, child. No, I will not." He glanced at the boy. "There's water in the well, down the path. Hurry along. I'm afraid I've got a bit of urgent business to do."

"For the surprise?" the boy asked.

But Rohan had shut the door.

ROHAN HURRIED FROM HIS HOUSE, letter in hand.

Nadi had been at the farm all day. He'd been letting her play there more and more, hoping he and Cerilla could find a way to convince the humans to stay.

They leave for a reason, you know. He heard Cerilla's voice in his head, and cursed. They leave because staying is unsafe.

He looked to the sky. Moonface, as they'd started calling it. The fullest moon. It would be tonight.

HE FOUND Nadi high in a tree—higher than it seemed a child should be able to go, her limbs hanging over the thin upper branches like she was a bird. Even more ironic when you considered that in a few more hours she would turn to wolf.

"Child, come down."

"Shhhh, Daddy. I'm waiting for Tessa to find me. You'll give me away."

"I could smell you," Rohan said. "Tessa will too."

"Nah," Nadi replied. "The humans are no good for smelling things. It's what makes hiding so fun. Especially before Moonface."

"Fun for you," Rohan said, glancing nervously at the setting sun. "Now come down, dear."

Nadi pouted.

"Uncle Brayton will be arriving soon."

"Really?" Nadi said, taking hold of a branch as though to swing down. Just as Tessa ran into the edge of the wood, her cheeks flushed.

"Found you," she cried.

"See, Daddy, you've spoiled it," Nadi said, tears pricking into her eyes.

Rohan shook his head, as the sun sat halfway over the horizon. "Girls, we must get you inside. The sun is setting soon. Tessa, where is your mother?"

"Cooking supper with the other women," Tessa responded. "But I don't want to go find her. She'll make me clean the pots."

Rohan bit his lip. "We really must get inside soon. I've heard a storm is coming."

"But the sky is bright," Nadi said. "And a beautiful purple."

Both girls gazed at the sunset. "When does Uncle arrive?" Nadi asked.

Rohan opened his mouth to say he wasn't quite sure, and that they needed to return to the house, but before the words could come out, the howling began. Not full wolken, but the start, the growls. He could feel the same type of sound, deep in his throat, aching to reply.

"Inside, girls," he said, his voice low and rumbling as he swept the girls into his bulging arms and ran for the kitchen.

The women were fluttering around, Tessa's mother in a panic, when Rohan deposited her daughter. "The howls?" she said.

"Andrae," he said to Tessa's mother, but any explanation he had was cut short by another round of howls, much closer.

"Councilman, what is this? What is going on?"

"I'm not sure," Rohan replied. "But it doesn't smell right."

"Doesn't sound right either," an older woman said, her voice cut with anger.

"Can you get out of here?" Rohan asked. "Without being seen?"

"There is a pathway, an old servant's staircase that leads to the cellar," Andrae said. "But these women won't leave their men."

"Those who have children need to take them, and run," Rohan said as the howls took on their full wolken sound. He shoved Tessa toward her mother. "I will see what I can do with the shifters."

At that moment, they both glanced at Nadi, her skin prickling with the beginnings of fur. He looked into the woman's eyes, pleading, as his own body began to shift.

"We cannot take her with us," Andrae said. "They will smell her."

"They will smell you too," Rohan said.

"But we will smell the right way. She will not."

Rohan closed his eyes and nodded.

"Your smell will mask her," Andrae said, glancing at Nadi. "The child just needs to find a place to hide."

The howls united as a battering ram struck a door in the distance.

"It's the old outbuilding," Andrae said. "That's where the men were gathered. All of them."

Tessa started to cry. "We can't leave Nadi, Mother. What if she gets hurt?"

Someone tapped on the door and all the women whirled toward it, makeshift weapons in hand. The door opened just a creak. "Rohan?" the voice said.

"Uncle!" Nadi squealed, as someone slunk through the door.

The women took a step forward, armed with pans and knives.

"Nadi," Brayton said in a whisper that he was trying to make sound calm, though he'd clearly been running and his voice was ragged. He held up both hands to show he was unarmed. "Just here for my brother."

"Take her home," Rohan said, pointing to Nadi.

Andrae looked from one brother to the other. "Did you know they were coming?"

Rohan didn't answer. "I will go help your men."

"Our women will too," Andrae replied. "At least those without children."

And they would. Rohan could see the fierce looks in their eyes—glinting to match the sharp cutlery in the women's hands. "Brayton, take Nadi—" But before he could finish speaking, they heard the sounds—bodies prowling around the house—animal-sleek, though twice the size of men, positioned at each exit point.

"Mama, we can't leave Nadi," Tessa said again.

Andrae's shoulders slumped slightly in the darkness. "I will take your child," she said to Rohan. "From the cellar we can try to make our way to your house." A loud crash as the shifters in the distance broke through some type of door or barricade.

"Thank you," he whispered. "Have Cerilla call the guard. I'm sure it's just a misunderstand—"

At that moment, a scream hit the night—the curdled sound of a man who would not scream again.

Those with children pushed their young through a tight opening to a narrow staircase. Andrae took Tessa with one hand and Nadi with another.

The remaining women raced through a dim corridor that had been dug into the earth, leading to the various buildings surrounding the farmhouse. Rohan and Brayton stumbled after them in the darkness.

"You knew," Rohan hissed, quietly enough that he knew no human ears could hear.

"I was trying to stop it," Brayton replied.

"But you knew," Rohan said. "There's a whole government that could have stopped it."

"Is there, Rohan? Is there?"

Their argument was ended by the war cries that rang out—the broken songs of the fighting and dying.

The women tore into the room with kitchen knives and heavy hammers, thrashing haphazardly, surprising some and injuring others. But seeing the shifters in their wolken form—nearly double the height of the humans, broader, stronger, faster—Rohan knew that the humans didn't have a chance.

For the first time in his life, he understood better the equality that his parents had been fighting for. And why the stone could not be shared by human and shifter.

Beside him, Brayton cursed as both of them hung back, pausing, watching, listening.

"I'll take the right," Rohan said.

"I know these men," Brayton interrupted.

"Does that matter?" Rohan asked. "They're attacking innocent human civilians."

"More importantly, they know me," Brayton said.

"Then use it, brother," Rohan said, a deep ache building in his head. "Use it to your advantage. My daughter—your niece—is trying to escape. Along with a bunch of other people."

~

Brayton

"Rjen!" Brayton said, walking into the room with bravado. "You left in such a hurry. How strange to find you here."

For a minute, the entire room paused, each face turning to Brayton. He cut an impressive figure—slim and sleek, his fur the color of the Grey, shining in the dim light of the room.

Rjen, he could see, was looking a little worse for the wear—snorting iron had apparently not been to his benefit after all. A human woman had him pinned into a corner, a deep cut across his forehead. His face, already pale from the iron poisoning, was now white under the fur.

"Good to see you, friend," Rjen said with his thin voice.

"Have you found what you were looking for?" Brayton asked.

"Are you going to help me, brother?" Rjen asked, sneering at the human woman who had not let him go.

"I am not your brother," Brayton replied. "Nor could we be considered friends."

"Comrade then," Rjen said.

Brayton felt the room turning on him, murder glinting in all their eyes—from shifter to human. Even Rohan turned.

"Business associate at best," Brayton replied.

"Of course," Rjen said, a bit of blood dripping to the fur of his muzzle. "In a deal made with the devil. I'm not sure you've got a single friend in this entire room."

"You might be right," Brayton said. "But I'm not sure you do either."

"Then we should band together."

"I think it's time I stopped making deals with devils," Brayton replied.

"Oh, it's too late for that," Rjen said.

In the pause, one of the human men began sneaking to the doorway. A shifter saw it and rushed forward, screaming hysterically, "He's got the stone."

He thrust his claws, long and sharp, into the back of the man as he was running through the door.

Rohan leapt to the man's aid, pulling him away from the shifter.

The shifter howled in rage, as Rohan started spilling out the contents of the man's pockets. "You see," Rohan shouted. "Nothing!" Rohan put his own body in front of the human's. "Nothing here. Leave him."

The shifter growled, but turned away, as Rohan tried to tend to the man's bleeding.

Brayton watched the chaos as it spun around him. Humans fighting and falling, and every once in a while, a shifter injured.

Rjen had managed to wiggle free from the human though she was still pursuing him. Without the moon-shift, it would have been a non-struggle. She was faster and stronger and smarter on every count. But as a human she was still at a disadvantage. At least on this night.

"They don't have what you want," Brayton shouted, trying to stop the fighting. It didn't work.

"They've got it," one of the shifters said. "We just have to find it."

Brayton was trying to fight the shifters without doing harm to them, but it was getting harder. He could see that Rohan was having the same problem.

"If they don't have it, we'll fight till they're all dead and we know for sure," Rjen said, taking a swipe at Brayton. "Unless, that is, *you* know, my friend. I mean, *business associate.* You always were good at picking the winning side." He stalked toward him, pushing him into a corner.

"No," Brayton said, blocking the shifter's arm as he tried to pin him against the wall. "I wasn't."

Rjen laughed, doubling over with a cough, just as the woman pounced on him, thrusting the long carving knife into his back and through his heart. His face, already pale beneath his fur, went white, his eyes glassy.

"See you on the devil's doorstep, *brother,*" Rjen said, sinking to the earth. The woman faced Brayton.

He held up his hands. "I'm on your side."

"Are you?" she asked. "Because our side is dying, and *you're* not stopping it." She held out the knife, still hot with Rjen's blood.

Brayton stepped back.

"Choose, shifter. Choose a side," she said.

Brayton expected her to thrust the knife into him—or at least try, but instead she tossed him a short dagger, before darting away toward another shifter who was attacking one of her friends.

Turning, he looked around the room. Half a dozen men and one woman lay on the floor, unmoving. Along with Rjen. The others were dodging and lunging and fighting. In a dim corner, he spotted Titri, who had been cornered by three humans.

Faces of shifters he knew, faces of humans fighting for their lives. But there was one face he didn't see. The face who had brought him here, as well as everyone else.

"The devil," he murmured.

◦

"The stone isn't here," Brayton hissed, rushing to Rohan.

"Whether it is or isn't doesn't matter if this doesn't stop," Rohan said, backing away from the group.

"It won't stop till they have the stone, or every man is dead. They're mad with greed for it," Brayton said.

"They're mad alright."

The humans had formed up along a wall in a trapped but defensive position, each of them holding their weapons in front of them. Brayton couldn't help but notice that it looked like a line of people about to be executed. The tallest human man stood at the center, an ax out in front of him.

"There's one creature missing," Brayton hissed. "The most important one. The demon who brought us all together."

"And where do you suppose he is?" Rohan asked.

"My guess is that he's hunting the stone. Which means if he's not here..."

"How do we stop them?" Rohan asked, interrupting.

"I don't know," Brayton said, "but maybe we can turn this band against the old devil, get them to look for him."

"How do you turn this band anywhere?" Rohan asked. "You can't reason with them."

"Oh, it won't be about reason," Brayton said.

◦

"The old man!" Brayton shouted. He didn't bother to position himself in front of the group. Instead, he stood to the side, looking through the exit into the distance.

A few of the shifters paused in their fighting, turning to look.

"He ain't here," Titri said, coming up beside Brayton.

"No," Brayton said, his voice heavy with meaning. "No, he isn't."

Titri cursed under his breath. "What are you saying, pretty one?"

"I think the old man has it." Brayton said it quietly, but not nearly as quietly as he could have.

He felt several members of the group turn to him.

"Shhhh," Titri murmured.

"You're lying," another said, as the entire group moved toward him. "You ain't even on our side."

"You're right," Brayton said, his eyes like ice. "I'm on my own."

He turned back to the door and then bolted—slamming the door behind him and racing for the woods.

The shifters stopped in their fighting. A collective pause.

Titri cursed again.

And in moments they were gone, chasing after Brayton, chasing after the dream they would fight to the death to get to see.

Rohan

ROHAN LOOKED around the room at the dead and dying. He called out to the remaining humans, giving instructions. Some listened, and one ran to call the guard. But others turned from him, hunched over their injured.

Rohan bent over a man with a deep gash along his gut. He put pressure on it, tearing his cloak with his other hand and shoving wads of fabric into the wound.

"Move," someone said, kneeling beside him.

Rohan looked up, surprised to see a wiry man, scowling at him. "If we can stop the blood long enough—" Rohan began.

"*We* won't be doing anything," the man said. "Now, go. You've no jurisdiction here."

"I'm not trying to have jurisdiction," Rohan said. "I'm just trying to keep some of these people alive."

"We can handle our own," the wiry man said, pushing Rohan to the side and cooing gently to the injured man. "How do we know you're not some traitor, like your brother?"

"He's not a—" Rohan stopped. He wasn't quite sure who his brother was at this point.

Rohan clamped his mouth shut and moved on to a man near the wall who had been throttled and lay in a heap, his neck a web of purple bruising—a man the others had passed over for dead.

Perhaps he was. Rohan traced a finger along the lines of bruising, then placed a hand on his chest to check for warmth, for breath.

All at once, the strangled man startled, his eyes popping open, as he sucked in a labored, broken breath. Seeing Rohan, he laughed. "You'll never find it," the man said, mistaking Rohan for the shifter who had nearly killed him. "You can't even begin to think of where to look."

The man's breath broke further, thinning with each inhalation. Rohan pressed his mouth over the man's mouth, trying to breathe for him. But the man's breaths only grew shallower, until they stopped coming at all.

Rohan looked down at the man. He recognized him as the leader of the humans—a tall man who had fought at the center of the room with an ax.

Surveying the room, he saw that all of the felled humans were the strongest and biggest, the ones you might assume would be hiding the stone. And suddenly he knew who had it.

And he knew she was being hunted.

"By the moon," he murmured, rushing from the room, back through the kitchens, down an old servant staircase, and into the cellar—now empty and completely dark. He felt along the walls in the darkness, meticulously, until he found it—the small line of a door.

Pressing with all his weight, he forced the old door open, and exited through some broken steps into the fallow fields.

ROHAN HAD ONE ADVANTAGE.

He knew the girls' smells better than any of the other shifters. Unfortunately, there was something besides their smell—something one who knew of old things would feel as well. For, under the full moon, which always made the shifters strong, Rohan could tell that one of the girls held that ancient thing, that ancient thing which sucked strength from him.

Rohan found them hiding, among stalks of grain.

"Girls," he whispered.

"Papa," Nadi whimpered.

"Yes, love. Come on, now. We've got to get away."

"We can't," Nadi answered.

"Of course you can," Rohan replied. "I'm here, and I'll help you."

"Mama told us to stay here," Tessa murmured, tears filling her entire voice.

"We will find her later," Rohan said, his voice urgent.

"She told us to wait," Tessa insisted. "Until she came back."

"Your mother is a wise woman," a gravelly voice responded from the shadows. "Unfortunately, she's also a dead one."

Nadi threw her arms around Tessa as the girl began to cry.

The shifter landed silently in the dust beside them. When the moon caught his face, Rohan stepped back, shielding both the girls with his body.

The creature in front of them looked like he'd been cut into pieces and stitched back together—scars running along his jaw and nose and ears.

Scars Rohan had heard about in the stories his parents had often told.

"I thought you were dead," Rohan whispered. "They all thought it."

"A great advantage to be thought dead," the shifter replied. "It allows one to move about much more freely. As long, that is, as he is not seen. Lucky for me, your parents made that easier when they trapped us all in our human forms for most of our days."

"You will not touch these children," Rohan said.

"Oh," he replied. "And who's going to stop me? A councilman who's barely raised a sword or claw in all his life? Your parents weakened you."

Rohan stepped back, the girls moving with him, in the shadow of his body. He could feel them clinging to his legs, Tessa's hot tears burning into his skin. "Just because I choose not to use sword and claw does not mean I cannot," Rohan replied.

It was only half a bluff. He had been taught, from practically his infancy, how to fight. Though, unlike Brayton, he had not much taken to the practice of it.

"Don't be ridiculous," the old shifter responded. "I can smell your fear."

Rohan planted his feet into the soil, solidly. "And I yours, old one. You've lived longer than almost all the others. You've hidden and scrapped your way through the woods and wilderness. Seeking the one thing you think will bring you back to youth."

"Not youth, child of the Greylord. But greatness."

"And how many members of my family have stopped you in your pursuit," Rohan said, though he knew in his heart he was only stalling. He had no plan, and Brayton was the one better able to think quickly under pressure. "Let's see, I believe it was my grandfather in the first place. In the days you were called Draden. Ah, and then my father. When you became the Night Hunter. You were stronger by then, but weaker too. A shifter held together by pain and revenge."

"That is only a strength, boy. And now I've outlived them," the scarred shifter replied. "Outlived them. And soon I'll outlive you as well."

Nadi peeked from behind her father's legs. "I know you," she said. "From Mother's stories. You were *not* strong in them." The night was still, though each time a small breeze caught, the sound of dry stalks scraped and shuffled, like the sound of ghosts stepping through the fields.

"Then your mother is a fool," the old shifter said. "Did she also tell you what one such as me would need to succeed?"

"You need the stone," Nadi said. "Which you don't have."

The old shifter smiled—a face uglier than it was before. "Correct on one count," he said. "I do need a stone. And one to carry it." He looked at Tessa. "But it looks to me like I've got both of those things right here."

With a movement swifter than seemed possible considering his age, he grabbed Tessa.

Rohan pulled a small blade from his boot and held it up.

"Ah ah ah," the old shifter taunted, holding the child in front of him, so Rohan couldn't hurt him. "Now if you'll excuse me..."

"I thought you said you'd need the stone," Nadi said, stepping toward him.

The scarred shifter took a breath when she did, as though a sudden wave of weakness had hit him. Suddenly, he looked hard into Nadi's eyes, his mouth parting as though he couldn't get quite enough air.

"Wolrijk," the girl said, mimicking her mother's voice. "A shifter stitched into a stolen body, so he could create a stolen life."

"So he could steal life," the old one said.

"How much difference is there?" the little girl asked. "But you won't steal mine, Father's, or Tessa's either."

Wolrijk clamped his teeth shut as Nadi took another step closer. The old shifter gripped Tessa's arms so tightly tiny pinpricks of blood sprouted where he held her. "Show me the stone, little human girl," he said to Tessa.

"Oh, she can't," Nadi said. "Which I know you've figured out."

"No," Wolrijk murmured.

"Mother told me I was stronger than you," Nadi said. "And I see now that it is true. The stone that makes me strong weakens you. And Father too. But especially you. Because you are old. And small of heart. Mother says the heart is what makes a person big."

"And as I said," Wolrijk replied. "Your mother is a fool. But perhaps I can give you your friend, in exchange for the stone."

"You need a human and the stone," Nadi said. "And Mama is no fool." The wind picked up, its gusts battering the leaves against each other, like the whisper of footsteps.

With that, Wolrijk let out a howl, more than a howl—a type of call.

Rohan could hear them in the woods—the band Brayton had sent on a goose chase—as they turned to the sound, as they began to run toward them.

"Will you fight us all?" the old one asked.

"I could," Nadi said. "With the stone. But that would hurt Father too."

The old shifter smiled. "Weakness," he said. "These connections."

"And besides, I don't need to," the girl said.

"Oh, you'll need to," Wolrijk said.

"No," the girl said. "Because connections aren't weaknesses. Please put Tessa down. You're hurting her."

"I'll put her down, and you'll hand her the stone, child," the old shifter said. "Otherwise, I'll shred her skin into ribbons even uglier than mine."

"If you put her down, I'll hand her the stone," Nadi said.

"Darling," Rohan interrupted. "This is not—" From every direction the other shifters could be heard making their way to them through the fields and grasses.

"It's okay," Nadi said. "It's what Mama would have wanted me to do." In the distance, a bit of grass moved, as though a mouse shuffled to safety.

Wolrijk set Tessa down, watching hungrily as Nadi moved a small pouch from her pocket and placed it into Tessa's hand.

"Your mother is more than a fool," Wolrijk said, lunging for the human child who now held the stone, the beginning of a howl forming on his lips.

A howl that was cut short by the blade that went straight through the old shifter's back, into his heart, and came out the front.

ELEVEN

Rohan

Cerilla pulled the blade back with a solid jerk as the Night Hunter sank to the ground without a single moan.

Tessa nestled into Nadi's arms, tears streaming down her face.

Rohan gazed at his pregnant wife in disbelief. "How?" he finally asked.

"I've been scouring the black market for traces of the Grey," she said. "I recently procured this blade." She held it up in the moonlight. "The tip is painted with a bit of the Grey. I was planning to use it for Nadi after the full moon. But this seemed more timely."

"My dear," Rohan said, but couldn't finish as a unified howl took up near the outskirts of the field. Nearby a stalk rustled.

"Your mother is not dead, sweet Tessa," Cerilla said. "So dry your eyes. But she is hurt. You must both get to your group. And quickly."

Tessa swiped a hand across her face. "But the other bad ones are coming. How can we move quickly with Mama so hurt?"

BRAYTON TUMBLED out of the tall grasses. "Rohan," he said. "They're coming and—" He stopped just short of tripping over Wolrijk's body. "By the moon."

"You're the fastest among us," Rohan said, speaking quickly. "I need you to get Tessa, her mother, and Nadi to safety. Now."

Brayton shook his head. "They've surrounded the farm. And how —?" He gestured to the body.

"Later," Rohan said. "There are passages from the house—and I'm guessing from most of the outbuildings as well. Cerilla, where is Tessa's mother?"

"She's in a cellar at the outskirts of the property. Truly, our old friend calling the other shifters to him may have saved her, as they were getting closer. Andrae has a way to leave through the cellar, but will not go without Tessa. And Rohan—" She turned to her husband. "—the humans have collapsed most of the exits. It's possible that is the last one available. It's also possible that they were unwilling to wait this long and collapsed it too."

"Take the girls," Rohan said to Brayton. "Tessa knows the way."

"They'll smell the human and follow me," Brayton said. "They want nothing more than that stone. All the better if they've got a human child to hold it for them."

Rohan closed his eyes, trying to think.

"Give me your coat, Tessa," Nadi said suddenly. "And I'll give you mine."

"What are you doing, child?" Rohan asked.

"We'll confuse the scents," Nadi said.

"It won't much matter since Uncle is taking both of you," Rohan said firmly.

"No," Nadi said. "He is going to take Tessa. I am going to stay here, in plain sight, and smelling quite human. Tessa got some of her blood on the sleeves from that horrible creature, so it won't be so hard."

"You will not stay," Rohan said. "You will go to safety."

"I am safe," Nadi said. "Here with you and Mother."

"You need the stone to survive," Rohan said to his daughter. "We'll bargain with the humans, beg if we must."

"Papa," Nadi asked. "Do you really think the humans will welcome me into their most secret spaces after...this?" Nadi held up her hands. All around them, buildings had been broken and ransacked. Somewhere in the distance a shed was on fire.

"You need the stone," Rohan said as though no other words would come into his mouth.

"No," Nadi answered. "I don't."

Another united howl broke the night, this time the voices much closer. They could hear the footsteps now, as they crushed the dried stalks and branches of the field.

"You can use it," Brayton broke in. "It has power for our kind. You even have a friend to help you."

"I won't use it, Uncle," Nadi said. "Now, please go. Tessa is about to start crying again." Nadi patted her back. "Don't cry, Tessie. Uncle is very fast. But you must hold the stone tight to you, so he can't feel it much."

"Rohan," Brayton said.

Rohan looked away. "The child has made her choice."

"She's a child," Brayton said.

"Would that we all were," Rohan murmured. "Now, go. Cerilla and I will make a stir, so you can get through."

"This is madness to let it go, to let your own child..."

"To let my own child save her friend?" Rohan answered.

"Her friend needn't—"

"Go!" Rohan shouted, as he turned with his dagger toward approaching footsteps.

"Please, Uncle," Nadi said, looking into his eyes.

"I could kidnap the child," Brayton said to her, "keep the stone."

"But if you were going to, you probably wouldn't have said that," Nadi said, reaching up to kiss her uncle's cheek.

Brayton nodded, a tight movement. Then turned from his niece, lifting the human child and holding her close.

"Thank you, Uncle," Nadi said.

Brayton didn't answer, except to sprint away toward the darkness of one of the few buildings that wasn't broken or on fire.

"Come, Nadi," Cerilla said. "Let's lead you into the moonlight, so they can see you clearly. So they can follow us. You'll be faster than they are, won't you darling?"

"For tonight, Mama, yes I will," Nadi said, wrapping the coat tight around her.

Rohan held his defensive position as his wife and daughter ran up a small hill. It was then that he heard the howls shift, moving toward the bloodied coat that they could smell, toward the child they thought was human—the hood concealing Nadi's beautiful face.

EPILOGUE 1

Brayton

It was well after dawn when Brayton trudged back to his own house, exhausted from carrying a child with the stone of source, exhausted from resisting the urge to run away with both child and stone, taking the power the old one had wanted, taking it unto himself.

If power it was.

By the time he got to the door of the cellar, it was only the memory of the glassy look in the old, dead shifter's eyes that had stopped him from changing directions, from running into the woods with more power than any shifter of his generation had held in his hands.

The look in the dead shifter's eyes, his niece's living eyes, and the knowledge of his own child, about to be born.

He'd released the human, who had run to her mother. He'd heard them move through the passageway, and then the small pop of an explosion nearby just a few minutes later, as the exit had collapsed behind them.

As for the other shifters, they'd run toward Rohan, Rohan and the child. But he had fended them off, acting as though they were madmen and he was just trying to go home with his shifter child and wife. The group had gone wild then—he'd heard it as he'd waited by the cellar—but they had no time to waste with shifters or even revenge when they were looking for the stone. And so they'd gone, following the sound of the explosion. Which had done them little good.

He wasn't even sure if they'd bothered to notice the dead body of their leader, left to rot in those fields.

AND NOW HE stood at his own door, half expecting to be arrested. For what, he wasn't quite sure. The piece of cloak that was surely hidden in the dead shifter's quarters, the farm burned to the ground by a group he'd been a part of, the body of the ancient shifter found dead in that field. Too many reasons to count.

But no part of the guard waited, only the pleasant trill of his own wife's laughter.

But who was she talking to?

He heard the clink of a glass as he opened the door—a teacup being set on a saucer. And then Shanna's voice, though he couldn't quite make out the words as Lili burst into a greeting.

"Home at last!" Lili said, standing with a smile, her growing belly bumping the table. "You've been gone a whole night longer than expected. I was beginning to wonder if I should send the guard after you."

"Oh," he said. "I stopped over at Rohan's. It was quite a night."

Lili looked at him suspiciously. "You look more like you've spent the night in drink than with your teetotaler of a sibling. Are you sure you were with Rohan?" She stopped. "Is Nadi alright?"

"There was a bit of an issue," Brayton said carefully. "But I think we've got it resolved. And she is safe. At least for now." He looked at his feet, now restored to their human form.

"I'm glad," Lili said. "That poor child. Do they need any more help?"

"No," Brayton said. "Not now." He sucked in a long breath. "But I believe I should probably wash up."

"Don't neglect the scented soap," Lili said cheerfully. "And then come back. Shanna has just been telling me some wonderful news."

"Wonderful?" Brayton asked, pausing. "I could use a bit of that."

"Oh, I can't wait," Lili said, stopping him on the way to the washroom and looking at Shanna. "Just tell him," she said.

"You may want to sit," Shanna said with a forced smile, slipping a small white envelope into his hand.

"Tell him, tell him, tell him," Lili chanted.

"I'm with child," Shanna said, trying to lift her mouth up in a way that failed to match Lili's smile.

"Oh!" Brayton replied, trying to read Shanna's eyes. "And you told Lili first? That wasn't very sporting."

"To be fair, she guessed it on her own," Shanna replied. "I've been quite ill."

"Well, that's wonderful," Brayton said. "Not the ill part, but the other bit. I, um, I didn't realize you'd found a mate."

"I haven't," she said curtly. "At least not long term."

"It's a new world," Lili said. "She doesn't need a husband. She has a wonderful job. And plenty of friends. Of course, I'll help out. The babies will only be months apart. Isn't it wonderful?"

Brayton fingered the envelope in his pocket. "Wonderful," he said, meeting Shanna's eyes, which held a careful, practiced look. "Are you hoping for a boy or a girl, my friend?"

"What I am hoping for doesn't much matter now, does it?" Shanna replied with that plaster of a smile. "But I'd best be going. It's been a long month."

"Why, yes, yes it has," Brayton replied.

"Oh, you have no idea, darling," Lili said, punching Brayton playfully in the side, "how long these months can feel for a woman."

"I don't," he said, "not at all."

Shanna met his eyes on the way out. They were dark, like an abyss she had fallen into.

AFTER LILI WAS SOUND ASLEEP, Brayton dug into his cloak for the letter. Slitting it open without a sound, he held it up to the moonlight.

"*We all make deals with the devil,*" it read. "*You made yours in joining that group. But the old man required something quite different of me. And now I am with child. I watched him burn the pieces of evidence one by one, including the bit of cloak that involved you. We are free, my friend. You and I. Finally free.*"

Brayton wandered into the kitchen, lit a candle, and set some water to boil. As it did, he held the missive over the candle, watching Shanna's own words burn away, trying to put the pieces of all of it together.

Free. Now that she carried the ancient shifter's child.

But were they?

EPILOGUE 2

Twenty Years Later

They met again at the river. Cerilla and Lili, their hairs turned to gray, waited at the bottom of the falls with their children, all of them weeping. Rohan could hear the sound from where he stood, ankle deep in the water, watching for the small boat.

"It didn't have to end this way," Brayton said, from the other side, his own eyes on the horizon.

"Didn't it?" Rohan asked.

"I almost took the child, all those years ago. The child and the stone with her."

"I admit I expected you to," Rohan answered. In the distance, a glint of gold struck the horizon.

"It wasn't a stone for children," Brayton said.

"It was exactly a stone for children," Rohan replied. "It wasn't a stone for us."

"It's a stone that could recreate us," Brayton said.

"It's a stone that could break us," Rohan replied. "And almost did."

"Does this not break us as well?" Brayton asked, as the watercraft drew nearer.

"You can never turn things back," Rohan said. "Not a world, not a choice."

"But perhaps we could get a new world, a new set of choices."

Both paused.

"The water is pushing it west," Brayton said. "I'll catch it."

Rohan only nodded, unable to speak, as his daughter's casket floated to them.

Brayton's arms flexed as he held the boat in place, Rohan splashing to his side.

"It feels too big to hold," Rohan said, looking down at the boat.

"It is much too big to hold," Brayton answered. "Why couldn't the humans have helped her—that friend she saved? Why did she never return?"

"We'd proven ourselves dangerous," Rohan answered, though he didn't sound convinced. "Or perhaps she did help when she could. There were days when Nadi seemed stronger. But if the girl came, or anyone else, we didn't see her."

"I sought the stone," Brayton replied, slipping the long weight into the side of the casket. "When she was weak and couldn't move out of her bed. I renewed my search."

"And with it your anger," Rohan replied, adding his own weighted rod to the other side.

"A bit," Brayton responded. "They should have come back."

"You know that you need more than a stone," Rohan said. "That's the thing about it. It can't be used with just our line. The line of humans will have to help."

"They seem easily enough forced," Brayton said. "Or that's what the Night Hunter seemed to believe."

"And we saw how that turned out."

Brayton didn't answer until they'd steadied the casket. "With the stone we wouldn't be doing this. Nadi would have lived."

"Until she died."

"Thousands of years later."

"It's still death."

"Tell me you wouldn't have wanted another thousand years."

Rohan quietly placed the flower wreath on Nadi's head.

Truthfully, he would have contented himself with another twenty years. The medicine may have made her live longer, but it had not made her live *long*. He grieved that, though he would have chosen these years again, his time with Nadi, even at the end when she required almost constant care.

Finally, he said, "The stone will only be of any good to us when we learn to work with the humans. And do you know the problem with that? We learn to love them too, just as Nadi did. To care for them like we do our own children. To want them to live, same as us. When we learn to do what the stone requires, we'll be unable to use it in the way we wish. Nadi understood that."

"Many do not," Brayton replied. "Even if I choose not to seek it, others will. Others do."

Together they sealed the final panel, covering the young face forever.

"Lili gave me this," Brayton said, holding up a small flask.

"Funeral tonic?" Rohan asked.

"Bitter stuff," Brayton answered, taking a swig. "Here's to living forever."

"Here's to living better," Rohan replied, shaking his head at the flask.

"You always were the stubborn one," Brayton said. They released the casket, watching as it crested the top of the fall, pausing, then tipping up before crashing to the waves below. The sound of the cries of their families built to a crescendo, then faded.

Both of them stood, the waters lapping at their ankles, until the sky began to turn pink.

"Our wives," Rohan said, taking his shoes, and heading to the path.

"I still hate the wailing song," Brayton said.

Rohan nodded as they both turned toward the path.

"After today, I'll be headed off on more business," Brayton said.

"Quite long?" Rohan asked.

"I expect."

"I had hoped you would join the Council one day," Rohan said.

"And once upon a day, I had thought that I might. But that was before all this. Your children, my children. Shanna's child."

Rohan nodded, as though he understood, though Brayton knew he couldn't, not fully.

"And when will I see you again?" Rohan asked.

"Likely when you don't wish to."

"I'll look forward to it then."

GREY WISH

A (LONG) SHORT STORY

He did not come to her until the third generation had passed.

Two generations longer than he wished to live.

When he had been king, he had sought for immortality, planned for it. But that was a different man—one with power over the world. Now he barely had power over himself. Scavenging through the woods in search of food, killing birds and rabbits and squirrels for scraps of flesh and scraps of leather for food or clothing. Learning the art of fire and food and raiment, while trying to forget the surge that used to hum from his fingertips, fill his body and mind, ignite the bauble atop his staff. That magic that had given him power over man, beast, and shifter. Over cities and kingdoms.

Now he set small traps for small creatures, and when he was lucky enough to capture them, he used every piece—meat and bones and skins and feathers. His tunic was stitched together of these various animals—some barely tanned long enough not to stink under the heat of the high white sun.

He would have looked to the sun with a curse, but it was too strong to gaze at while shaking a fist. And so he hunched forward, looking to the ground for weeds or bugs or rodents to heal his hunger and thirst, though nothing could ever quench the deep heat that always burned at the pit of his stomach. It had started as an ache for revenge—against the woman Sadora, against his own daughter, his own son, against the human boy and the disgusting dog.

That first generation the flame inside him had blistered like the heat of the hot stone walls of the head city. The walls that held him away from the new world that human, shifter, dog, and wolf had built up around themselves. A world they thought would be perfect. They were children still in that way, for one thing he had known as king and still knew. No world was perfect. No matter how new.

The second generation the flame inside him had cooled from blue to orange—burning still, but softer, almost warm at times. He had outlasted them—those children who'd usurped him. They'd grown old and died. He alone had mastered the wilderness. He alone still lived. He alone could rise up and conquer.

Only he could not.

New leaders ascended, and soon a system of queen and council was appointed to lead. They did not crumble as Crespin expected. Not quickly anyway.

Most of the wolves returned to the wilderness. He heard them howl at moon's first light, a song different than that of the dogs, and —to him—more beautiful. And somehow, he could understand them still—the meaning of their sounds, even though the words had been lost.

The wolves roamed around the places where he camped and lived, avoiding him, though knowing of him.

As for the dogs, most of them still lived near the humans, offering support and services when they could. The humans lived more decadently than they had ever deserved and that fanned the flame of his rage, but the shifters had been brought down to the humans' level—just what they deserved for cowing to the methods of that first ruler, Sadora. Their sameness brought him some satisfaction, as did the rumors that occasionally floated along on the howls of the wolves, speaking of the dissatisfaction of some, of their desire to return to the time that once had been.

Though as the years wore on, more and more of the shifters seemed more and more content to live as equals with those whom they had once despised.

At first, the once-king did not even consider the race of the cats—where it had gone or what had become of it. After all, he'd spent most of his reign removing them from his sight, from his thoughts, from his concerns. Why wonder about them now?

Yet, as the second generation began to die off, as the city rose up stronger and more beautiful than it had been even in his day, as his bones began to weaken, but refused to crumble, as his body began to bow, but refused to break, as age ate at him piece by piece without ever fully consuming him, he began to ask himself: What had happened to the cats and the girl who had once been their mistress —the girl that was half of him, and half of another? Two powerful and opposing forces.

On the morning he first arrived at the wood—her wood—he told himself that he'd gotten there by chance. Searching for shelter in the trees that grew thick as shadow, dense as stone, dark as midnight.

Once there, he found no well-worn path leading to its edge, no path at all really. Though his feet must have remembered the way, or perhaps a memory that went deeper than the muscles of his body, reaching down into the joint blood, the kinship he shared (whether he wanted to or not) with the girl that had been—the tea drinker, the prophecy giver.

Surely she had died with that first generation. Surely the only things that lived here now were moss and worms and mushrooms— the tokens of death—a thing he had begun to yearn for even as his ancient body insisted on withholding it.

An idea struck him.

Ignoring the forlorn forest, he gathered the fungi, the maggots, the decaying dirt, and stirred them into a pot with water. If she was no longer here, then he would create his own tea, his own death. Perhaps with her perverse sense of mercy and justice, she had left these elements here for him—the ingredients to finish the life that had grown much too long.

After the tea (more of a sludge, really) had steeped overnight, he drank it down. Forcing it to stay there, though his stomach retched and threatened to remove it.

And stay it did, settling deep into his bones, leaking into the recesses of his mind, calling up visions of his first wife—so long since he'd thought of her, so long since the tones of her name had left his lips. Loerwoei. Now, however, he found them again, calling to her, begging.

And then a memory of the other—the woman he had tried to forget—the servant who had left him, the one who had birthed the girl, nursed her to childhood, and then died.

And with the final rend of the final syllable of her name, the shadows of the trees parted and the woman came toward him, white shimmering gown, her hair pulled back in a moonlit weave. "Have you finally come for me, Andaya? To release me from the prison of my life? To make right what was always wrong between us?"

"Oh, don't be a fool," the voice said, the clatter of its tones nothing like what he'd expected. "You've gone and eaten too many mushrooms and now look at yourself."

THE OLD MAN looked down to his stitch of animal skin rags, to the weathered, wrinkled hands and age-pocked skin, to the sweat that dripped from every pore, soaking his thin hair.

The woman poured a tonic into his mouth—a different tea. When she did, the sludge in his belly seemed to thin. When he opened his eyes, the night was no longer lit by the moon and the trees had somehow closed around him.

In the darkness, he could see that the woman's hair hung gray, not white, over her shoulder, that her dress was a dingy yellow, her laugh a mocking sound. And those eyes. One brown as the dead leaves he'd crumbled into his own tonic. And one bright and living as the green buds that hung from the trees.

"The next few days will not be nice," she said.

He noted that his own kettle now swung from a rope at her waist.

"But you'll get through." She laughed, the tones grating against his bones. "One thing you'll always do is get through."

THE NEXT FEW days were *not* nice.

For every ounce of vomit and fluid he lost, she plied him full of a variety of homemade teas—some sweet and soft, most bitter and strong. "We've got to work it out of you," she'd said.

"Why?" he'd asked. "I wish to die."

"Oh, no sort of mushroom can do that for *you*," she said. "Not anymore. Death, my king, is a privilege of the fully living. And you had that honor taken from you when Sadora altered your course. Or rather, when you altered it, by using the Pallium to try to heal yourself. You're just lucky it turned out as well as it did."

"I used to wish to live forever," the king murmured.

"Of course," the girl said. "And that is why you are here now. Those wishes, some of them survive. Perverse really, the way they turn on us."

She was not old as he, though she was—just a little bit—older than she had been. "How are you not dead?" he asked. "How are you still young?"

"I suppose that's a bit of a gift from you," she said. "My werewolf father, my human mother. Winding me up into an odd sort of girl."

"But you do age," he'd said.

"Quite slowly," she said. "As the shifters of times long past. My body—unusual as it was—was not altered with the changing of the suns. One day I will die, but that day is far, far away." When she said it, he heard a touch of sadness in the words, a sadness that he felt reflected in his own heart.

"You also wish to die?" he asked.

"Not exactly," she replied. "But it is difficult to keep living when no one else does, now isn't it?"

"The purest form of torture."

"Dramatic," she said. "But it *does* get lonely."

"It is not dramatic when you have decayed as I have, but continue to live. You at least have your youth," he said.

She cocked her head to the side, regarding him. "I have the life I built for myself. As do you."

He growled at the words, at her impudent pride. Same as always.

"And how are you feeling today, King?"

"Do not call me that."

"Then what would you have me call you? 'Father' still doesn't really seem to fit, does it?"

It did not.

"Call me my name, girl. That will do."

"Very well," Zinnegael answered. "But in that case, you must also call me mine."

He had never let the syllables of the child's name leave his lips. But now, in the hunger to hear the tones of his own name, he nodded, working out the sounds with his parched mouth.

BY THE END of his fourth day, his stomach had cleared, though he could barely sit up to eat.

The girl, Zinnegael, fed him with a spoon dipped into honey and grains. It tasted better than anything he remembered eating. When she left to tend to her garden, a gray cat came to sit with him. No, he reminded himself. Not to sit with, but to stand by—to guard him. Though this particular cat was quite young, with a little burst of white on her chest. "And what is your name?" he grumbled, taking the steaming cup of tea the girl had left, his hand shaking. "I suppose you've got one."

"And why wouldn't I?" the cat answered.

"Well then?"

"*The name your child has given to me,*

The counterpoint to harmony," she answered in a rhyme.

"We're doing riddles now, are we?"

"My mistress said it would be good for your mind."

"Your mistress would drive me to madness," the once-king answered.

"Do you not know the term?" the cat asked. "It is a simple one in musical theory."

"Do you know how many years it has been since I heard music?"

"Music is all around you," the cat answered, adding another rhyme.

"*In every song the morning brings,*

Of beast and purr and wind against wings."

"The counterpoint to harmony?" Crespin grumbled, and the cat seemed to nod, as though to encourage him.

"Melody, I suppose," Crespin said. "The main line of the song."

"You needn't call it 'main,'" the cat replied. "It is but one of many lines."

"It is the most important one," the once-king answered, "and there is no use denying it."

"It is lonely on its own," the cat said. "And fuller with others. More beautiful."

"So it is," the king murmured, wondering if the riddle had been about more than the cat's name.

And with that, the small cat curled next to him, warm at his side, the hum of her own voice vibrating in a way that caused his eyelids to grow heavy, his breath to come deep and warm.

～

From that point on, the king returned every few months, sometimes bringing the girl, Zinnegael (the name still felt rough against his throat), thistles for her teas or milkweed for medicines.

She never thanked him exactly, but at every visit had just happened to prepare a batch of muffins or pan of cookies, which she then coated with honey or a wild berry syrup.

He never bade her goodbye and she never asked when, or if, he would return. Though a few times, the cat, Melody, followed him into the woods and remained with him for several days. Often the creature would drag a fat pigeon or rabbit to him, and together they would eat—he from the cooked flesh; the cat from the raw.

After nearly a year, when the sun rose softer, leaving a chill in the air, he returned to the wood. "My bones ache," he said to Zinnegael. "Ache like they should break."

"I've several teas that will help with that," the girl answered.

He grunted. "They'll hardly help in the way I want them to."

"And what way is that?" she asked.

"Do you not wish to die?" Crespin asked yet again.

"Perhaps one day," she replied. "When it is my time."

"And what will make it your time?"

"I'm not quite sure," she answered. "Though I trust when it comes I'll know."

"Well I know now," Crespin said. "And now is my time. But the woman Sadora cursed me to live on past that time. So what now? Do you have a tea that will fix that?"

Zinnegael raised the eyebrow over her green eye. "*The woman, Sadora*, became your daughter-in-law, brought two sons and a daughter forth from her union with your son. Did you never wish to know them?"

"I don't see how it matters if I did or not," he responded.

"And that, good Crespin, is exactly your problem."

"I do not see anything exact about it," he replied.

"Your problem is that you don't know what you want," Zinnegael said.

"Of course I know what I want," he responded. "I want to die."

"And what did you want before that?" she asked. "When you were king?"

"I wanted immortality," the king said. "But the immortality of a god, not a skeleton."

"Is that really what you wanted?" Zinnegael asked. "No wonder you're here. Did you not wish for love or companionship, for your sons to grow old and bring you children, for your life to be filled with laughter and love?"

"Loerwoei was gone," he answered. "That made it hard to think on those things."

"Even before your wife was gone, you struggled to know what you wanted. If you'd only cared for your wife and only wanted her to live, then you would not have formed a union with any other woman, and I would not be standing here right now."

The king grunted in a way that would have been a growl if he still had his wolken form.

"A piece of advice, my dear Crespin. Figure out what you want, why you want it, and what will happen if you get it. Figure it out before another eon rolls away with you stuck in the bones and wishes of a man who never bothered to think about what might actually make a life that was worth having."

It was just why he'd never come to her before—the know-it-all of a girl. Find worth in a half-baked life, in the body that was collapsing beneath him but wouldn't let him go, in his mind that swirled around and around about what might have been—that mind lighting upon a thought.

The stone, the stone of source.

Perhaps nothing natural in this world could kill him, but there was one thing that certainly could.

Turning in the direction of the nearest gate, he made his way toward the city. He would camp there overnight, would watch for the merchants who came and went. Inquire about those who had survived, the children of the lord of the Grey, the shifter who had taken this land and turned it on its head. Ask what had become of the thing that could save a Greylord and kill everyone else.

His mind scrabbled to find the name of the child—his own child—the one who had usurped his kingdom. Had it been so long that he had forgotten?

Wittendon.

He hadn't thought the name for so long, not since he'd watched from his hiding place in the woods as his son's dead body had tipped over the falls and to its final rest.

His daughter-in-law, on the other hand—Sadora. That name he remembered, for he cursed her every morning, in the way that some men prayed. But his own son had nearly slipped from his mind—the sounds and syllables of his name becoming foreign, almost lost.

He dipped into his memory, saw Wittendon as a child, and Kaxon so much stronger. But also more impulsive. The thing that had destroyed him. Destroyed him, but perhaps saved him too. Kaxon had also sacrificed himself for the woman—the hateful woman.

She'd taken down his entire family—seducing Wittendon into loving her, tricking Kaxon into saving her, and then ruining him, Crespin, in his own box at the tournament.

Crespin took a moment to curse the woman again, but underneath the curse, he still felt the name of his son, and thought on the words of Zinnegael.

Wittendon had had two sons. How long ago must it have been now? Decades, perhaps even centuries. Easy to lose track of time when it did not kill you. Those sons would have had their own sons, perhaps daughters.

Would they be purebred? Would they even be shifters? His blood boiled at the thought—the thought of his own grandchildren being anything less than the power that he had once fed.

And in that thought, his legs grew weak. He sat with a plunk.

He had nothing to eat except for the kettle-flask of tea and a small cake the girl had insisted he bring. No sugar or honey on this one, but a solid, stiff crumb that wouldn't break in travels.

He ate it, and slept.

IN THE MORNING his body flashed awake with the sense of another creature touching him—perhaps his Loerwoei waking him for breakfast. After all, the hands—yes, they were hands, not paws—were nimble and soft, feeling their way across his tunic, plunging deep into his pockets.

He sat up with a jolt, whipping his staff around. In a quick movement, he knocked the young thief on the head, so that the youth fell sideways.

Crespin stood, walking toward him, ready to strike another blow.

"Leave off, you old man," the boy said. His face was full of young scruff, like a mangy wolf. "You've not got anything worth taking anyway."

Crespin lowered his head to the fallen boy's level. He smiled, showing teeth that had long decayed, some half broken so that they looked again like fangs. "Lucky for me, you do."

He helped himself to the young man's money sack, and the boy kicked out at him.

Without thinking, Crespin stepped to the side, then he struck the young man across the back with his staff, pulling at a sleeve of the youth's coat. With a quick turn, the coat came off and Crespin saw that the boy was not wearing a shirt underneath.

"You're nothing more than a bag of bones," Crespin sneered.

"And you're even less than that," the young man answered, facing him, ready to pounce.

Not ready enough.

Crespin blocked him with a flick of his staff, tripping him almost at his first step. It was then that Crespin caught sight of the bare back, and the large mark that stretched along his left shoulder.

Much had changed since his reign, but it seemed that some things hadn't. "A prison rat, are you?" Crespin said, circling around him. "And a dangerous one."

"You've gone senile."

"I see it on your shoulder, boy. The marking. Turning you in would be worth four times the sum of the money in this bag."

The young man lunged at him, but Crespin whirled away. He might be a crumbling bag of bones and aching joints, but he had spent nearly a millennium fighting as a king. He could move his way around a prison rat.

"I'll kill you first," the young man said, spittle flying from the edges of his mouth.

"Yes, you're doing quite well with that," Crespin replied.

The boy gritted his teeth. "You can keep the coat, but I need the money back."

With a firm whack, Crespin swung his staff against the backs of the boy's knees. The youth crumpled to the ground, moaning.

"Other old men's money?" Crespin said.

The boy did not deny it, though he got up on his hands and knees, wobbly still, but trying to make another go for the money sack.

"And why would I let you keep it?" Crespin said, lifting his staff over the boy's head. With a swift enough movement, he might be able to bring it down and crush the boy's skull. He wasn't sure if he still had the strength, though looking at the young man, he could tell that the boy wasn't sure either.

"It's for my mother," he said quickly.

"Your mother," Crespin answered, lowering the staff, while still holding it firmly in front of him. "Well, if that's not the sweetest lie I ever heard."

"It's not a lie, good sir," the boy said, swallowing his spittle and sitting up.

"I am neither good, nor one to be called 'sir,'" Crespin responded. "As well you know."

"She is ill." The boy rocked back, watching Crespin.

"Of course she is," Crespin replied. "How else would the story go? And why, may I ask, is she ill?"

"Why is anyone ill?" the boy replied. "She has grown old."

"How old?" Crespin asked.

The boy seemed to count in his head. "I've lost the number, but a good fifty years beyond my own."

"That *is* old to have a child, at least since the sun shift," Crespin said. "Go on. I always enjoy a good tale." Crespin pulled the kettle from his belt and took a swig of tea. The child stared.

"She did not have me by birth, but took me in when I was young and roaming the streets."

"It looks as though you've repaid her well for her kindness," Crespin said, waving his staff to the boy's shoulder marking.

"That was not my fault. In some sectors the streets grow wild. I was accused unjustly."

"Hmmm, like now?" Crespin answered. "And here I thought the humans were the superior race," Crespin clucked. "Not common thieves."

The boy looked at him, narrowing his eyes, eyes that yellowed slightly at the edges with pus. "And how do you know I'm human?"

"Oh, but an old man like me does forget. I suppose now we must wait for the moon to show me your true nature, and all that. But do you know what, boy? You *smell* human." He smacked his lips on the words.

The youth tipped his body away. "Well, you smell like a rotting sack of flesh, old man. "

"A correct assessment," Crespin replied, tucking the bag of money into his cloak.

"I need it," the boy said, sitting crookedly and favoring the side that Crespin had hit.

"Oh, I know. That's why I have a little task for you." He tossed the jacket back to the boy.

"What do you want?" the boy asked, his eyes flitting to the lump of money under Crespin's cloak.

"Well, since you enjoy a tall tale, I thought you could do a little research. There is something I want to know."

It took three sun cycles.

Crespin heard the boy on the third morning. The child was still far off, but he had a distinct step, one leg dragging slightly after the other. A step that would have sounded guilty even if it wasn't. And one that usually was.

The young man stopped at several points nearby, and the once-king listened—eyes closed, chest rising and falling as though still asleep. He noted the number of steps between each point, and the closeness of the boy's noises. The youth had set two traps.

Under his cloak, Crespin held his staff, waiting for the boy's guilty shuffle to approach. When he was near, Crespin rolled to the side, as though just waking.

"The stone is lost," the boy said, flopping onto the ground in front of him.

Crespin worked his way up, nursing his old bones. For that part, he did not need to pretend. In fact, this morning, with the boy so close, he felt even weaker than usual.

"Vanished generations ago," the boy said.

"Lost?" Crespin asked, running his hands through a bit of grass and then dusting them off into an old handkerchief. "And this determined in three turns of the sun. I think perhaps that you have not looked very hard."

"The stone was taken by a human, then sought by the sons of the Greylord, then lost again, or perhaps never found. The records are unclear."

"Records?" Crespin asked.

"What did you expect me to do?" the boy replied. "Find a cat and demand a prophecy?"

Crespin turned to the prior night's fire, one he had shared with the little cat Melody when she'd come bringing two fat, dead squirrels.

He blew the embers into a few thin flames, while the boy watched the fire carefully.

"I expected you to find information on a stone, just as I asked."

"I gave you information," the boy said.

"So you did," Crespin replied, dropping a match and a few pieces of dried dung into the struggling fire.

The boy grimaced with disgust at the smell, then glanced quickly at the ground around Crespin.

Crespin added sticks, watching the boy through the flicker of light and smoke.

"I got a squirrel last night," Crespin said, gesturing to the carcass where flies were gathering, ready for their own breakfast. "Two actually, but I already ate the first."

The boy didn't move.

"Suit yourself," Crespin said, swatting the flies away and sliding the corpse expertly along a spit he'd made from a green stick. "Now I must admit that when I asked for information on a stone, I'd hoped you would do more than waltz into your quarter's library and inquire of the elderly woman at the front."

"I had no need to inquire," the boy responded. "All know the stone is lost."

"Except he who keeps the lost." Crespin said, turning the spit. "Do you mean to tell me that in all your unsavory circles of prison brethren and sisters, you've not got a single tip from a single dark market about its whereabouts?"

"I told you I was falsely accused. I don't run in dark circles." As the boy said it, he fingered something tucked into his palm.

"Well, if only I'd nearly had my pockets picked by a librarian, we could have skipped the middle man." Crespin patted the pouch of money he'd positioned beside him. "Unfortunately, with only this much information—information that, by your own admission, "all" know—we can't do business at this time."

Crespin plucked the hot squirrel from the spit and began to eat, waving the boy away.

The boy didn't move.

Crespin started with the head, swallowing the chewiest bits slowly.

"I did know someone," the young man said, watching the bag of coins instead of Crespin's breakfast. "Someone known for knowing the unknown."

"And how did he come into this...knowledge?"

"Because it was his job to kill those with information."

"And was he good at his job?" Crespin asked.

"Very," the boy said.

"Hmm. Better than others are at their jobs, it seems." Crespin set the squirrel down and flicked a small coin from the bag to the boy. It landed with a puff in the dry dirt, and the child placed a palm over it.

"This prison mate," the boy said. "He was sent to find the great-grandchild of Councilman Wittendon—he who protected the stone."

"And did this man succeed? In killing the royal grandchild."

"Not exactly," the boy said. "But there was this human girl, a girl whom the shifter protected."

"And your prison mate—this knower of things unknown—he killed her instead?" Crespin asked, tossing another coin, which the boy caught.

"Oh no, sir."

"What did he do then?"

"Married her."

Another coin.

A stiff breeze blew through the air, rustling his clothes and stirring the fire.

"And *then* he killed the great-grandson of Wittendon," the boy said. "Being a little jealous and all."

Against his will, Crespin felt his throat go tight at the news. He tore at a bit of grass, which then tumbled away. "A dramatic story."

"But the girl didn't like that, the killing of the shifter—complicated, it was. So she goes and turns in my prison mate."

"Complicated indeed," Crespin said, noticing the scent on the wind. "And where is the girl now?"

"Protecting the stone."

"How convenient. And where might that be?"

"Nowhere, sir. See, that's the thing. She up and vanished, and her little baby too." With each 's' a bit of phlegm flew from the youth's mouth.

"Her baby?" Crespin asked. "What *kind* of jealousy caused the death of Wittendon's great-grandson?"

"A complicated kind," the boy said. "That's why I don't pay it no mind. But, like I said, the stone is lost."

"And like I said, 'except to those who keep the lost,'" Crespin replied.

The breeze blew again and the boy cast a quick glance at the ground.

"Tell me," Crespin said, taking a deep breath. "Besides this unlucky great-grandchild of Wittendon, do any other of his progeny live on?"

"But surely you know," the boy responded. "That's the type of information people don't have to pay for."

Crespin tossed him another coin. "Humor an old man. Did I not tell you that there was more than a shoulder scratch keeping me out of these walls?"

"The great Wittendon wed the mighty Sadora," the young man replied, as though it was the most boring story ever.

Crespin spat when he heard Sadora's name, but the boy didn't even pause.

"From these came two sons—both mighty, and in the way of siblings often at war with each other."

Crespin leaned forward slightly, sure not to miss a word.

"Both sought the stone to be used in their own ways. Both claimed his way to be the best. And both lost the stone in the end."

"To a human," Crespin said.

"Some would say that the humans are the only ones that could hold such a thing anyway." He licked his chapped lips.

"Some would say that," Crespin replied. "Only if they had not met a Lord of the Grey. Do none remain?"

"In myth, if not in blood."

"An unsatisfactory answer," Crespin responded.

"How could they be located with the mines sealed up and the Grey all gone?" The breeze had died down and the air sat hot and still around them.

"How indeed?" Crespin answered. "And with the mighty stone lost to all."

"That's okay," the boy said, the sunlight dancing on his face like he was a demon. "'Cause I won't be needing the stone now. And you neither."

"Is that so?" Crespin asked, gripping his staff lightly, and waiting for the flick of the thing in the child's palm. It did not take long. With a quick strike, the match in the boy's hand lit, and the flame fell to the grass. The thin line near Crespin's feet ignited, forming a circle around him.

"Canningum powder," Crespin said. "Quite clever. Heavy until ignited, when it expands and lightens, spreading." As he said it, the line of powder seemed to widen and grow, the flames leaping up as tall as his shoulders, the circle where he stood narrowing.

"It's not a fire that blisters," the boy said.

Crespin looked at the black smoke. "No. It's a fire that chokes."

"You're smarter than I thought, old man," the boy said. "A fire that chokes until people talk. You wanted information from me. Now

I want something from you. Something more valuable than a bag of old coins."

"That's unfortunate," Crespin said. "Since I left them for you." He nodded to the purse of coins right by the boy's leg. Then set his dusty handkerchief on fire and tossed it toward the sack.

"Coins don't choke," the boy said.

"But children do," Crespin responded as the bag burst, throwing the boy back. Granules of the powder settled along his pants and in the crevices of his jacket, crackling and smoking as they ignited.

"I'm not a child," the boy said, trying unsuccessfully to dust the flames away, before ripping a satchel from off his neck and tearing it open. When he did, a delicate white powder flowed around him until the heat caught it and it fell, suffocating the flames.

Crespin jabbed his staff through the fiery cage, sweeping the remainder of the white dust toward him. "The antidotal powder. Opposite in every way from canningum," Crespin said. "Light until ignited, when it becomes heavy and dampens the fire, clearing the smoke."

Crespin stepped through the now-ashen opening he'd created. "Now, child of Pietre," he said, looking at the boy who stood charred in front of him, his shoulder marking glistening with sweat, "Why did you really go to prison?"

"Because I seek treasure," the boy answered, a wild light in his eyes, as he fingered the long line of something sewn into his jacket. "And sometimes I find it." He removed a dagger from his cloak. "Just a little paint on the tip—that's all it has."

Even though Crespin had known it was there—even though he'd felt its drain on him since the boy sat down—Crespin felt his blood go cold.

"But it's not worth the half that you will be when I bring you to the head city."

"Ah, but you are a human—the race has hardly changed since my time."

"I thought it was a myth. We all did," the youth said.

"And how do you plan to prove them wrong—with this ragged man you drag from the woods?"

"Most ragged men have secrets. Now tell me where she is?"

For the first time that morning, Crespin was caught off guard. "She?" he asked, confused.

"The tea drinker. The prophecy giver—you old fool. I found a sachet of her medicine in your pockets on that very first day. Her head is worth thousands of pieces of gold in some circles."

Crespin tipped his chin back and laughed. "And here I thought you were after a king," he said, looking at the Grey-tipped dagger the boy had stolen.

"A king?" the boy asked, confused.

"Of course," Crespin answered. "Can't you tell? Can't you see it in my eyes, my royal posture, the square of my shoulders, the sharp of my teeth?"

"You could barely remember the name of Councilman Wittendon," the young man said.

"And to think I would have called him 'prince,'" Crespin responded, watching the young man as he circled with the dagger. Crespin could still feel it draw from his strength, even after so much had changed.

"Where is she?" the boy asked, waving the dagger closer to Crespin.

"*You* could kill me," Crespin murmured, his eyes following the Grey tip of the dagger.

"I won't have to if you tell me where the witch hides," the boy replied.

"I wouldn't even need the stone," Crespin muttered. "A deep enough wound to the heart with the Grey." He dove toward the boy, who leapt back, whipping the dagger away and looking at Crespin as though he'd gone mad.

"She's put a spell on you. Any who try to find her seek their own deaths instead."

"Oh, don't be ridiculous, you idiot of a child. I've had more than a spell torturing me for centuries."

"You're not the only one who is tortured," the boy replied.

Crespin noticed the froth at the corners of his mouth, the gray pallor of his fingernails, the crusting pinks of his eyes. "The seeping sickness," he said. "But how? It was all but eradicated hundreds of years ago."

"The hovels feed it," the boy said.

"So it is not your mother who needed help?" Crespin replied, leaping again toward the boy, trying to pierce his own heart with the dagger.

"My mother is dead," the boy spat. "She gave me this disease and I watched her crumble to dust and slime at its touch."

"Yes," Crespin replied, stepping toward the boy, trying to see into his eyes. "That is what it does. Dries the skin, plumps the organs. Eventually they rupture, spilling from the cracking skin. It is a disease that can be healed with exposure—" He stopped. With exposure to the *moonburst*. The time of day when the two moons hung across from each other, bringing in the night. A time of day that no longer existed.

"If you go to the witch girl, she could help you," Crespin said.

"I need her bones," the boy replied. "Everyone knows that ground to powder they can heal any wound."

"Everyone knows, eh?" Crespin murmured. He had never felt sorry for a human before, but found a slight pulse of pity in his chest. He pushed it aside, watching the tip of the Grey dagger.

The boy parried around him, looking for a place to stab him that would not kill. Crespin ran at him again, feeling already the weakness from the Grey, like his blood was thinning, his bones cracking. He managed to graze the tip, scratching his sagging bicep. It bled, and did not stop. For a moment, Crespin paused. Truly, it had been so long. He touched the blood, held up a finger.

"And more of that, if you don't tell me where she is," the boy replied.

"I won't tell you where she is," Crespin said. "You'll have to kill me."

The boy bared his teeth, spittle dripping from them, and ran at Crespin, aiming for his chest. It was then that Crespin noticed a different feeling—bold and icy. It came from his shoulder, the shoulder that had once been healed by a metal more powerful than the Grey.

Crespin frowned, whipping his shoulder away from the dagger.

"Tell me," the boy screamed, plowing a deep gash along Crespin's side.

"Beautiful," Crespin whispered, feeling his breath thin at the loss of blood.

The boy swung again at his shoulder and Crespin spun again away, not wanting his Pallium shoulder to resist the blade.

"Ah," the child said. "A weak spot."

"You hardly know what you say," Crespin answered.

"Tell me where she is," the boy growled. "Better yet, take her to me and I'll split the money with you."

"You'd split something," Crespin muttered, dodging another attempted stab at his shoulder. "Hit that shoulder and you'll regret it for the rest of your life."

"That won't be long if you don't tell me where she is," the boy said. "For you or for me."

"A better deal for one of us than the other," Crespin replied, trying to position his ribs to take the full force of the child's blow. If he could just puncture a lung.

It was then that Crespin spotted the tiny gray cat, the sun of white on her chest.

Melody watched from forest edge, as though she'd never seen a crazed human in her life. Daintily, she began walking toward them. Crespin willed her to go back.

She moved forward.

Crespin jumped in front of the boy, blocking his view of the cat.

"Take me to the witch," the boy said, his eyes fully bloodshot from the exertion of the fight.

"I can't," Crespin responded, trying not to glance at the cat. "She, I'm afraid, has become what all myths do. Extinct."

"You wish to keep her to yourself, now that you know her worth," the boy roared, stabbing the dagger toward Crespin's shoulder.

Crespin sprang back, remembering the thrust of a blade such as that into his shoulder all those centuries ago, remembering the weakness, the loss, and then the healing the Pallium had brought—a healing that had taken from him everything he thought he'd wanted. And more.

"The Tea Maker is dead," Crespin said. "I killed her myself."

"You didn't," the boy said, moving closer. Crespin felt the Grey from its tip, felt it in his skin, his bones, his throat.

"I made her," Crespin said. "And I destroyed her. It is the way of the world, is it not?"

"I need that money," the boy said, jabbing forward. "I need the medicine."

Crespin felt the wound in his shoulder burning, as though the Pallium were still there, pushing against the Grey.

"The witch is dead," Crespin said. "Kill me and take the medicine I have in my pocket. It's all that is left."

And then a different feeling—satin and soft. The cat wove between Crespin's legs, dropping a slip of paper at his feet. An envelope?

The boy stumbled back, his limbs flying in all directions as Melody delicately turned to him.

"*Foolish child,*" the cat said. "*A lack of mother has made you wild.*"

Crespin felt the hot blood in a stream from his side. Without thinking, he put a hand to it. "Step back, Melody. The boy is mad."

"*He is not the only one, to lose his sense before fight was won.*" She faced Crespin, looking disapprovingly at his wounds.

Crespin scooped her up as the boy dove forward, cackling wildly and holding his own side, as though his stomach was about to burst.

"I don't need you anymore, old man. This beast will lead me to the witch better than a mangy rat like you any day."

Melody looked around, licking her lips like she was in search of a rat, as the boy thrust the blade through Crespin's back, so that he dropped the cat, who landed expertly on her feet.

"Run back to your mistress," Crespin murmured, sinking to his knees. "I've gotten what I came for."

"*Alas, I have not,*" Melody replied. "*Organs burst and heart to rot.*" She pushed the little envelope in front of Crespin with a delicate white paw.

"I can't read it just now," Crespin replied.

"It's not for reading," she hissed, ceasing her rhyme, and nodding at the boy, just as he sprang at the cat.

Crespin blocked the boy with his body. "Leave the creature. She's brought a thing for you." Crespin nodded to the small envelope.

"Trying to keep the demon for yourself," the boy shrieked, plunging toward Crespin's chest, so that he could kill him and take the cat.

Crespin felt the ache of the shoulder, the deep, cold pulse of the old wound. He also felt Melody's danger—as she stood, so small and helpless, in front of the maddened boy.

The boy seemed to notice Crespin's gaze fall on the cat. Staggering, the boy switched direction, diving with his dagger toward Melody.

Crespin swore. There was only one way to save the cursed cat. And so, turning his shoulder toward the boy and his dagger, Crespin lunged in front of her.

"If you stop—" Crespin said, his voice hoarse from weakness, from loss of blood.

The boy laughed, driving the tip of Grey deep into Crespin's shoulder.

CRESPIN FELT the thrust as it threw the boy back—some remnant of the metal that had both saved him and destroyed him—the Pallium. A perverse metal, as it always had been. The boy fell back, his head striking a boulder, a small line of blood trickling from his ear.

"What?" he murmured. "What have you done?"

"I suppose," Crespin answered, feeling the remnant of Pallium course through his new injuries, healing them. "That I have saved one creature at the cost of another. Strange the ones we choose in the end."

Melody sat on her haunches, gazing at the boy with her head tipped to the side.

Crespin staggered to his feet. "I told you to leave my shoulder alone," he muttered to the boy.

The boy moaned, holding his head. "At least you have released me from it, the sickness. You wicked old man."

Crespin looked at his human-ish hands, his hairy arms. "Sleep, boy. And maybe if the gods find you they will teach you to recognize a king."

THE CAT HELPED Crespin cover the boy with his coat. He closed the child's eyes, and Melody dropped the packet of medicine on his chest. "*Perhaps someone will give this medicine use, if not this most unfortunate youth.*"

"Better to hide it," Crespin said. "If they know what your mistress can do, they'll never stop hunting her."

"My lady does not fear the hunts of men."

Crespin picked up the blade tipped in Grey. "I don't suppose that this will be of any use to me now?" he said.

"I suppose," the cat said, working on her rhyme, "*That the blade thrust into old wounds, No longer holds much gloom.*"

"You think the Pallium has disabled it."

"Likely destroyed," the cat replied. "As it does," she finished, looking at the boy.

"Yes," Crespin said, looking at the youth with a sense of sadness. "It takes from you that which you most wish to have."

"Though it always gives something in return," the cat replied.

"Something perverse," Crespin replied.

"Something revealing," the cat added. "You took pains to protect the location of my lady."

"I only wished to die. What better way than to anger the child?"

"Still, it was an odd choice you made at the end, wasn't it?" the cat said without looking at him. "I came to help you, you know," she added after a pause.

"Well, you didn't. You ruined my death."

The cat looked at him, like that was exactly what she meant by helping.

Crespin gathered his things, leaving the boy's money sack.

"*The fact remains...*" the little cat began, as though waiting.

Crespin finished for her, "*Spared by a metal that contains. Again.*"

"Admirable rhyme," the cat replied. "Except for the end bit. Now come. My lady has something to show you."

"Did you find it?" Zinnegael asked when he arrived in the clearing.

"Find what?"

"Something of worth," she answered.

"The stone?" he asked.

"Not at all," she answered. "Something of real worth. Something you give instead of receive."

"What would anyone who knows me wish to receive? The smelly rags off my back, the calluses of my feet, a bit of pheasant to chew as they walk?"

"I was not referring to an actual item," she said.

"Then what?" he rumbled at her. "What would I find? What would I give?"

"That is for you to figure out."

"Why? It is you who reads the tea," he shot back.

As he said it, her kettle whistled.

"You knew I was coming," he said.

"As you have so eloquently stated, it is I who reads the tea." She removed several leaves from jars. "Though in your case, I simply made an educated guess based on the absence of young Melody. And the, uh, smell as you say, of the rags on your back. They're quite pungent and give me the exact amount of warning I need to get the kettle on."

"I almost succeeded," Crespin said, the anger wearing into his voice.

"At what?" the witch asked.

"Dying," he answered.

"And at what did you actually succeed?"

Melody curled up at his feet, falling asleep with a paw against his foot. Zinnegael glanced down without comment.

"What must I give up to die?" Crespin asked.

She took a leaf with a stringent odor and crumbled it in her hand.

"Will that kill me?" he asked.

"Hardly," she answered, taking several dried pieces of fungi along with a flat black leaf that looked like it had molded.

"A brutal death in those leaves," he grumbled.

"Ah, you wish for it to be sweet."

"At this point, I simply wish for it to be."

"Do you?" she asked, pulling a few fresh sprigs of peppermint from an earthen pot. "Fresh leaves don't crumble nearly so well, but they will do."

"It smells foul all together," Crespin grumbled. "Even the sweet things are tainted by the odors of the other ingredients."

"So now you wish for prophecy to smell nice as well."

Prophecy. He stopped talking and simply watched. She poured the steaming water into an old dogwood mug, holding the kettle high above it, so the water cascaded in a steaming stream—so close to her skin he was surprised the steam did not burn her. The water in the cup swirled from the movement of the pouring, and into the swirling waters she dropped the crumbled and crushed herbs. He was surprised to find that it did not, in fact, smell foul, though it did not exactly smell sweet.

Another metaphor she undoubtedly wanted him to notice.

The steam drifted. The leaves rose and sank and spun. He held his breath, then let it out slowly. "Will my line live on?" he asked, after she was done.

"Shhh," she responded. "You'll disturb the waters."

When the steam was gone and the leaves had settled, the peppermint drifted lazy and green to the top, surrounded by flecks of black and brown. "Ah now," she said. "That *is* fitting."

"What is?" he asked. "When will I die?"

"One good deed," she said. "One truly good deed done not for you or for your kind. But for those whom you have despised. Those who will live on if you do the deed, and who will die if you do not."

"I've just done a good deed," he grumbled. "Or tried to."

"This must be done for those whom you truly despise," she clarified.

He cleared his throat, glancing away from Melody. "I must save my enemies?"

"Not just any enemy," she answered. "You must perform an act for the lines you most despise: the boy Pietre, the dog Humphrey, and the one who helps them—one whose blood flows with the kindness of the Lady Sadora."

"Then I will not."

"Won't you?" she said. "Because Sadora's bloodline is now mingled with your own. They cannot be separated."

Crespin bared his teeth.

"Without your help, the lines of Pietre and Humphrey will become extinct—the thing you've always wished—but also the thing that has cursed you to remain alive this long. With your help, they will thrive."

"You curse me in your prophecy, Tea Reader."

"I give you access to that which you wish."

"You give me access to nothing, because I will not help them to live when they deserve to die."

Zinnegael shrugged. "Your choice, my king."

He growled at the term.

"Crespin."

"This I will do, and this only. I will see that the line takes care, that it hides well enough to not be destroyed. But I will never, never save it if it is about to die."

"That is your choice," she responded. "But remember my words. One good deed."

GREY FLOWER

A (LONG) SHORT STORY

From the forest surrounding the head city, the wolves howled. From the southern belly of the city, shifters brawled while groups of humans and halflings placed bets on the outcomes. Further north, the wealthy hosted dinners and galas, sumptuous meats and sweet breads served in tiny golden bowls.

The moon shone like a lantern over the entire city—each star glittering around it like the swish of a ball gown.

Anjei felt the sway of it, the swagger of the people, the sashay of the sky, all from the safety of her small house at the outskirts, near gate eleven, where humans had once flooded the city at the final Motteral Mal.

Next to her sat a sand-yellow dog named Bo, and together they ate a traditional Moonface meal of round cakes with white butter and honey. Her uncle had begun encouraging Bo to eat in a spot away from the table because he said the animal made too much of a mess. In truth, Bo made quite a bit less mess than Uncle and, without the privilege of speech, could not speak with his mouth full either.

Anjei set another cake in front of Bo, not on the floor, but at the traditional spot at the table—to the right of the head. As Anjei watched him lap up his cake in one bite—not a single crumb dropped—she suspected Uncle's new thoughts about dogs and meals might have more to do with increasing his social standing than keeping crumbs off the table.

In some wealthy circles it had become quite popular to set a place for the dogs on the floor with the excuse that it was more comfortable for them there. But Bo seemed perfectly content standing at his spot beside her. At age sixteen, Anjei had begun to wonder why the races always sought to put one below the other— quite literally in the case of the dogs and their meals.

Anjei let a bit of the sweet butter melt on her tongue and watched Bo gaze at another cake. Clearly he wanted one, though she knew he considered barking loudly rude and would never do it. What torture to not be able to ask for what you wanted. She reached over and took one.

"Finish your first one," her mother chirped, almost automatically.

"It's for Bo," she replied, and her mother blinked like she hadn't thought of it. It's a wonder they'd been approved to house a dog at all, though as the years flew on, she'd heard her parents murmur about how the application process was getting easier. Fewer humans were willing to take on the expense and responsibility of their speechless friends, even if the dogs helped with hunting or other chores.

Personally, she thought Bo did more than his share of the work. He helped her father every fall with the hunting, pulled heavy sleds of food from the market in the winter, and—Anjei's favorite—always warmed her feet at night while she completed her studies.

Looking into his dark eyes on those nights, she knew that bit of service was of mutual benefit, and often she would read to him from her books.

She favored law, which her mother found intolerably dull and her uncle thought unprofitable. Her father, however, continuously bought her books from the thrift shops on the fringes of their sector.

Bo, she thought, from the sighs and snorts, particularly enjoyed history and she always read him her favorite parts.

On the night of Moonface when the shifters took to hiding or carousing, and the wolves gathered in the wood in their ritual of howling, she read Bo tales of the human Pietre and his dog Humphrey—their friendship and then governance together—Pietre's time lasting much longer than Humphrey's.

For, in addition to the lost speech, or maybe because of it, the lives of the dogs had shortened as well. Anjei had come into the world four generations after Pietre, while Bo was a full twelve removed from Humphrey. She knew Bo would not live even close to as long as most humans.

Already, at age ten, his muzzle had turned from blond to white. And this made their lost language seem even sadder. Because of this she had also taken to requesting various medical books, especially those that specialized in the health of the dogs.

Her mother had told her that Bo's age wasn't an ailment, and thus couldn't be healed. Her father had told her to enjoy the friendship for what it was. And Uncle, of course, had told her to be grateful that the dogs still had a place within the city walls at all.

Standing up from the table, Anjei removed her plate as well as Bo's. "I'll start the washing," she told her mother.

"Thank you, my love."

"And what will the dog do?" Uncle grumbled. "Finish off the cakes so no one else gets any more?"

But Bo had already begun trotting after Anjei into the washing room. While she did plates, he would carry linens to Mother's wash basket for cleaning. It was more than Uncle did.

Anjei ran water into the bucket, gazing at the bright yellow moon. "It's a different color every night, isn't it, Bo?"

He gave his response, a humming growl that Anjei had come to recognize as agreement. "And always a little different on Moonface.

Often yellow, but sometimes nearly white, and occasionally even pink."

Bo came to her side and together they gazed at the moon, fat above the wall of the city. But also fat above the woods, perhaps even across the sea in other lands. A hypnotizing thought. "Uncle says you are lucky to still be welcome in these walls," Anjei said. "But sometimes I think it's the walls that are the entire problem, and that you should be free."

Bo did not answer this time, and in his silence, she knew he wondered the same thing.

The next morning was best for shopping since prices always dropped slightly the day after Moonface. "Take Bo to the market," Mother said. "He can carry the bags over his back. I'll be needing flour and seedmeal, as well as several dried fruits and nuts. They're quite heavy."

"When do you need us back?" Anjei asked.

If the question surprised her mother, she didn't show it. "As long as you're here by sunset meal."

They took the long route to the market, walking the periphery of the wall, stopping at gate eleven, then beyond, all the way to gate one—ancient openings, now sealed off and replaced by modern gates and bridges—contraptions only the queen and her guard managed. A protection against the forest bears that had overpopulated since most of the humans had moved within the walls of the head city, or created other cities of their own.

And a protection against the wild man, the once-king, who roamed the woods, tearing at his clothes and screaming at the sun. The man who waited in the shadows, hair bound up in knots, for his next meal to wander past—whether rabbit or quail or wayward child. At least that's how the stories went.

Above them, a scream shook the skies. Anjei jumped just as a hawk screeched again and dove for something outside of the gates. She laughed. "And I thought I was too old to get spooked by stories," she murmured.

Bo pawed at the bronze statue that now blocked the old entrance —a seven-foot rendering of the brave Damian—the first human to come through the gate on the day the humans changed the sun, creating the free world. And there, behind the noble Damian's right leg, a bit of the old wood from the old gate had worn away. It looked almost as though the wood had been intentionally broken, some of the soil dug out.

"Perhaps we're not the only ones who feel trapped in the city walls," Anjei said, though she'd never heard of anyone leaving through an old gate.

Bo pushed against the remaining wood with his paw. More gave way.

Anjei looked at him. "We have till sunset meal."

Bo dug at the dirt, Anjei wiggling the loose boards above it.

A few minutes in the wilds—that's all they wanted—and a few minutes could not hurt.

It did not.

Except that afterward, Anjei found herself dreaming of it—the open spaces, the animal paths, the holes for rabbits and foxes, the berries and flowers and the smell of growth and decay bound up together. Dreams of freedom. Especially for Bo.

In her dreams, she led Bo through the woods to a strange place— a line of trees she couldn't pass. A place of words and tea and promises. And in the way of dreams, she somehow knew that beyond that line lay a clearing she'd read about in her history books, one inhabited by an ancient apothecary (some said a witch), who had once brought language to a few select dogs on a few select nights of the year.

Of course, most of the lead historians no longer believed such an area or person existed, and some questioned if she ever had.

Certainly, even if such a person had existed, she wouldn't anymore. At least that's what Anjei told herself every day upon waking from her dreams. After all, even in the dreams, the path always ended just before they got to the wood.

Once the dreams began, she tried to stay away from the exit (though she'd begun to think of it as an entrance), creating diversions for herself, tasks, extra studies.

Still, she found herself wandering through her sector, closer and closer to the gate with every passing day.

At the end of the second week, she stood in front of the statue, looking into Damian's bronze eyes. Bo stood beside her, but she had no way to know if he felt the same draw—the desperate pull toward the high white sun that called to her through the dense green trees, the smell of fresh dirt and weeds, the cool of the shadows contrasted by the heat of the clearings. He could not tell her if he did.

"We must not go through it," she said to Bo, though he was making no move in that direction. "What would Mother do?" she asked, her own feet stepping closer and closer to the opening, the exit-now-entrance. And then, somehow, she was out, just like in her dreams, wandering a path, hypnotized by the buzz of insects, the cooing of the birds, the ripples of water and wind.

Bo drew her back, pulling at the hem of her skirts, shaking her from the path, from the head fog that had taken her.

A head fog that persisted for days—beating against her skull in her sleep as her mother brought cool cloths to soothe her burning skin.

"It haunts me," she murmured to her mother who spooned broth between her lips while Bo draped wet rags over her feet.

"They are just fevered dreams, child—whatever you're seeing. They will flee when the heat does."

Except they didn't.

She knew the city could no longer hold her because she knew the city now as a thing that *kept.*

At the next Moonface, she heard her mother whispering to her father. "I fear since the fever that she has lost a part of her mind, and that if we are not careful a madness will take her."

"It's that dog," her uncle interjected. "The way she coddles and pampers it, as though it were human and not beast. Perhaps he should be removed to a place where others of his kind live."

"Hardly more than hovels for those who aren't fostered," her mother murmured. "We could never do that to her."

"Would you rather the madness took her?" Uncle asked.

And with those words, the madness did.

The next morning, she could not be found. Nor the next day, nor the next. The animal was missing too. Search parties roamed the city day after day, and none found the child or her companion. One did find the gate, fresh dirt filling an old hole, though he naturally assumed that to be the work of the gatekeepers. Perhaps if he had examined it a little closer he would have found a scrap of orange fabric caught on an uneven bit of wood.

The search continued for nearly two weeks, and the searchers grew weary. The child, they said, had likely fallen into a well, the animal following behind in an effort to save her.

The wailing drums beat for a day, and then their quarter fell into an hour of silence.

ANJEI, staggering through the woods miles away, felt that silence, that mourning—the lamentation for her lost soul. Felt it even though she could not hear it. For the woods grew quickly deep and windingly dark, slithering into her heart, gobbling her up piece by piece.

Beginning with her body.

She had not known which flowers or leaves to eat and which to avoid, and so had eaten nothing at all, only drinking at clear streams. At least for a few days.

But hunger is wilder even than the woods. And in time, she was swiping at berries, digging through thistles.

One night, when Bo dragged a rabbit to the clearing, she did not care that there was no fire or even some salt, she took pieces, and ate.

Bo consumed most of it, and that was for the best, because by morning a sickness had taken her—sickness of both stomach and bowel.

After that, the forest took her mind—her thoughts wandering the corridors between dream and reality, catching in wavy lines as she stumbled along after Bo, who brought her to water, who pushed her head into it, making her drink, even when she resisted, especially when she resisted.

The woods soon found her thin, ragged, and nearly dead. Bo, however, had caught a pattern through the trees, a pattern she followed with him. A pattern that wound from one ash-scarred patch of ground to another.

After days of this, when she felt she could not take another step, her mind finally cleared. She found in that clarity, the darkness of the night and the silence of her city sector. It brought peace. "I will die tonight, Bo," she told the dog. "You find the apothecary, the witch, and she will protect you."

She closed her eyes, feeling the cool of the earth under her back, the blanket of the sadness that stole into her mind. A blankness, like an ancient, unused scroll.

And then that scroll unfurled, the clouds peeling off the moon, the wolves taking up a howl, their voices far to the south, though one voice curled close—a voice like an old man's growl—ash and fire reaching up into its rumbling tones.

She blinked her eyes open. Moonface. The full moon gleaming so white as to be nearly blue, a christened child of a moon.

And from that moon, she heard another voice, soft, hissing. Were the angels now come to receive her?

My lady finds a bag of bones,
   To stitch together, then send home.

.   .   .

Anjei batted her eyes. Bo growled.

Follow *if you wish to live.*
   Or sleep and die, like sand through sieve.

And then Bo grabbed Anjei's collar with his teeth, pulling her along the hard ground until she stumbled to her feet.

One and a half more days she walked, Bo dragging her when she stumbled, endless rhymes tumbling through her head, sometimes studded with the low, gravelly voice of a man.

She woke to the smell of rosewater, felt the cool of it on her forehead. Dappled sun floated in emerald lines through the trees.

"I believe I've died," she said aloud.

"Should you be so lucky," a gruff voice muttered from a nearby table.

She leaned back into this place of seeming afterlife, and then a tongue licked her cheeks. "Bo, have you perished too?"

He lay his head against her stomach, those doleful eyes peering at her, always like they had something to say.

"No, I suppose not," she murmured. "But then, where are we?"

"In a witch's wood," the rough male voice answered.

"A witch who has not been disturbed for many a year," a young woman's voice added, the clink of a teacup hitting the saucer. "But now that he and Noley have brought you to me, I suppose something must be done."

The witch rose from her chair, and Anjei strained to see her, expecting a crooked old woman, bent from years of work. Instead, she was greeted by a wisp of a young adult, just a few years older than Anjei herself—bright skin, mismatched eyes, thin wiry hands. The only sign of age was the long gray hair draped over her shoulder in a tight weave that reached past her waist.

"Who has brought me?" Anjei asked

"One of my cats," the young woman said. "And someone else. Someone who is just leaving."

Anjei heard the scrape of a chair, the drag of a heavy body. "The girl cannot be rid of me so easily."

"Of course not," the woman murmured. "Why ever would someone want to be rid of such a ray of sunshine as yourself?"

"I will see you at the solstice," he replied, and then his feet stomped along the earth, pulling his body into the forest.

The woman turned to a large pot of water that boiled over a raging fire.

"Do you plan to eat me?" Anjei asked, looking at the long metal ladle the woman dipped into the liquid.

"Only if you are made of chocolate, child." And with those words, the woman set a small cup at Anjei's bedside. "Eat. Or drink, as it were. Until you have the strength for more."

Anjei took a sip and then a gulp. "I need a witch," she said.

"Don't we all?" the woman replied.

Anjei risked a longer stare. The woman moved like the branches of a willow—all limbs and hair. Her cheeks were bright patches of pink near lips that laughed without making sound. She could not possibly be the ancient Pietre's witch. "Unfortunately, it seems you're not the right one," Anjei said with a sigh.

"Unlikely," the witch replied.

"And why is that?" Anjei asked.

"Because I am the only witch."

"Then I suppose my witch has died."

"Perhaps she will simply never die," the woman replied. "For all practical purposes, at any rate."

"You are too young," Anjei replied.

"As are you," the woman answered. "To be out in the woods alone and lonely. Dangerous things roam here."

"I wasn't alone."

The dog wiggled his head under Anjei's arm.

"Those with such loyal friends never are," the witch said with a sigh. "Ah, but I do miss them. The boy. The dog. Now tell me why you've come."

"To set him free," Anjei said, sitting up and pointing to Bo. "Uncle spoke of returning him to the places meant for un-fostered dogs."

The witch dipped her head slightly in a nod.

"And by restoring his language," Anjei continued. "Which is a thing I've read that a witch such as yourself can do. I imagine that would make Bo more valuable to Uncle. Then we will have to keep him."

"Hmph," the witch replied. "Do not count on that flower before it blooms."

Anjei tipped her head to the side, regarding the witch. "Do you," Anjei asked, carefully, swirling her nearly empty cup, "have any more tea?"

"Of course I have more," the woman replied. "What type of witch would I be otherwise? Noley—get your tongue out of the cream. It's for our guest." The orange cat called Noley slunk away. "A naughty one, that. Now where were we? Oh yes, tea."

"And language," Anjei said.

"Impossible," the witch answered. "The dogs gave it freely, and it is gone."

"The books speak of others whom you have helped."

"What books?" the witch asked

Anjei did not answer immediately and the witch raised an eyebrow above her green eye. "Fairy stories, are they?"

"Not exactly," Anjei answered. "They just lack citation."

"Hmmm, I suppose they would," the witch grumbled. "And have you met any of these speaking dogs?"

"I have met but few dogs in general," Anjei replied. "You must foster them, or they live in hostels."

"I see," the witch murmured. "And so the world turns."

"It is unfair," Anjei snapped. "The least greedy of all the races. Why should they suffer most?"

"Their sacrifice was not meant to be fair. That is not, in fact, what the word 'sacrifice' means at all."

"They hunger for words," the girl said.

"Perhaps it is you who hungers for them," the witch said.

"Nonsense," Anjei responded.

"Is it? You have a connection with the animal, and ache for more. Regardless of what it might cost. Practically the definition of a human."

Anjei did not reply, stirring her tea and gazing into the golden liquid. "I feel shame in the way we treat them. And I feel shame in the loss of it, their language."

"It was freely given," the witch repeated, though her voice was softer.

"And freely taken," Anjei sighed.

"Not exactly true. You do your forefathers a disservice. It is true that the dogs often gave while the inclination of the humans to take has grown in recent years. Think on that, child, before you make a request of an old witch. As the privilege of the humans grows, so does their hunger for more. Is it your great privilege that now makes you wish for the animal to speak? Or your true love for him and his needs? After all, an animal with an ability to speak might find himself hunted by those who, these days, consider such things unnatural."

Anjei had no response.

"Noley, the cream!" the witch scolded.

Bo placed a paw on Anjei's arm, then settled his body against her as the light faded from the trees.

"Think on it," the witch repeated.

Anjei nodded, then looked into the black eyes of the creature who'd been her closest companion since childhood. They nuzzled closer together and—to the buzz of the night insects and the groan of the wind—fell into a deep sleep.

～

IN THE MORNING the table was set with biscuits and a variety of butters flavored with fruit and honey. A rosemint tea steamed from the pot.

"Eat, child," the witch said. "For this morning, you must depart."

"I will not depart until I get the thing I came for," Anjei said.

"Well now, that's just bad manners," the witch replied.

"Please," Anjei said, buttering a biscuit and adding a mound of fat red berries. She handed it to the witch. "Consider it. I know it's been done before."

"And did it benefit the dogs?"

"I cannot know," Anjei replied.

"Then ask the dog," the woman said. "If you want him to speak so badly, look into his eyes and ask him if language is something he needs to have."

Anjei felt suddenly afraid to look at Bo. Perhaps the witch was right. Perhaps she'd dragged both of them here because of her own selfishness.

Fortunately, at just that moment Bo answered for her. Or at least, he put his forepaws on the table, looked the witch in the eyes, and barked.

Anjei had to smile. He looked almost like a human defending a friend.

"Very well," the witch said, looking from Bo to Anjei. "If that is how you will have things. But it is very difficult. More so than it was in the early days. Many years ago the moonflowers bloomed along almost every path, opening on the night when the moons hung high. Now the bloom has become rare, opening only once every year."

"When?" Anjei asked.

It was the orange cat, Noley, who answered.

"When the time comes to leave your room.

The flower you seek opens to longest moon."

"The longest moon?" Anjei asked.

"Several months hence. There is no room for error," the witch replied, standing and motioning for her to do so as well.

"Can you give me an exact date then?" Anjei asked, as the woman pressed her toward the edge of the clearing.

"Do not tell any that you come here," the witch said, ignoring her question. "Except for those you most trust."

"A simple request, for I do not trust any."

"An interesting quality in a girl. And useful. You can follow Noley back to the city."

And with those words, the woods seemed to close in a curtain behind them, a path to the south opening up. The cat Noley pranced ahead, sniffing occasionally at mint grasses, her tail in the air.

WHEN ANJEI RETURNED to her sector, the bells rang out, all the races dancing in the street, her parents weeping. Even Uncle smiled.

"What happened, Anjei?" her mother asked.

And, not willing to break her mother's heart, she replied, "The fever took me, and I wandered, lost outside the gates."

Her mother clutched her heart.

"But Bo came after me, found me," she added quickly. "And brought me back as soon as he could."

Her father placed a hand on the dog's head. "We shall not lose you again," he said, looking at his daughter.

"Of course," Anjei replied, looking nervously into his eyes—eyes that saw more than her mother's.

"Definitely not," her uncle added. His eyes were the most alarming of all, for he saw much, but only what he wanted to see.

THAT NIGHT her room was locked, the house boarded.

"Are we now prisoners?" she asked her mother.

"Prisoners?" her mother answered. "In our own house. How could you say such a thing?"

"Mother," Anjei said.

And her mother must have heard it, the threat of escape in her tone. "Your uncle suggested this precaution. Your papa and I—we weren't sure what else to do. What if you wandered again? For the woods hold horrors you cannot comprehend."

"And miracles," she said.

"Only to a fevered mind," her mother replied, preparing the beans for evening meal. "Now come help your old mother."

Anjei obeyed, snapping ends off the vegetables and wondering which of her mother's herbs might be added to cause sleep—the type of thing only a witch would know.

ONE NIGHT ROLLED into a week rolled into a month, rolled into four months. Beans, books, morning and evening cleaning. Little else. Bo grew thin, and then stiff, the white of his coat deepening so that it covered his entire snout and most of his legs.

"I must leave," she told her mother.

"Of course not, child. Such words."

"I must leave," she told her father. "Bo is tired, and my mind grows weak here."

"Stick to your studies, daughter. And you will do great things."

"When, Papa?"

"When the time for great things has come."

She nodded. "Yes," she said. "Yes, you are correct." Then, kissing him on the cheek, she made her way up the narrow stairs to Uncle's room.

She knocked three times before he answered, limping across the floorboards. "I will leave, Uncle. Or I'll grow mad. Perhaps *you* already have."

"This is how you speak to the uncle who only wishes to keep you alive."

"This is not living. And it is about to kill Bo." Her eyes flashed a look that matched his, and then his shoulders slumped.

"You do not know what you speak," he said with an edge to both voice and eyes. "I have no ill wish against that dog. But there are some..."

"Some what?" she asked.

"...If that dog had come back with language—and there were rumors, girl, spoken in whispers at the edges of the town—if he'd come back with language, the sector would have killed him."

"You lie," she said, her voice narrowing.

"They spoke of it while you were lost. Ask your father if you wish to know. We hear what you do not."

"But why would they wish to harm a dog, just because he could speak?" Anjei asked.

"Why do they wish to harm other men, who have power or skill they do not understand?" Uncle replied. "Fear, I suppose, of the thing they are not."

"But men can speak," Anjei said. "What do they lose in sharing it with the dogs?"

Uncle shrugged. "I only know that this was the talk in the pubs and eating houses when you were gone. Men have begun speaking as though dogs must find their place."

"Surely you know that is wrong, Uncle."

"Do I?" he asked.

"Surely," she repeated.

"Surely I know that a fever didn't lead you into the woods, not a normal one anyway. You'll stay in this house until you have grown. And by then I hope you have sense for grown things."

"By then I will, Uncle."

~

BUT NOT NOW.

For now, the days grew shorter, and with them her opportunity.

She had promised her uncle madness and madness was what she would deliver. It was easy, for every day her mind grew wilder.

First she pulled up the boards of her floor, stashing papers filled with nonsense under each. Then she broke her mother's dishes—one by one, though never in a rush of rage or passion—chipping away at them in secret until each one spidered with lines of disrepair and her mother wept, not knowing from whence the cracks had come.

After that it was her clothes—small tears that she pestered until they grew—always looking natural.

She clipped off bits of hair—her own, her mother's, her father's, even Bo's—all while they were asleep. Uncle had none to clip, so she snipped at his wily eyebrows. She found bugs, which she planted in the corners of her cupboard, the foot of her uncle's bed, spiders which she ushered out of corners and into the main house. And if they grew too many, she doused them with vinegar so that they died in droves along the floor and counters.

"The gods do not smile on us," her mother said.

"Perhaps we do not make enough of our own smiles," her father added, trying to lift the corners of his own mouth and cheer them.

"The gods have never smiled on humans," Uncle said.

Under their newest shifter queen, the city all around them grew rich, while they languished on broken furniture, eating molded bread off chipped plates.

"I only just set the bread to rise," her mother moaned. "How can it already be thick with mold?"

Because Anjei had been feeding and harvesting moist spores from the corners of her damp room.

Why she did it, she could not be sure. Perhaps she hoped that one day her uncle would finally thrust her from the house. Perhaps she prayed that something in the damage of her actions would wake them up. Perhaps she wished for her mother and father not to miss her when she finally found a way out. Or perhaps, perhaps the need to leave had driven her to true lunacy.

Lunacy.

Lunar.

She played with the word on her tongue, remembering all the fat moons of her life, and knowing that somehow, she needed to find one more.

PERHAPS HER ACTIONS would have continued until the entire family went mad if Bo had not fallen ill. His stiffness took a turn. Now he could barely mount the stairs for pain, barely stand at his spot at the table for the ache in his haunches.

"He grows old," her father said. "So it goes with their race."

"Only because the humans have ruined them," Anjei spat.

"Oh, sweet girl. I feel for your mourning."

"You feel nothing of my mourning." She tore from him, past Uncle, headed to her room, in the hope of finding webs and cloth worms in the trunk—something with which to sabotage her mother's kitchen or her uncle's bed.

"Stop, Anjei," Uncle said, trailing after her. "Dogs die."

"I will not stop," she said, turning sharply to face her uncle. "If he dies, I will as well."

"And kill your mother with you?" Uncle hissed.

"I know a place that can heal him."

"A place in your dreams," her uncle snapped.

"It feels that way now," she murmured.

"Then how will you get there?"

She folded her arms, face set in a sharp line. "Perhaps a madman will lead me."

"A plan only a madwoman would accept."

"Yes."

"If your mother dies of grief, it is on your head."

"She will not die. Nor I."

"Then go. And take your madness with you."

"I come back sane."

"See that you do," Uncle said. And with his words he stomped on the floor, flipping a loose board, so that one of the papers fluttered to her feet.

WHEN THE TIME *comes to leave your room.*
The flower you seek opens to longest moon.

LONGEST MOON. Shortest day. The winter solstice. Three days hence.

The last time it'd taken her a month to stagger into the witch's wood. Now she had only a few days. And that with Bo stiff and growing worse by the minute.

"Is it a thing we can do?" she asked the dog after Uncle had left. "Or have we lost already?"

Bo growled in answer—a throaty sound—a howl all his own. He knew a way.

BO STAGGERED on stiff legs from one ash pit to another throughout the woods—all of them burnt out, their fires long cold. His bones practically poked through the flesh—swollen at the joints, brittle everywhere else. Yet, for two days, he pushed on, tripping and limping and leading the way. Ash pit to ash pit.

"That's how you found the witch's wood," Anjei murmured. "The first time."

Bo did not answer, not even to look into her eyes.

At the last ash pit, they found not only a fire, but a scruffy man to go with it. He looked himself like the woods—covered in trees and twigs and bugs, though not smelling nearly so sweet. "So you've come back to die?" he asked.

Bo stepped forward, growling, his knees shaking from the stiff-sickness.

"Oh, *you* have," the old man said.

"Please, sir," Anjei said. "We're looking for the witch."

"It will cost you," he interrupted.

"How much?" she asked, opening a small purse.

The wild man laughed. "Oh, that's no good to me. I need a child."

Anjei stepped back, preparing to run. Bo stepped forward, preparing to fight.

"Two actually," the man continued. "One of your race, and one of his."

"What will you do with them?" Anjei asked.

"Do?" the man cackled. "I'll do what all old men always do with children."

Bo leaned back on his old haunches, ready to spring, his entire body shaking from the effort.

"Nothing at all," the man crowed. "For doing things with children is women's work. But when you're done and have grown old, and that mutt too, I need you to return, and tell me of the lines—yours, the ancient Pietre's. And his, the dog Humphrey's."

"And why do you need this?" Anjei asked.

"Quite a few questions for a girl whose dog is about to die."

Bo growled again and the man turned to him.

"If you must know," he said to the dog. "I ask it, because the witch tells me that one day I'll need to find them."

"You answered him?" Anjei said.

"It would have been rude not to," the wild man replied.

"But, I mean, you understood him?" Anjei said.

"Well of course I did. And you did too."

"Perhaps," Anjei said. "But not…"

"Not with words, you mean. The animals hear me yet," the wild man said. "Attuned to my call. And they smell me—my throne."

That was definitely not what Anjei smelled, though she didn't say so.

"And why do you need them?" she asked. "The lines of Pietre and Humphrey."

Again, the old man cackled. "It would be wonderful to kill them, for together they ruined my life. I'm told, however, that if I destroy them, they'll ruin my death as well. And it's been so long, so very long already." The madman gazed into the line of dark trees. "One day," he said. "One day it is prophesied that I will call away a great danger from them. And only then will I find peace."

"Well, there are many yet of those lines, so you needn't worry," Anjei replied.

"I need a promise," the old man said. "That you will not let them die—your line."

"An easy promise to give," she replied. "For why would I let my children and grandchildren die? I will do everything to protect them. My whole life long."

"Oh," the wild man said. "I shall need it to be longer than that. Many generations past."

"But how could I protect them past my own years?"

"That is your problem, not mine," the man said. "The dog has already sworn it to me—the last time you were here."

Anjei looked at Bo.

"He was quite concerned for your welfare when you were unwell."

"As I now am for him," Anjei said. "But what if I don't succeed?"

"Then your precious dogs will lose what little speech you have granted them."

"But how?" she asked.

"You think the witch is the only one with access to the moonflower?"

"With access to its power, yes," Anjei answered.

"She has power to give. And she does. But every point needs a counterpoint. The witch and I are a balance. And so I have power to take." He hooted madly. "The flowers will soon cease their blooming. Already they dwindle. You come for the final bloom, and the night grows old. The flower begins to close." As he said it, she saw that it was true. Through the woods, she noticed a dull light, pale in comparison to the flickers of his fire.

"I need a promise of you," he said. "If you wish to pass." He pulled out an old staff, a broken bit of sharp glass at its tip.

"I promise to do my best," Anjei said, stepping back.

"Promise more," he said.

"We all die," she said. "I can't promise that we won't."

"I can only hope that we all die. Now, promise it," the madman hissed.

Anjei shook her head, confused.

"The last bloom closes."

"You wish to die?" she asked.

"All wish it. They simply do not live long enough to realize it."

"I will protect the dogs—the line of Humphrey."

He waited.

"And my own line."

"Very good," he said. "Hide them—your children. And carefully."

With that, a howl took up from the East.

The wild man called back, his fire dying out as a shadow within the wood brightened—a dull light throbbing, like a candle flickering, about to go out.

Anjei raced toward the light, Bo staggering after her. The shadows of the trees shifted in front of them, drawing them in.

At the place of a cluster of downed trees, a small flower grew along an old trunk. Closing. Just like the madman had said.

"But one breath is all you'll need.

Of glowing bloom and soft moonbeam."

Noley stood near the flower, her mistress beside her.

"Come, child," the witch's young voice commanded.

They could barely see her in the shadows.

Anjei stepped forward. Bo attempted to follow, but stumbled over his arthritic forepaws, crumpling to the dirt, his breath heavy.

The flower continued to close, its light growing thinner.

"You must hurry, child."

Anjei bent, attempting to drag Bo, though his limbs seemed to have frozen in place, the final stage of the stiff-sickness.

"No," she murmured. "We're so close."

"I cannot pluck the flower and move it," the witch said. "He must be here."

Anjei attempted to lift Bo, though he was much too heavy. She attempted to drag him by the scruff of his neck like a mother would, but his old skin only pulled and threatened to tear. She shoved him from behind so that the roots dug into his fur.

Finally, she stopped, sitting beside him, hot tears burning at her eyes.

It might be possible to move him, but it would hurt him, rip him, break him. The dog looked into those eyes, then lay his snout on her lap as he had done every day for every year since she was six. Those sweet, black eyes.

Anjei rested a hand on his head and he settled in, his breath slowing, the flower fading. He shifted his head to the side and gazed at her—glad, it seemed, for the soft lap in these final moments.

Anjei moved him, made him comfortable, dusted the dirt and twigs from his fur. "Ah, friend," she said.

For these last months, her sight had been set only on leaving, on returning to the witch, on granting Bo speech and extended life—so that he could be like her, talk to her, live like her.

Perhaps the witch had been right. Perhaps that had been something more for her than it was for him. Perhaps even when he'd fought and worked for it, it had been because it was something he knew she wanted so badly—knowing without words in the way of the dogs. Working without words in the way of the dogs. To help her accomplish her goal. *Her* goal.

The tears spilled over now, hot lines along her cheeks. And Bo—even in those last moments, even as the final petal of the flower began to close, even as the beams of the moon narrowed—he reached up to lick the tears away.

She laughed, bending down, her cheek to his face just as a soft ray of moonbeam fell across them. A line of gray light that seemed to flow through their bodies on its path to the last light of the flower. "Oh, how I'll miss you when you're gone."

They took a deep breath together, the final scent of that final flower.

The flower closed—Anjei felt the brush of its petals—the moonbeam vanished, and Anjei laid Bo on the soft earth.

"You needn't miss him," the witch said. "For it is done." The witch turned away, an ornate staff in her hand that Anjei had not noticed before.

"Done?" Anjei asked, glancing down at Bo. He breathed steadily, his side rising and falling, his coat beautiful in the night. "He is not yet gone."

"Nor will he be," the witch said. "Not tonight. Not for many years to come. It is *done,*" she repeated.

Anjei looked to the closed flower as Bo sat up, stretching his legs, his back, then standing, turning a circle.

"You've healed him?" Anjei asked.

"Not I," the witch replied. "Or at least not I alone. The moon, the flower, and you—both of you—you giving up your biggest wish as your two hearts came together."

"Is it that simple?"

"The best things are," the witch replied. "But also not. You must keep your promise. Or many other things will be lost."

"So I'm told."

"It is a promise that will not be easy to keep," the witch said.

"I will keep it," Anjei said.

"I know," the witch replied. "Or the king-grown-old would have killed you."

Anjei gazed at Bo. She could see now that he looked a decade younger—his fur soft and golden, his back muscled and strong. Straight, sleek snout, shining nails and white teeth. "You're so handsome," Anjei said. "Young again."

"I am whole," the dog responded, and when he did, Anjei buried her face in his fur, weeping.

The witch stood in the shadows, her dress and hair gray with the remaining moonlight. "His youth will remain, as least as long as it did with the dogs of bygone days. But his voice—"

"Only at moon's full light," Anjei finished for her.

"Yes," the witch said, looking into Bo's dark eyes.

"It is enough," Anjei replied, pulling away from Bo to look at the witch. "Thank you."

"Do not thank me yet," the witch replied.

"I will thank you," the girl said stubbornly. "Today and always."

"And I as well," the dog added.

For the first time, the witch smiled, a few lines forming at the edges of her eyes as though she had aged when Bo grew young. Anjei found that beautiful too.

ANJEI WALKED THROUGH THE GRASS, her dearest friend beside her, both of them surrounded by the soft blue of near morning.

For the last few hours of the night, she and Bo had talked in the woods, the pain in his jaw and limbs gone.

Together, they'd walked from the shadows that had swallowed the witch, from the flower that had shriveled into a papery husk. Now the light of the moon dripped toward the horizon.

Neither of them could know, would know, what difficulties their promises would contain. One child lost. Another gained. One kingdom fractured. Another sealed. Their own lives shattered. So others could live.

For now, they saw only the moment, and the moment was

happy. Anjei ran with Bo in spurts, talking in bursts—childhood memories, jokes about Uncle, questions about the history of their land.

Finally, as the morning light began to overcome the sky, Bo murmured, "You must hide me."

"I will," she said as they stood, making their way back along the line of ash pits where the wild man had camped. "But in plain sight. For the rest of our journey, you will run and jump and chase the night. Until we pass through the gates, when you will stagger and limp. As soon as I leave my parents' house—and that will be soon—you will die, and I will mourn. But that eccentric Anjei, she'll find another dog, of the same yellow coat. She will tell them that she got it from a dog hostel in a distant sector (and for no small price), and she'll give it a different name. And always when the dog she fosters dies—*her dogs* they'll call them—she'll find another. Oh, it might have darker paws or a patched eye. But nearly the same."

"Yes, so nearly as to be practically identical," Bo said, laughing.

They paused on a hill, looking across the distance to the walls of the head city. "Ready?" she asked.

"I'm ready," he replied, as the moon hovered just above the horizon. "And thank you."

"We will have many more years," she answered, just as the moon dipped below the horizon, its light blinking out, and with it, the dog's speech.

THROUGH THE FOLLOWING day and into the night, they walked back to the city.

When the dawn of the second day broke, they could see the gates, flags blowing in the wind. Anjei stopped, glanced at Bo standing tall beside her. She thought of the humans in the city, the hostels for the dogs, the food dishes placed on the floor to bring one race lower than another.

"I was wrong," she said suddenly. "Wrong again. Selfish again. You must not playact in my role. You should stay here, where you are free, free to be strong."

Without the full moon, he could not answer, and even in his renewal, Anjei felt the loss of that.

But then he nudged her. She followed his gaze. The final ash pit, long cold.

Bo walked to it. He lifted a paw, dipped it into a bit of the white ash, and shook it.

"Gray," Anjei said, and he nodded.

"Is this what you want?" she asked.

In answer, he dipped another paw, graying it.

She smiled. "You old coot." Anjei scooped up a handful of the cinders.

Bo looked at her, the black eyes clear.

She spread the ash along his snout and legs, the tip of his tail, graying his coat once again. He hung his head so the bright eyes and healthy teeth would not be noticed. He limped and staggered.

"Oh, it will not be long now," she said. "Before the poor Bo will die from age and sickness."

He hobbled along for a moment before casting a mischievous glance at her, running full speed, soaring high over a log, and landing perfectly.

"Just like the ancient Humphrey was said to do." Anjei said.

He tipped his head up to the city.

Together, the two of them walked silently down the hill, heading to a life that was about to be reborn.

GREY FALL

A NOVELLA IN TWO PARTS

PART ONE

GREY FALL

Some say it happened on account of her hair, which ran in a black river nearly to her knees, smooth and thick, the type of waters one fell into. Who wouldn't want to weave such hair with the colors of the earth? Adorn it with the shimmer of the stars?

Which is exactly what Queen Aemalia did. From the beginning of her reign, laborers dug deep into the mines of the land, searching for the brightest ores, which smiths and designers then fashioned into trinkets to be hung from their queen in various ways. Thick bronze bangles reaching from wrist to shoulder, heavy copper chains in rows around her neck. Sharp golden studs with various gems through ears, nose, cheeks, even the tips of the smallest finger of each hand. At first it was diamonds only for her hair, twinkling with every movement, every nod of her head. Then gold beads, connecting in lines that dripped like rays of the sun through the long, straight locks. Though sun alone was not enough. Set upon the throne at the impossible age of sixteen, the girl soon tired of gold and platinum, rubied lips and garnet-studded cheeks; now she desired to harness the beauty of the moon as well. "Surely," she said, speaking to an elderly member of the council—one who had fumbled into her presence at just the right moment. "Surely it is time for a change."

"I couldn't agree more, M'lady," the old man said, bowing his head, eyes low.

"But what exactly would be the perfect thing, not so boringly common as all this?" She gestured to the emerald beads that fell in a rope from her waist.

"Common indeed," the old man said.

"But it seems we've used everything," the young queen pouted.

"Quite nearly so," the old man responded.

"Quite?" she asked.

"Well, of course. Although it is hardly my place to say, as you have surely learned of these histories in your lessons, but there is but one metal as yet *uncommon* in such a wealthy court as this."

"And what, Councilman Rodolph, is that?" the girl asked, tapping her metal-ringed fingers upon her throne.

"Surely you have heard talk of it," he said. "From sources besides myself. An ancient mine, nearly forgotten, once forbidden. But then—"

"Forbidden?" she interrupted, intrigued.

"The metal so scarce, so scarce."

Her eyes glittered at the word.

"Though it can be dangerous too," he continued, folding his hands as if in penitence. "But only to some. And fewer now than in days long past."

"How could it be dangerous?" she replied, waving for her pen and signaling for her royal seal. "It's not like we'll be using the ore for weaponry."

"Of course, my queen. And it would be seen as a source of power, just as much as beauty," the old councilman said.

And so a movement was made to open a very old, very fragile mine, though as soon as the news carried to the council, many objected. One could almost say 'all.' Almost.

"This was not the intent," the older members of the Council, both shifter and human, grumbled when she first made the request to open the Grey mines. They grouped together, drafting and signing a petition for the queen, just as Lady Sadora had instructed in the early days, at the beginning of the Sun Change, at the time when things seemed clear, if still complicated. In those days, there were no queens, human or otherwise. Only a Council. A Council, which remained, though now underneath the bejeweled thumb of a human magistrate.

"You cannot open the mines," the youngest councilman said bluntly. "It would release the Grey."

"Release," she laughed. "Of course not, my dear Councilman Taamani. Merely repurpose."

"A lethal purpose," the shifter insisted.

"M'lady," several members of the council chimed in.

She held up a hand, each finger ringed in metal and stone. "I am in need of repose," she said. "To think this through. The Council is dismissed."

"But we are not finished," one of the oldest councilwomen objected.

"My darling," the queen said.

"You may call me 'Councilwoman Anjei,'" the woman inserted. A yellow-haired dog stood tall at her side, and some said that on nights of fullest moon, the animal spoke to her, though most believed that to be the talk of children's tales.

"Of course. My darling Councilwoman Anjei, I cannot now think with so much new information."

"That you cannot now think I have no doubt," Anjei muttered.

The queen smiled, each garnet band studded into her cheeks shining against the fire lanterns that lit the hall.

"You will leave one of your members to discuss it with me in private. Perhaps in this way I can come to understand. After all it's so difficult with so many voices chiming in. Surely you understand how a simple mind like mine might struggle, Councilwoman."

"You wish then that I remain?" Councilwoman Anjei replied, lifting a bushy eyebrow.

"Perhaps in the future," the queen replied. "But tonight I think I'll benefit from someone closer to my own age. Councilman Taamani, you shall remain."

"Me, M'lady?"

"I see no other."

He nodded and the members filed out. Councilwoman Anjei squeezed his shoulder and whispered, "I'll wait in the hall."

"You've no need," Taamani replied.

"Then I will leave Leonii to wait and accompany you home," the woman replied, nodding to the dog who seemed to nod back.

When the council was gone, the queen rose from her amethyst throne. "Come," she said, motioning Taamani forward.

"I shall remain on the floor of the council."

"Then I will come to you."

With a swish of gown, made heavy by the gold and brass sewn through its fabric, the young queen descended the steps, moving close to Taamani.

He began to speak before she arrived. "As laid out in article 527, the mines of the Grey shall remain closed so long as shifter and human remain in quarters together..."

"Hmmm, I like the sound of that last part," she said, leaning toward him.

He leaned back. "...as the metal of the Grey and even the gasses of the mine can prove dangerous to full-blood and halfling both."

"We should discuss it further," she said, inching closer to him. "I am in need of an advisor."

"I am too young," Taamani replied. "It's quite clear in Ordinance 1724, where it states—"

"—And quite fresh," she replied, ignoring him. "Who better?"

"The mines are dangerous," he finished. "We wait for a vote. This thing must not be."

Queen Aemalia inhaled, smiled.

Taamani stepped back. It was the day before the *Moonface* —night of fullest moon, and he was aware of his musky scent, that his shoulders had broadened and were pressing against his robe, teeth just beginning to sharpen.

"Like diamonds," she said, leaning forward, gazing into his face. "Your kind. A bit rough perhaps, in need of faceting, but so beautiful."

"If we are to be compared to diamonds, my queen, then I prefer to think of us as unbreakable," he replied, adding, "and I am not in the market for faceting."

"And I am not in the market for a petition," she replied. "Yet here we are. Bring me your petition overnight. I shall hear the details of it then."

"Overnight will not work," Taamani replied. "As you very well know. The moon already begins to rise and will soon grow bright. Many of the Council must seek darkness."

"I did not ask for the Council, only that you bring me the petition. And darkness is something that I can supply." The ruby studs that lined her lips glinted in the paling light.

"My queen," Taamani replied.

"If you wish your petition heard, meet me in my chamber after evening meal."

"This thing cannot be," he responded. "It is dangerous."

"Perhaps I like danger."

"You do not know what you like."

"Oh, but I do. That is the one thing I do know."

"I must not come at that time, my lady."

"Ah, but you must. I have commanded it."

"I am not a circus act."

"A circus is not what I am after."

"I will send Councilwoman Anjei. She is human and more well-versed in the law than I."

"I am interested in neither a woman, a human, nor the law. Meet me after evening meal, or I will deny the petition."

"It is not a thing that can be denied. There must be a vote."

"After evening meal. In my chambers. The guards will let you in."

But after evening meal, he did not come.

The queen paced, then raged, demanding that her midnight-black locks be brushed 1000 times. One thousand. A number to count on. The number of ages.

The next day, the Council again adjourned. Queen Aemalia read the petition, or at least began, then patted her ruby-studded lips in a yawn, and tore the paper precisely in two. Her lips clicked when she did so—metal and gem clacking together.

"You must read it," Taamani demanded, his shoulders narrower, fingers slender and soft after Moonface. "It is the law set forth by our Lady Sadora and the honorable Councilman Pietre."

"Well," she said, her gaze flitting in his direction. "We do not always do what we must, what has been commanded by the mouth of the law. Is that not so, Councilman?"

"That was not the law."

"Your petition is denied."

"It must be read," Councilwoman Anjei said, joining him, as well as several others.

They pressed forward and the queen's guards tightened the circle around the throne. One shifter, his mind still fired from the previous night's Moonface, raised a hand, revealing sharp, yellowed nails. His human companion pulled a rapier, and both rushed the guards. Others called out for them to stop while the guards thrust copper spears, moving toward one of the humans until Councilwoman Anjei —skin sagging, hair thin and white, but with arms strong and tight as wires—reached out and grabbed a spear. "Enough," she shouted.

The Council broke into confused groups, but the other guard rushed her, aiming for her neck. The dog, Leonii, shot forward, biting the guard in the calf, as the entire room broke into fighting.

The queen's reign might have ended there—pierced to its conclusion on a sharpened dagger or spike of wood or wrung breathless by a powerful hand—had a small voice not risen from the din.

Those who thought of it later would wonder how the old man had even been heard—his voice trembling with age, with deference. "Calmly, now, my friends. Dear friends."

People slowed, turned to gaze at the old man. He held a paper in his hands and wore small spectacles atop his crooked nose. "Now wait, good people. Yes. There is, you will note, a place in the old laws. An addendum, I believe it is called."

The old man, Councilman Rodolph, shuffled forward as the members of the Council lowered their weapons, just a bit, but enough. The jolts of emotion that had run along their spines and ignited their blood—these feelings settled at the sound of the gentle voice.

They stepped back, embarrassed at the rush of adrenaline, at the wild behavior that had propelled them forward. Most nursed wounds, though all still lived.

"Our lady queen," Rodolph continued, "need not hear the petition if presented by an imbalanced number. Human and shifter must be equally represented."

"Are we not?" Taamani asked. "The nature of the Council is balance, and all have signed."

"Care has been taken," Rodolph quavered, a guard holding out an arm to give him support as the old man lifted the torn petition from the floor. "Unfortunately, not enough. The shifters on this petition outnumber the humans."

"How is that possible?" Taamani asked, making a snatch for the petition, though the old man moved it with surprising deftness.

"Yes, here. Councilmen Bernase and Kanoi are not included. In fact, they are not in attendance today either."

"Where are they?" another councilmember asked.

"I do not know," Rodolph replied. "As far as I know they were last seen carousing night past with a group of shifters from this council."

"What do you imply?" Anjei asked, Leonii opening his mouth in a silent growl.

"Oh, nothing, good woman," Rodolph replied. "Only that they must be both included. And present. Which they are not."

"Then we will find them," she replied.

"Likely drunk in their beds," another added.

"But if we cannot find them?" Taamani asked, the hairs at the back of his neck rising, though he tried to tell himself it was just a side effect of the recent full moon.

"Well, then," the old man said, snuffling and clearing his throat. "I suppose the petition cannot stand—for a vote, or otherwise."

The Council turned in on itself, folding, the edges smoldering.

The queen waved a hand and a stream of guards poured in. "The Council," she said, "is dismissed."

"For now," Taamani replied. "Until the missing councilmembers are located."

"Of course, of course," Councilman Rodolph replied, hobbling with his cane and the assistance of a guard to the side of the queen. "Of course."

UNFORTUNATELY, the councilmembers were not located. Not that night, or any other. The petition did not stand. Nor could another be organized as the two new members of the council refused to sign it. And so, within six months' time, excavations began, ancient places cracking open, places that had the power to break a race.

Though even in times like this, life moved on. Councilwoman Anjei introduced Taamani to her oldest grandchild—a halfling woman with hair the color of wheat and eyes the blue of the softest skies. They were married within four moon cycles, and by the time the first cart rolled down into the abandoned and dangerous mines, the woman was with child.

The queen was betrothed as well. How convenient that her ancient advisor should have a handsome son of perfect marrying age

—a man sought by women across the land, though until that point he had never shown any interest in women at all.

Dangerous things, children and politics, love and war.

The queen, of course, wished to be married with threads of the beautiful Shining Grey woven through her hair. And at this point, most of what the queen wanted she got. It was the trembling advisor who made the announcement—so very old to have such a young son. "The Grey will be smithed for our lady only, due to the queen's most precious wedding wishes. All scrap will be returned to the mines, so no need for anyone to worry." That crumbling voice, diminutive stature, gentle tone—who could have sensed a threat? "For such an amount is nothing, nothing at all, in the large picture of things. And, after all, the Council exists for the support of her lady highness, not in voice against her."

The members bristled, the shifters indignant, many of the humans too. Though there were some humans—new members of the Council—who were privately relieved to have the mines reopened, secretly thrilled with the queen's latest wish, and deeply pleased at the rumors that hummed of an underground market where scrap might be bought—laced with iron to be sure, but with enough of the Grey remaining that the humans could hold a little power in their own two hands. For it was no secret that on the night of the fullest moons, many of the shifters were prone to drown the pains of the shifting in liquors and drug—an act that may have reduced their own suffering at the cost of the barmaids and business owners, or anyone else with the unfortunate luck to cross their paths on the night of Moonface.

Several members of the Council complained. The mines would need security, they argued. Taamani himself presented the newest petition, though he knew that the numbers were not balanced, and that as such, it could not legally stand. Not without the additional signature of the queen.

"Do not worry," the kindly advisor replied. "Your queen and I will find a solution to protect you from those who might wish to abuse the power of the Shining Grey."

The trance of his smile.

Taamani nodded.

"Now back to your wife," the old man said. "I hear you are soon to be blessed with child."

"It is many months still," Taamani answered, "though my wife grows often hungry, and sometimes sick."

"Such is the way with women," Advisor Rodolph said.

Barely a fortnight flew by before a solution was indeed presented, although when Taamani received the news—second-hand, for the Council had not been notified beforehand—he was not sure that *solution* was the word he would have chosen.

From this point forward, the law read, *all those of shifting blood will be required to remove themselves from public places during the precarious time of month, known in common terms as Moonface. Those shifters not in compliance shall be subject to the fullest weight of the law, no less than one year's time in the newly re-opened dungeons of the ancient palace.*

"It is illegal," he said to his wife—Simone—pacing the tile floor of their apartments on the western hill.

"It is inevitable," she replied. "Can't you see it? The queen marries within the month. Soon the Grey will flood the court, the bourgeoisie adopting whatever the queen does."

"Impossible," Taamani replied.

"Is it?" Simone asked, and it was all she needed to say.

Several shifters arrived at the palace the following morning to object. The advisor, Councilman Rodolph, appeared this time without the queen. "Our lady prepares for her upcoming nuptials," he said. "Now what is the problem, my children?"

"We are not children," the oldest shifter replied.

The advisor smiled, like a platinum sun hung from his mouth. "Ah, then, let's hear what problem you councilmembers have come up with now."

"You make it sound as though it is a problem we've created," Taamani said.

"But of course not," the advisor replied. "Now speak. And I will soon supply a solution."

And soon he did.

In order to avoid the trouble of prison, or even the temptation to approach such trouble, whole families could be moved into special zones of the city—concrete housing where they would be sheltered from the moon, and protected from themselves.

The Council objected, though its voice had grown weak. Several human members had vanished during the last Moonface, and it was decided by the advisor and his most trusted aides that for every human councilmember who vanished, two humans would replace him.

"That is not just," Anjei spoke out.

"But of course it is, good lady—"

"You may call me Councilwoman," she replied.

"As I shall," he responded. "If one race of those on this Council cannot be trusted to protect the others, then we must balance the numbers in our favor, weak as we are."

"We are not weak," she replied.

"You perhaps," he answered, his voice cracking, head bowed.

At the next Moonface, Anjei was found crumpled in a heap at the side of the road, her throat crushed, scratch marks across the neck. Nearby, a trail of red blood dragged into the woods—the only remnants of the dog, Leonii, who had been her friend for so many years.

The entire city grieved.

Taamani's wife wrapped herself in layers of black so thick she could barely move, and ate only for the sake of the baby within her.

"This violence," Advisor Rodolph said. "This is enough. From this point forward, the shifting members of the Council shall be disbanded." He no longer bothered to attach the queen's name to his decrees.

"You cannot," Taamani said.

"Then bring a petition," the old man challenged, his voice losing its tremor.

But of course Taamani could not. Most of the humans would not sign it, and only some of the halflings. *We are the last link to the Council,* the halflings said. *The last bit of voice you have.*

Taamani raked a hand though his hair; they were not wrong. Even some of the shifters hesitated, though in the end all agreed. "We must stand," Taamani said. And so they did, though all knew that it would likely be their last stand. The petition was not balanced —most of the signatures from shifter, a handful of halflings, and only two of their human companions.

Just before the Council met, one of those—a girl with shimmering eyes and a mouth that usually laughed—pushed a piece of paper into Taamani's hands. "There is a place," she murmured. "Anjei knew of it. Deep in the wood. If a place becomes necessary— one that is not made of stone." She tried to push the corners of her mouth back into that pleasant smile. "Though I'm sure it will be fine."

It would not be fine.

And on that night, the remaining shifters of the Council were dismissed, though it was agreed they would be replaced with halfling, not human.

On the morrow, the wedding bells tolled and the queen descended from her throne, hair and gown cascading with slivers of Grey, like drops of the moon down her back. She took the hand of the most handsome bachelor of the land and they were wed with foreheads bent together. To commemorate the event, the queen asked that a small rod of the Shining Grey be pierced through her forehead. And so it was. One knob through her scalp at the hairline, the other just between the eyebrows. "Beautiful, my lady," the advisor said.

"Beautiful and strong," she replied.

"But of course."

"And no longer to be called by the antiquated name of 'Grey,'" she said. "From henceforth this metal will be known as 'Silver.'"

From that day, despite any old promises to the contrary, the fashions of the court changed, each member adopting a bauble of Grey—little bits the queen now called Silver—leading the court as she wound it through her hair, along her fingers, even in circlets about her toes.

From the strength of the metals that now burst into their culture, many of the oldest shifters grew weak, along with those of the purest shifting lines. Smoke laced with it billowed from the smithies, and many sensed it trickling into the waters of wells and gutters, as those who mined and formed it cleaned their tools and discarded the smallest shavings.

Several shifters fled of their own accord to the concrete houses, now called camps, where they could live in the protection—if not comfort—of the stone. Even the halflings began to feel the effects, sleeping poorly, falling ill with ease. While the humans grew strong.

Taamani himself did not feel its effects, as he had known he would not. But his wife grew pale, her muscles overly soft, just as her belly rounded into a distinct 'O.'

"I am not well," she said one night when the moon hung heavy and fat, almost at Moonface. "Perhaps we should consider the camps, just for the duration of my child-months."

"Perhaps we should consider...something," Taamani replied, tapping his tongue against his teeth, thinking of the queen's words from all those months ago. Like diamonds, she had said. So strong, so rough. And how, a short while ago, they'd taken a "stand."

As though names on a parchment could be a stand.

He felt for the paper in his pocket—one he had carried since that last night on the Council. "There is a place," he said, holding the shoulders of his wife, pulling her in against his chest, feeling the new smallness even as her stomach had grown big.

∽

THE WAY WAS NOT STRAIGHT. At each turn or turnaround, he positioned a small stone—nothing more than a pebble, though on every one, he had worn one side out, creating a small indent like the waxing moon. He had not told many; it was too dangerous, but there were some— parents ailing, children dying. These he knew would wind their way after him.

The way was also not swift. His wife, heavy with their child, seemed to grow sicker at every step. Her face, always pale, seemed ashen, never flushing or changing. Her lips, never pale, now were. Her hair, once silk, had turned to straw. And her eyes, those beautiful mirrors of the sky, had misted and fogged.

"My energy simply goes to the child," she said, patting her belly and sitting on a stump—the fourth time she'd done so within the hour.

It took nearly a month of searching before they came to the wall of trees. *The Walking Forest,* Anjei had labeled it on the paper, though he could not understand why. The forest in front of him seemed so thick as to be impossible for anyone to walk through, especially his wife.

"They've poisoned you," he growled, his voice harsh.

"Is it me that has been poisoned?" she asked in response to his anger. Just then, both of them noticed a slight movement among the trees, a flicker of white.

"Bird?" Simone said.

Taamani shook his head. "Guide."

OF THAT, good one, you are correct.
   At least for those sans circumspect.
   The river flows to place of peace,
   For those whose path my lady seeks.

"A CAT," Simone whispered. "I've never seen one."

"Yes," Taamani replied, watching it suspiciously. The animal was black and sleek as the night save for one diamond-shaped patch of bright white on her back. "Though I believe it used the word 'circumspect' as a noun rather than an adjective."

"You're going to criticize its grammar?" Simone asked.

"I wasn't—" He stopped and looked at the cat, who had turned with its tail up and was walking back toward the thick wood.

"Now you've offended it," Simone hissed.

"Me? It should just be glad the humans haven't learned to put them in cages on display," Taamani whispered back, following the cat.

"*The humans*?" his wife asked. "Many of those *humans* have been your friends."

"Those men and women are gone. Vanished in the cloak of our new democracy."

"They have sons yet. Daughters too."

"Mind-washed."

"Really, Taamani." It was what she said sometimes. He never liked to hear it.

"Come on," he whispered, following the cat. He took her hand, helping her over the rocks and branches of the path. She panted from the exertion, though just a few months ago she could have run through these fields for hours. He tightened his grip on her hand, and she squeezed back as the cat stopped in front of an enormous tree. At least Taamani had thought it was a tree. Standing directly in front of it, he saw that it was only shadow, and the three of them slipped through.

They wandered in that way, coming to obstacles that suddenly weren't, following the white patch on the cat's back that glowed like a lantern. Occasionally the cat would stop and clean a paw, and Taamani couldn't help but notice that it was always just as Simone's strength was about to give out and she most needed a rest.

"I thought your poem was nice," he said, trying to patch up any hurt feelings from earlier.

"Ah, but you are correct. The proper word would have been 'circumspection.' Such, however, is the way with art. One must occasionally break the rules."

"I suppose one must," he murmured.

When they had walked what appeared to be three identical circles, another shadow opened up to a clearing where the sun dappled, dancing along the pathway until it reached a crooked hut that sat at the center of an enormous garden, heavy with herb and flower.

"Well now," a woman's voice called from the hut. "This is a change, isn't it? I used to be sought by humans and dogs and halflings. And now here we are gone half circle, maybe one quarter—it gets confusing—and I am sought by lord and baby and one who is called halfling still. Hello, my dear. Are you well?"

"She is not," Taamani answered for her.

"Tea-drinker," Simone said, removing the hood of her cloak to reverence the woman. "Health-giver."

"Yes, yes," the woman replied, blinking her mismatched eyes. "Refugee granter, and all that. You may simply call me Zinnegael."

The woman called Zinnegael leaned forward, pinching Simone's cheek. "You've no color at all, my dear."

"It goes to the child," Simone replied without skipping a beat.

"Well, perhaps the child can spare a bit. I've just put the kettle on so we'll see what we can do."

"They tell tales," Simone began.

"Of an old woman who never dies."

"But heals," Simone replied. "And saves."

"Hmph," Zinnegael grunted, turning her brown eye toward the hut. "Tries to save."

"Tries?" Taamani interrupted.

"There are many determined to go, even when they say they're not," she answered. "And some are simply too far gone by the time they reach me." She glanced at Simone, who looked away.

"And you, my lord, how have you found me?" She shot a green-eyed glance at him.

"A woman," he answered. "A human called Anjei."

"Lovely creature," the Tea-Drinker replied. "She and the dog visited us oft."

"Now gone," Taamani replied. "Both of them. I am sorry if you had not heard."

"My cats bring me much news," Zinnegael answered. "Much of it sad. Most of it true. Just as they told me of your arrival, they told me of her departure. The dog himself tried to reach me. He did not succeed, my lord."

"You need not call me 'lord,'" Taamani answered. "I have never been one and now am not even called 'councilman.'"

"You do not need to be called 'lord' for it to be so," Zinnegael replied. "You whom the Grey cannot touch."

"A title of old times, and perhaps best left forgotten."

"Most things from old times are *not* best left forgotten," the woman replied. "Though we don't have to go repeating them."

A tall, gray-streaked cat brought out a tray of biscuits, balancing the plate on its head. Zinnegael lifted them up and breathed in the scent. "Glazed with berry sugar, children. Now try one."

The biscuits were stacked so high it was difficult to see around them.

"I admit that I expected a whole group of you to arrive," Zinnegael explained, as the tea kettle whistled.

"Now I suppose we'll just have to eat more than our fill."

Simone giggled, but Taamani looked to the shadows of the trees. "You may have many guests yet. Things grow difficult in the head city."

"Opened the mines again, have they?" she replied, crushing leaves into the cups and pouring the steaming water over it.

"For baubles," he replied. "The queen's couture."

"Hardly," the woman replied. "They've opened the mines

because one more clever than the queen has willed it to be so. And now here you are; his cleverness is paying off. For a time."

"He wishes to eliminate us?" Taamani asked, thinking of the ancient advisor.

"He wishes to grow strong, and that is difficult to do with a thriving and balanced council. For one man to grow strong he needs imbalance, unrest. Otherwise, the people govern themselves much too well. And so these people who wish to be strong—hardly understanding what the word really means—" She glanced again at Simone. "—they create trouble, much like the burbeon plant grows a fungus to attract the sting beetle that it then eats. Marvelous trait in a plant; less charming in a human."

"Much," Taamani replied as the gray-streaked cat returned, sitting on the empty chair at the table. Taamani watched closely as Simone drank her tea, a bit of peach returning to her cheeks, a sense of peace settling over him that he realized he hadn't felt for months.

OTHERS DID COME to the clearing. Many. Though not nearly so many as Taamani had expected.

"They wait in the camps," one of the newly-arrived shifters explained—a man the others called Balt. "Too frightened to venture into the unknown of the woods. Though those able to wait in camps grow fewer."

"What do you mean?" Taamani asked.

Balt shrugged. "They vanish," his companion replied. "Perhaps to the dungeons. Some flee to the woods. Some join packs of wolves —not exactly a place of safety, but not one of danger either. Others do not flee at all, but stagger from the city, preferring a speedy death at the cold teeth of a bear than the slow drain of the Grey."

The cold teeth of a predator. Moonface was nearly upon them. He felt the sharpening of his teeth, the boiling of his blood.

Even Simone did better just before Moonface, though tonight her time of child-giving neared, and she sweated and panted out the hours. He had left her only once that day in order to meet the newest arrivals, most of them as pale and colorless as Simone, but not weighted with the holding of another life in their bodies. In fact, most were men.

"Should we organize, Councilman?" Balt asked, and Taamani realized he had not been listening.

"Organize into what?" Taamani asked.

"A rebellion, of course. Like in days of old."

"My wife," Taamani replied. "She is close to the time of child-giving."

"Well, go to her, man. But think on it. If this keeps on, our kind will soon be no more."

"And where are your own women?" Taamani asked, as he turned to leave.

"Many are dead. Some given into the queen's courts to brush her hair and wind it with the metal."

"But it weakens them. Why not have the humans do it?"

"It is a punishment, Councilman. And something more."

"What is that?" Taamani asked as the nearly-full moon began to creep above the trees.

"A way to find them," Balt replied. "The daughters of the Grey."

"And what of the sons?"

"The queen does not wish sons of any kind near her husband. He enjoys it too much, and she grows jealous. Besides, it is believed that the lords of the Grey are no more. While the women hide it better."

"And when these daughters of the Grey are found?" Taamani asked, his back to the shifter.

"I pray that they are not."

Taamani nodded. "Doubtful that they will be. Masters of the Grey are few at the best of times. Perhaps they are already extinct."

"Have you ever known one, Councilman?"

Taamani paused. "No," he replied. "Of course not." He wound his way through the camp to the room in Zinnegael's house where his wife lay...dying. Or birthing.

The line between seemed very thin.

~

SIMONE DID NOT DIE that night. Though she did not properly recover either.

For months she hovered between the two—life and death, feeding the child when she could, and allowing Zinnegael to supplement the baby's nutrition when she could not. In what seemed like no time at all, the child—called Lilycup after her mother's favorite flower—crawled, then walked. She did not, however, talk. Silent as the flower for which she was named.

On the night of her first birthday, Lilycup presented her mother with a flower and a soup.

"What's this?" Simone said, laughing. "*I'm* supposed to be the one giving you a gift." With an effort, she pushed herself up to sitting and presented Lily with a small package. Inside lay a bronze brush with thin, soft bristles.

Taamani noticed that Simone made a great show of holding the brush and showing Lilycup how to use it in long strokes through her hair. He also noticed Simone did not touch the soup. By the time a cake had been brought out, carried on the head of the gray cat, Simone had drifted into a troubled, tossing sleep.

~

A SLEEP that held her for most of the days for the next six months.

"Why did the Grey affect Simone so much, Tea-Drinker? It's been over a year since her exposure, yet still she suffers. And she is a halfling, not even of full shifting blood."

"Is that so, Lord Taamani?" Zinnegael asked, crushing leaves for a tonic.

"Do not call me that."

"Pay attention to the question."

Taamani watched his daughter sway among the lemongrass, reaching out her arms to feel the vibrations of their stalks. "The women hide it better," he murmured, thinking of the words of the rebel.

"Women have learned to hide many things, especially when it is in their favor to do so."

"She was not halfling," he answered, tasting the fact.

"Nor granddaughter to the human Anjei," Zinnegael responded. "However, halflings do not pose a great threat to the queen—even beautiful granddaughters of powerful humans. She does not solicit them to be her ladies or her servants. Quite convenient to become a halfling, is it not? Anjei had no grandchildren of her own, none she raised at any rate, and managed to happen upon a child in need of protection. A mutually beneficial situation."

"And how has Simone hidden it during Moonface?"

"Moonface," Zinnegael answered. "The easiest time of all, since the halflings shift on occasion, and since *you* go into hiding."

"I would not want to hurt someone."

"I know," Zinnegael answered.

"Who are her parents?" Taamani asked.

"Perhaps that is a question best for her."

"She dies."

"What better time?" Zinnegael asked.

As Lilycup danced for Zinnegael, Taamani dragged to his wife's quarters. He could hear her breathing through the walls, labored and thick.

"She told me you would come," Simone said without opening her eyes.

"And how did you know it was me?" Taamani asked.

"How could I not?"

"And why would I not come to the wife who can recognize my footfall?" he answered.

"Because you are afraid of what you will see."

"I'm afraid of everything these days." He settled in on the stool beside her, stirred the tonic Zinnegael had stewed. He lifted her head, held the spoon.

"No," she said.

"You must drink."

"I cannot," she replied. "It settles in my belly, the poison from the Grey."

"Odd trait for a halfling."

She smiled, closing her eyes again as he lowered her head back to the pillow. Her neck was narrow and thin—all sinews and skin.

"Took you long enough."

"Why didn't you tell me?"

"Because at a time when the queen could open a deadly mine, such information seemed dangerous. The less you knew about the things I hid, the better."

"Better than what is happening now?"

"What is happening now would have happened whether you knew or not. What was happening then, with the dismissal of the shifters—that was troubling. Still is."

"And so you tell me now?"

"I didn't tell you. You figured it out. And that is just as well. At this point, you can't be troubled more by any secrets I have kept."

"A full-blooded shifter."

"But hardly a Greylord," she said, gazing at him.

"I wish you had been instead of me." Perhaps he should have been angry at the secret his wife had kept, but she was right—why wouldn't she keep secrets in a land that was eliminating her race; why wouldn't she hide things that might hurt those she most loved? Him, Anjei, the child.

"I'm glad it is you who lords the Grey," she said. "I'm glad you'll be here with our little Lilycup."

"Now is not the time for such talk."

"Now is the perfect time for such talk. I will go, but the child will live."

"You ate up the Grey poison for her."

"I did."

"And who was your father?"

"The one you know him as."

"Your mother?"

"Long dead, as I shall be. Anjei raised me. A convenient union with her grandchildless and me motherless."

"Strange, these trades. Stranger that she had no grandchild of her own."

"She had one once," Simone replied.

"I had not heard this," Taamani replied.

"Few have," Simone answered. "The mother died in birth."

"And the baby soon after?" Taamani asked.

"No," Simone answered. "But her mother was quite young."

"Anjei would not remove a grandchild, even to avoid embarrassment."

"No," Simone answered. "She would not." A wave of pain swept through her. Taamani leaned down, massaging the area around her belly, wishing he could pull the metals out and make her well.

"But she might remove one for other reasons," she murmured when the largest of the pain had passed. "And that is what she did."

"But why?" Taamani asked.

"So the bloodlines would run long. That's what she told me. And now she is gone. And soon I will be too. So perhaps she was right."

"Not you. Not tonight."

She put a thin hand on his cheek, and said nothing.

"Shall I tell Lilycup that she is a partialling?" he asked, changing the subject.

"Such ridiculous words. Tell her she is a child to two parents who are master of the Grey. One a lord; the other a protector."

"Absorber," he finished. Very different, and so much worse.

"Tell her that her mother loved her enough to do that."

"I will," he replied.

"I know," she said, and after that no more words followed. Her breathing grew heavier, as though weights pressed against her lungs. Then sparser like the weights had been replaced with a stopping stick.

LATE THAT NIGHT, the queen's own child was born. Trumpets blew so loudly from the head city that they could hear them deep in Zinnegael's wood. Firestars floated from the palace and drifted down in red-hot coals. People sang and drank and ate roses dipped in honey.

And late that night, Simone died, eaten up by a metal the queen had wound through her hair and pierced into her face.

The wood of the refugees fell silent.

The few women in the clearing wound flowers together while several of the men crafted a bier. And just before dawn, when the ash from the firestars hung as dust in the air, the friends of Simone lit flames beneath the bier. Taamani held Lilycup in his arms as the shell of the woman that had been his wife drifted back to the moon.

The following morning, the announcement came from one of the few halflings left on the Council, carried on the mouth of one of the cats. "In honor of her lady's newest child, and in light of the discovery of a pink ore the queen has named 'rose gold,' the mines to the Shining Grey, now known as Silver, will be resealed."

"Strange how fashion works," Zinnegael said. "Coming and going as it does." She fed the messenger cat a small fish on a plate. "I suppose both court and council have gotten all from the Grey that they wished."

"Court *and* council?" the rebel named Balt asked. "I hardly think the Council—even as it now stands—cares much for the fashions of the court."

"Which is why one might do well to consider why a Council led by the venerable Rodolph gave its blessing to the release and then *re-closure* of the mines."

"The queen demanded it," Balt replied, and Taamani stirred slightly at the reference.

"The queen's fashions, yes, of course," Zinnegael replied, sipping an amber tea.

"They've used it," Taamani said, looking at her, then Balt. "Just like you said earlier. Used it to root out the masters of the Grey."

Balt sat at Zinnegael's table, breaking pieces off a corner of his cake. "And if they feel they need it no more," he finally said.

"Then those who lord the Grey are dead," Taamani finished.

Zinnegael looked at Taamani for several long moments before chirping, "I suppose the good news is that the shifters can finally return. If they choose."

Very few chose.

~

TAAMANI DID NOT NOTICE who left or who stayed. He only noticed the absence of his wife and the silence of the child, who had now learned to dance to the quiet rhythms in her head, to sway with the energy of Moonface, who smiled with a mouth full of beautiful white teeth, though no sound ever escaped her lips.

One month after his wife's death, he sat perched in a tree, watching Lilycup trip and twirl among the pansies and lavender and lilies, passing over any with stripes of poison in the petals as she'd been taught. She reached out her arms to feel the stems, the trunks of the trees, the breezes.

Zinnegael came out, a cup of tea in her hand. She paused a moment, watching the girl just as he had done, then looked up to him in his tree.

"Perched like a bird as usual," she said.

"Birds sing," he replied, swinging down and landing with a soft plunk beside Zinnegael.

Lilycup swirled in front of them, her skirt swishing.

"You realize," Zinnegael said, as Lilycup paused to pluck a small flower from the grass, "that the child does not hear."

He had known for months now, but had not spoken it. He hadn't wanted his wife to worry. "How appropriate not to hear in a time when our own voices fall to the deaf ears of others."

"Perhaps with the mines resealed, more good will come to your kind," Zinnegael replied with a sip.

"A fairy story," Taamani replied. "Since we both know Rodolph would open them again in a blink if it served him. And with any suspicion of a Greylord among them, it might serve him."

Zinnegael watched the girl run her fingers along the tree trunks at the edge of the clearing. "Perhaps." She emptied her cup. "Stay as long as you need."

He did, for two more years.

ON THE EVENING of the birth of the queen's second child, which soon became the night of the death of the queen's child, no firestars flared, no trumpets sounded, no voices sang.

The decree went out and the city tumbled into a forced silence that lasted for days. In the midst of the mourning, a ruckus broke out along the west gate. Several shifters, trying to return to their concrete camps after hunting in the woods—some say seeking an escape with an ancient witch and not finding her—were blamed for the death of the queen's child. How they could be blamed when the child had come into the world small enough to fit in the palm of a human hand mattered not. For when a mob grieves, it doesn't look for reason—only a place to land its grief.

The following day the bodies of those shifters hung from ancient gallows, re-erected, as the funeral procession snaked in black through the head city.

At the next Moonface, the killings began. Always at the western wall. And every month. Soon, no humans ventured outside the walls on the night of Moonface, save a few brave huntsmen, who sometimes died, and occasionally lived. Those who lived did so only because fear feeds best on panic and rumor, and the white lips and scratch-scarred faces of the hunters who returned supplied plenty of both.

In another time, Taamani might have tried to stop such killings, begged his own kind to display mercy, equanimity, justice. Now these seemed like the high virtues of those who had time and energy for such things—for people who did not sit on their own grief, caring for a young daughter in the relative safety of an ancient witch's wood.

"Most do not remain here forever, good lord," Zinnegael said one morning.

"I am neither lord nor good, as we have discussed. Would you have us leave?"

"That is not what I said."

"Then what do you wish?"

"I wish nothing. I only hope. For movement, progress. You have something beautiful and living to love."

"And nowhere else beautiful and living to raise her."

"Then create it."

"Where?" he asked, "How?"

"Answers for you, not me," she replied.

But he had only questions.

He taught the child her numbers, the markings of her name. Then other written words. She learned quickly, grew strong with long legs like the flower of her name and hair bushy and wild like his own. He taught her to climb the trees. And she still danced, now with more purpose—stretching her legs, leaping, creating patterns that she would practice and follow.

"You should find one to teach her," Zinnegael said and he only grunted in response, though he did wonder if there was another place beautiful enough for such a creature. But then he caught her silence in the air and knew he could never find such a place, not with so much ugliness in his own heart. That was the way with things. You found what you sought and he found beauty only in his child and these woods. If ever the child or their refuge was gone, he would be left with only the ugliness, for everything else hung dark and damp around him.

It did not take long for the shifters who found their way to Zinnegael's hut not to recognize the former councilman, even though it had only been four and a half years since the Disbanding of the Shifters. When men and the occasional woman arrived, he called himself Timane—a blending of his name with his wife's. And none questioned it.

Shifters came and went from Zinnegael's hut. Sometimes to seek peace; sometimes war. He stayed. Until one day, the child herself wandered off. On the night of Moonface. He knew the feeling, the way her blood must have boiled, her skin itched, her teeth—small as they were—sharp as needles.

The cats told him of the wandering child. Then he and they flew in separate directions. After many hours, he saw her small form—a great distance away, at the place of the western wall—piles of old bones left to bleach in the sun. Warnings, talismans. And she among them, sifting through, tilting and twirling as she did. Her hair grown full in the moon, teeth long over pink lips.

He saw her, holding a bone, holding it up to her hair, like it was a comb. Then he heard the creak of an ancient gate, something she could not hear and would never understand if she did. With all his might and with the power of the moon, he ran to her. But not fast enough.

The gate to the wall opened, the horses stampeding through, ridden by the king and his closest men. It did not take long to see the reason why.

A group of shifters in full change waited in the shadows of the wood, advancing as quickly as the king's horses. And she, his Lily, in the middle of them. Innocent as a moonflower. And just as clueless.

He continued to run, hopping over fallen trees, crossing the clearing, but he was much farther away than the king, and not in possession of a horse.

Seeing the child, the king swooped down and scooped the girl into a sack, as though she was a harvested crop.

And just like that, the king tossed her to his servant. Not even valuable enough to keep on his own horse.

The howl sounded, long and shrill, though not from the shifters in the shadows. No, from one standing under the full glow of the moon. Both parties of the battle—shifter and man—turned to the cry. The sound of a soul torn to a thousand pieces.

At that sound, many of the horses, trained to fight shifters, whinnied and bucked. The humans who remained on their mounts turned to retreat, but not quickly enough. A thunder of feet, swifter than any thought possible. And then a new sound—the tearing of flesh. The king first, followed quickly by all of his men, save one.

The man with the sack remained, his horse racing back to the closing gate as the howling shifter ran for the opening. The horse's eyes wild and bulging, sweat streaking its fur. Its rider was pulled off in a scream, though the small bundle remained and the horse ran on, pressing faster and faster toward the gate. The scent of blood rose up. More howling. All from one voice. A voice connected to a body who had killed them all.

The horse tore through the gates as they closed, the shifter following, his fists thundering against the wood.

Until the war horns sounded, until the other shifters surrounded him, pulling him away, back into the shadows of the wood, back into the darkness of his heart.

~

Every month at Moonface, the howls returned to the western wall, the thundering fists, till even the bravest hunters didn't dare cross through that gate, even on days when the sun shone bright and the birds swooped through the trees.

New rumors formed of a phantom who drifted through those woods—hopeless, ragged, no more than a broken shadow with razors of teeth, so many teeth. A rumor that was not wholly wrong.

And every month at Moonface, when the howling and pounding of the Phantom began, a small girl of the queen's court felt the tremble in the floorboards while brushing her lady's hair. The rhythm of a broken memory, one that dimmed over the years, but remained the saddest rhythm she had ever felt. On those nights, the child would weep, and the queen—lonely with one baby dead, husband gone, and her remaining child in the tutelage of her highest advisor—would ask for a thousand brushstrokes. The number of ages.

The queen counted each stroke, relieved that despite the traces of Silver her advisor insisted she leave in her hair for *safety*, the child never grew ill and died like some of her other maidens had. The queen was so relieved, in fact, that she failed to mention the girl's health to her advisor.

Quite to the contrary, she insisted the rod be removed from her forehead and all the Silver replaced with her favorite rose gold, as she tired of the poor girl growing ill.

A lie as harmless as the moon. On most nights.

PART TWO

GREY SECRETS

Every day.

Before sunrise meal. Before the queen called to her for morning ritual. Before anything or anyone entered her small chamber. She wrote. Seven symbols, one word. A name for which she could no longer remember the rhythms.

From the first morning after her injury to the first year. And every day for every year since. The same symbols, long spindles of letters with tight curls of vowel woven among them.

Lilycup.

She was now seventeen. Thirteen years spent in this room, writing the symbols, working for the queen. Four years from the *before*. A time she couldn't remember, though pieces of it flew to her in sparks. Flash of bone, flash of moon, flash of pain as her head bumped along in the darkness of that thundering rhythm. A thunder followed by still, by silence, by cold.

The memories blurred in the ache of her head—a head that thereafter would struggle to recall things from that night and the time before.

Until another spark lit and a small memory returned. The stamp of guards' feet, the pauses that followed when she knew they must be calling to each other. The swoop of her stomach as someone hoisted her onto a fresh horse—a horse with a different rhythm, and one that was clearly laden with armor. Its gallop was steady—incredibly fast, but nothing like the reckless rush of the animal that had brought her here. She and that animal the only survivors. If, in fact, the steed had survived. Then the groaning vibration of a smaller gate.

Followed by calm. So much that in the cramped space of her sack prison, she wondered if such calm was really there to hide a turbulence underneath. Or maybe she'd never wondered that at all—maybe those were the thoughts that came to her in the years that followed, in the times when she tried to put it all together.

Again she wrote her name, her real name. A flourish under the final letter. Something that wasn't possible with the new name. *Zara.* Favored of the queen—that's what it meant, and it was true.

That night, that first night she'd arrived, everything in the court had been quiet. Even to a deaf girl. From the roses to the swish of skirts to the strum of a stringed instrument to the steady strokes through her mistress's hair. She had felt them all.

At that moment, memory began.

The time before—those flashes of things—they were all she had in the gray cloud of forgotten patterns.

The queen had dismissed the servants that night, that first night, and had asked her if she knew how to brush. Of course she hadn't heard. She could only watch the red clip of the queen's bright lips. Mesmerizing.

When she hadn't answered, the queen had pressed the brush into her small hand. "Can you count, child?" she'd asked.

Lilycup—not yet Zara—had not understood, but in a moment the queen had. Taking a paper and charcoal, she'd written *50,* then touched the brush.

And so the girl becoming Zara had brushed. Fifty strokes. Precise, from the top of the queen's head to the very bottom of each strand.

She did not know how or where she'd learned such a skill, could not remember in the throb of that night, but when she was finished, the queen dipped a white cloth into a cold basin of water, then dabbed at the bruise that laced from the right temple to the top of her skull.

And so they went on. Quiet days. Quiet nights. Until Moonface every month.

On the night of Moonface the guards assembled to set the locks into place. To wait for the howling that always began—a sound that traveled from the soft moss of the wood to the roots of the garden to the stones of the tower to her own feet. A sound she knew though she couldn't know sound. Because on those empty nights, it was the rhythm of her own heart.

She'd read the queen's account of the monster who had killed the king and all his men, who had felled every horse save one. The tale of the monster who'd gone after her, an innocent child of the city who'd wandered of an evening. The Phantom. His rhythms waves like an ocean of tears.

She knew she was one of them—the Howlers—those whom her lady called Shifters, though the name was changing. Every Moonface, her small body manifested her nature, and in the reflection of her lady's tall mirror, she marveled at her own hair, the fangs that hung down from an extended mouth. What did the humans write it as—'snout.'

Her lady was teaching her to write more letters and words, and together they developed a system of symbols they could make with their hands. This, the queen said, must be kept as an utmost secret. Easy enough since no one ever visited the lonely chamber during brushing time. But not good enough for the queen. "When you come with me to the courts, I will not be able to gesture to you, and so—" She had gazed hard into Zara's blue eyes. "—and so we must learn another way."

Soon after, the queen began combining the hand symbols with the direction to watch her mouth, in the hopes that Zara would learn the words through the movement of her lips.

Such an exercise was enchanting with the queen's painted mouth, with the rubies stuck through and the satisfying click of her lips that Zara could feel when her mistress was near. And soon, Zara could read the queen's lips as well as any symbol on paper.

"Such a bright child," the queen mumbled, soothing her skirts. "But do not let on," she admonished. "Never let on."

Zara wondered if she had known secrets before this place. Were they a thing all creatures *kept*—a funny word for a thing that couldn't be held in a chest or even a hand.

Whether she had known them before or not, she knew many now. The way the king had died, but the queen had not seen him often anyway, the fact that the queen had begun to wonder if he loved her or ever had, the way her mistress's skin now ached and pulled from the metals that hung from it, the way the queen's advisor insisted she keep up her appearances though both appearances and gemstones had grown dull to the queen. The way the advisor never grew old—well, older—the way the queen had had almost no education until now when she found it in old books stolen from her very own libraries. The way the world was shifting. Another strange word since it shifted away from her own race of shifters. Or so the queen said. And it seemed to be true.

Zara could not help but notice that fewer shifters wandered the streets than they had when she was small, that the halflings slunk away when the queen walked past, that the dress of humans was far finer than anyone else. She noticed, too, that though the queen held her gem-adorned head high while she was outside, it drooped once she came back in. For the queen—so powerful and beautiful—she was the loneliest creature Zara had ever known.

Except, of course, for herself.

THE FIRST TIME Zara met the princess, Rosebeth, it was clear why the queen had grown lonely, why the queen hired help for something as simple as brushing her hair. For Rosebeth was not the type of child to alleviate solitude, at least not in the way a person wished it eliminated. At age ten Rosebeth began attending matters of court. At age twelve, she began participating in government. And no one—not the packs of wolves in the forest, not the ravaging bears, not even the howling Phantom himself—could make quite so much fuss as the princess could.

Zara knew, for she—nearly two years older than the princess—attended these events also. But always at the back of the queen, holding her lady's gowns so they didn't trail in the dust. She was meant to be neither seen nor heard, and she was quite good at both.

This much she could say for her princess—the girl created quite the rhythms in court, from her voice to the stomping of her feet, and Zara appreciated a good rhythm. Zara felt the vibrations of the princess through the floor, the walls, even the curtains.

"I chose the wrong flower," the queen said, looking into the big mirror in front of both of them so Zara could see her lips move. "Lilies must be softer than roses."

It was the first time since her first month in the palace that the queen had made reference to her true name—the name she had come to think of as only a word of a name instead of a name itself.

"Roses have thorns," the queen continued, making the pinching gesture in their hand language.

Zara nodded, though she knew something the queen didn't. For though lilies carried no thorns, their petals often hung with poison. How she knew such a thing, Zara could not recall, though she had a foggy memory of being told not to eat them. At any rate, from the feelings of her heart, Zara suspected this was the case with her—laced with a poison others ought not touch. She didn't tell the queen though. (Another secret.) Such a sad woman had no need for facts like those.

～

THE NIGHT of Zara's birthday—or rather her *arrival day*, which is what the queen celebrated—coincided with Moonface. Zara waited (could it be said eagerly) for the howls and banging of the gate. It began that night like a western wind—a thin vibration, a chill. She felt it through the open window of the brushing chamber. With the rise of the moon, her skin rippled, fur covering her body, protecting her from the cold.

The still of the city, contrasted with the stomp of soldier feet.

And then a different tremor. Instead of the pound of the heavy clicks of the western locks, another sound broke into the chamber— it shook and pulled, the entire floor shaking with it.

"They're opening the gate," she murmured, her words mushed together so that few people besides the queen could understand her. "But why? How?"

It was meant to be spoken into the darkness, but at that moment, the queen strode in. "They have found a weakness," the queen replied. "The Phantom does not harm children, especially those of your race."

"How is this a weakness?" Zara asked.

The queen did not answer.

"How did you know he had a weakness for children?" Zara asked, shifting her question.

"He has taken several," the queen replied, looking straight into her eyes. "Or so it is spoken. On the early touch of Moonface, before the howling begins, children have started to disappear from the camps."

"And they are sure it is him?"

"His purposes are nefarious—do not think him kind in his taking of them."

An answer to a question Zara had not asked. "Of course, M'lady," she answered.

"They are bringing a group of children to the clearing of the western wall, hoping to distract and then kill him. My daughter's suggestion. Perhaps you heard it in court."

Zara looked to the queen's lips.

"Ah yes, I suppose you were behind me, and could not make it out."

Zara did not point out that she was always behind her queen and could make out only what the queen told her later. Which was generally quite a lot. This detail seemed to have been intentionally forgotten. "But what of the parents of the children?" Zara asked. "They will not want their children used in this way."

The queen looked at her, glancing at the window before looking back. "No," she said. "No, I suppose they probably did not."

The gate crashed into its final position. Zara felt the sound in her bones, followed by the smaller tremors—children's feet. "Good lady," she whispered.

"Hush, girl," the queen replied, her lips clicking with each word.

"But..."

"I asked for silence."

Zara turned to the window, stared into the darkness, one hand to the wall, her feet shoeless against the floor. About twelve children marched outside the city. It was difficult to see, even with the moonlight. She could only make out their shadowy figures, tiny hooded silhouettes in the night.

She could not hear them weeping—such a thing would have been impossible; and yet, it seemed as though she did. She heard the distinct knocks and bumps of the horses' gallops, the vibration from the voices of men. Her senses even more keen than usual during Moonface.

And then, a thunder. They came at the Phantom from all directions—a circle of soldiers closing in, like a noose cinching. She could feel the way the vibrations moved. Tightening.

The children were definitely crying now—she could not mistake the shrill vibrations—they must have been screaming, shrieking. One tripped. Zara held her head at the soft plunk of the small body. But then, the noose of the circle broke. One horse fell—its powerful body down, and underneath it...

The queen held an eyepiece to her face. "By the moon," she murmured.

"Please tell me," Zara gestured, moving her mouth to form the words as the queen had instructed her.

"A horse has fallen. On a man. They've broken ranks."

"Are the children crying?"

The queen didn't answer.

"Well, are they?"

"Of course they're crying." The clack of her lips was angry, or perhaps just something closer to what Zara felt.

"But he—it—is prowling around them, the children," Zara said, for she could feel the vibrations of his heavy footsteps.

"Our men hesitate." The queen lowered the eyepiece, turned away.

Zara held out a hand for the viewing glass.

"You will not want to see it."

Zara did not remove her hand, but still the queen did not pass the viewing glass.

"It is a chilling thing."

Zara felt another thud—a man fallen from his horse, it seemed. The stampede of his horse toward the gates, and then the vibration from earlier. "They're shutting the gates," Zara said. "Shutting the men out with the Phantom."

The queen lifted the glass to her eye, did not reply.

Another man fell—his scream so shrill, the vibration of it made it up to the walls where Zara's hand rested. His horse stampeded toward the woods. Others broke rank now. Zara felt the pounding, the confusion of the feet—both man and beast, but not children. They stood still.

"Have the children shifted?" Zara asked.

"Yes," her mistress replied, and that was all.

"And grown quiet?"

"Yes."

"Are they beautiful, mistress?" she asked, her own fur rippling with the touch of the moon.

"Of course, Zara. Of course." The queen paused. "Four men have died. Four of twelve."

"I know," Zara replied. "I feel them fall."

"Uncanny your senses on this night."

"Another just went down," Zara replied. "A heavy one."

"Two," the queen corrected. "Struck down as one."

"Have they harmed the Phantom at all?"

"Perhaps a scratch or two—the tip of a sword against the leather of his skin."

"They're going to die," Zara said. "All the men."

"I fear so."

"You cannot stop it?" Zara asked. "Tell them to open the gates."

"He will come in. It is not worth it to risk the lives of the people of the city."

"You should not have taken the children."

"Do not correct your queen," the queen replied. "Besides, it was not I who took them."

"Your seal. Your word."

"Yes," she murmured, the glass to her eye as another scream trembled up the wall.

"I hope the children close their eyes," Zara said.

The queen laughed—a sad sound. "Their heads are covered, my child. With sacks, not hoods."

Zara watched the lips of her queen, long after the speaking had ceased. They trembled, the rubies, shaking against the skin that Zara realized had grown old.

THE QUEEN HAD ALWAYS BEEN GIVEN to moods. Zara knew this—it had become part of her job, perhaps her entire job, to still these moods. But what had often come to the queen as rage when Zara had first arrived in court, now came to the queen as darkness. Some said that she'd been poisoned by the many metals she pierced through her skin, but Zara knew she was only poisoned by whatever had pierced her heart.

What Zara was not supposed to know, though she started to get a sense for it, was that the queen knew she had ruined a kingdom—not through evil or malice or cunning, but through vanity, sightlessness, and ignorance. Who knew such weaknesses could ruin a court? And yet the queen talked of a time when the Council had been balanced with shifter, halfling, and human. When the land had been cleaner, brighter, even richer. "Can you imagine that?" she had asked.

Zara could not.

"Shifter married human and human married halfling. Now all have gone to their own races. We've lost something, my young Zara. And in so short a time. My reign." She'd laughed harshly and dug in the basket for the brush, thrusting it into Zara's hand as though that would fix things.

It seemed now that the queen was determined not to do any more damage. She stayed in her quarters unless her presence was required in court or council, and she had given her seal almost entirely to her head advisor, Councilman Rodolph, who was also her father-in-law and her only child's grandfather. Princess Rosebeth studied under his tutelage for almost all her waking hours. Councilman Rodolph seemed a logical choice, this man born old, this man who would never die, but Zara did not trust him. Her queen, she suspected, did not either.

"Why did you give him the seal?" Zara asked, combing the tangles from the queen's hair on the morning after the slaying of twelve men—as the people were calling it, though Zara tended to think of it as the *saving of twelve children*. All through the court, the council members spoke of his evil intentions toward the children, although if they were so very concerned, Zara couldn't help but wonder why they'd been so willing to use such small creatures as bait.

"You know why I gave him the seal, Zara, dear."

"You could choose better than he," Zara replied.

"The people no longer think so. At least now he will be blamed for any mistakes."

Zara thought this quite unlikely. In fact, she thought it quite the opposite and part of Councilman Rodolph's overall agenda. She was trying to decide if she should say so or not when the queen spoke again.

"Additionally, I've decided to give Rosebeth the throne on her twentieth birthday."

Zara asked her mistress to repeat the words, watching her mouth closely. The princess was nearly two years younger than Zara, which meant she'd be queen in about three and a half more years. A terribly short time.

"My lady," Zara said when she was sure she had understood.

"Do not reprove me," the queen replied sharply.

"I do not," Zara said, bowing her head.

"Ah, but you do. You just do not say it with words."

Zara had no response for that.

It started as a contest. A declaration made by Rosebeth ten months after the slaying of the twelve men. The ancient advisor, her grandfather, at her side as she announced, "The time has come, at last, to avenge my father's death. Any man strong or cunning or brave enough to conquer the Howling Phantom—he who batters our walls, terrifies our citizens, drags away our children—any who can conquer this beast will be awarded a prize of 100,000 gold pieces." A gasp rose from the gathered crowd. It was a sum worth nearly a quarter of the kingdom.

But Rosebeth wasn't finished. "As well as a place at the head of the council." The crowd broke into chatter, some young men suiting into armor right there, though the gesture struck Zara as ridiculous since Moonface was nearly three weeks away.

Rosebeth, however, smiled at the enthusiasm and then finished, saying, "In addition to the greatest prize of all..."

The crowd paused, holding a mutual breath. Zara knew what was coming—the queen had warned her. Yet even she waited, watching for the movement of Rose's lips.

"...My hand in marriage."

Women and men wept openly. Young men ran in circles whooping and slapping each other. Girls stood nearby, wearing faces of stoicism, while the boys they cared for cooed and crowed at the chance to marry the princess. For, besides being powerful and brilliant and rich, Rosebeth was dangerously beautiful. Hair and skin like her mother's had been, the strong lean limbs of her father, sharp features that softened into thick lips, round eyes and the curves of womanhood. No better prize existed in all the land. At least, if you wanted a pounding of rhythms for the rest of your life—thundering heart, racing blood, stomping feet, a whip of words—sharp and cruel, with shrieks of mood that shook and rumbled.

As for Zara, she found that she preferred a softer rhythm. A quiet breakfast of bread and tea alone or with the queen was better than all the wit and rumble of her princess. Princess, but in some ways practically sister.

Zara stewed on the thought that afternoon as she moved through her exercises for the day—first lengthening and loosening the muscles of her legs, then finding the patterns that her teacher had shown her—half dance, half worship. All with only the music of her heart to guide her. The queen had told her that, years ago, after Zara was brought through the gates and left at the palace, she'd barely moved for days, only standing to brush her lady's hair, only drinking a flowered tea.

Then, one morning, the queen had come in to find her stepping around the small table, though it was more than steps—the movements of her feet following a rhythm, a pattern.

"How did you learn that?" the queen had written to her.

And Zara—still mostly Lilycup—had shrugged. Soon thereafter, the queen had put her into lessons. Dance, though the more she practiced and the stronger she grew, the more she realized the dances she learned were also part war—leaps, kicks, and thrusts. It was different than the thing she'd known as a child, different than the flashes that battered against the locked vault of her memory. But it was good enough.

After the dance, she made her way to the stables, chose her favorite horse, and mounted without saddling.

No one had expected her to love horses. But love them she did, almost as much as she loved the queen. It didn't hurt that the Princess Rosebeth was afraid of them, and because of that could never be found anywhere near the stables.

Years ago, rumor from the kitchens (the best place for rumor to grow) had murmured that Rosebeth had once been thrown as a small child, just a few years after the coming of the Phantom. That horse had been killed, of course, but ever since then Rose had refused to go near the horses. Instead, a single cart had been invented with moving parts to transport her from place to place.

From the time the rumor came to Zara—she must have been just seven or eight back then—she began to frequent the stables. It didn't seem that it would have been a quiet place, with the stamping, snorting rhythms of the huge animals. But somehow Zara found the rhythms steady and quieting, a nice contrast to the moods of her mistress, the tantrums of Rosebeth, and the beating, arguing fluctuations of the court.

It hadn't taken long, all those years ago, for her to find the animal that had rescued her and borne her to the queen. She'd known it by its scent, and by the contours of its back. Even if she had not been able to smell or feel it, she would have known the horse by the pounding of its hooves, its unique rhythm.

"The fastest one we've got," the boy at the stables had told her.

"I know," she said, and he looked at her like he was pretty sure she couldn't know anything of the sort.

"Only creature in this whole city who's survived the Phantom," he'd added.

"The only?" Zara had asked.

"Well, sure. All the men and the other mounts died that night."

And that much was true, but this horse had carried another—not a man or a horse. And for the first time the girl who was now called Zara realized that the servants and guards and people had only seen an animal return, an animal with a sack on its back. The only ones with knowledge of her deliverance were the queen, her advisor, and perhaps the head guards.

"What a brave, sad thing," she said to the horse, who whinnied and snorted away from her.

"She ain't that brave no more," the boy said.

Zara had come every day after that, always bringing a treat—a bunch of carrots, a handful of sugar, a scoop of oat grains. In time, the horse no longer shied or shimmied away, though it always watched her with those bulging eyes, knowing who she was, as only a few in the entire city, the entire world, did. "You see," she whispered to it one day. "Even you have a secret."

The boy had taught Zara to ride, though never on the shivering back of that swift horse. It bucked and swayed too much at the saddle. "She don't like nobody on her these days," the boy said, patting her hide.

And so the stable boy chose a gentler horse. At least at first. And Zara learned well—this different type of dance with a different type of partner. Over time, the horses the boy brought to her grew faster, wilder, and more aggressive, until finally she was allowed a ride on that swiftest of horses.

"Do you think it's a good idea?" the stableboy, now her friend, had asked.

"Perhaps not," she'd replied, before hoisting herself onto its back. It neighed, then broke away, galloping through the fields, once again as though it was trying to shake loose of a weight it hadn't asked for. When she returned to the stables, her hair a whip of tangles, her skirts dirtied and torn, she dismounted from the creature, buried her face in its coat and whispered in her muddied tones, "Thank you, dear one. I will not need to ride you again, but I did, just this once, to see if I could."

After the ride, the horse settled, always trotting to see Zara when she arrived.

"Guess she's come to like you," the stableboy said.

Now Zara rode through the fields until the horizon turned to pink, then orange. She wondered, gazing at the color, what it would have been like in the time of the purple sky and the red sun—the time she was told was so different from now because the humans had been held down by another race, forced to do things in exactly their way. The hair prickled at her neck when the sliver of moon rose and she thought that perhaps it hadn't been so very different after all, just a little flipped.

The pop of an idea burst into her head and she returned as quickly as she could to the stables—driving the animal until it trembled, though she never drove it past that point—never to the place where she had once ridden with an animal whose heart was about to burst.

The stableboy waited to help her dismount, though she jumped from the horse without assistance. "Boy," she said, noticing suddenly that his face had grown scruffy, his voice deep, and then realizing that her own legs had also grown, her muscles long and strong. She shook such observations away, remembering her goal.

"How old is the horse? The one to survive the fury of the Phantom Howler."

"Ah, she's getting on now," the boy-turned-man said.

"Can she still have children?"

"I guess I ain't—" He cleared his throat, correcting his words. "—I hadn't ever thought about it."

"Please do," Zara replied with her most queenly posture and the best tones she could manage.

SHE ARRIVED to the brushing chambers—clean and still shining with the moisture of her bath, just as her lady arrived. The queen nodded at the basket with hair tools. "You must weave in the beads," she said. "For the contestants will begin applying tomorrow and I'm wanted at the ceremony."

"Applying?" Zara asked.

"Of course," the queen replied.

"Moonface happens but once a month. We must have only the best applicants at the ready. Otherwise, it will take years to defeat the beast."

Zara found, as she wound the threads of the queen's hair through the bits of metal bead, that she hoped it did.

"M'lady," she began, weaving in a golden bead. "My arrival day is approaching." Not a proper birthday, but even so, on that day her mistress often brought her something bright—a coin from the treasury, a basket of candies wrapped in papers that held in a twist without a bow, a new book of blank pages wrapped in leather, scented and soft against her fingers.

"Yes," the queen said as Zara lifted another soft strand of the spider-black hair, this time selecting a copper bead. "Do you know the old horse, the one called Mist?"

"I do," the queen replied, and in the click of her lips, Zara felt the knowing of the queen.

"Can this horse still bear?"

"She grows old," the queen replied.

"She runs still," Zara replied.

"But won't forever."

"Exactly."

"You wish for her baby?"

"In celebration of my arrival day," Zara replied.

"I shall check with the stable master," the queen said. "It is not ideal, a horse of this age."

Zara thought that it would be quite ideal indeed.

"And the father, if such a thing is even possible—what traits do you wish in him?" the queen asked.

For a moment, Zara paused. She had not even thought on the father and almost replied that it didn't matter. Almost.

"I wish for the father to be as steady as she is swift," she said.

"A wise request, if not a bit wishful."

"Is such a thing not possible?"

"A difficult request from a male, especially a horse able to produce seed. They buck and rear and fight—these stallions."

The queen gazed into the fire.

"Was your king a stallion?" Zara asked. "If my mistress does not mind my asking."

"I do mind," the queen snapped, her reflection clear in the mirror. "Such an impertinent question from the brushing girl."

Zara fell into silence.

"And, no, he was no stallion. Not for me anyway."

"A good thing then," Zara said.

"Neither was he steady. At least not for me. You make a wise request, if an impossible one." And that was all she said on the matter.

At the bottom of the basket, Zara found the three small ceremonial beads of the Silver, as she always did for large events. Zara knew the instruction of the queen—to thread them deep into the queen's hair. After that, Zara was supposed to take to her bed, refusing food and often drink—too exhausted to move.

As a child, she had hated those days, those requests. She was never sick, even though she was supposed to act as though she was. She got tired of staring at the ceiling, her mouth dry, her stomach growling. However, as the years had worn on, she'd become aware that there was something special about this demand of the queen— one of the deepest secrets that she must keep.

A MONTH after the first contestant was chosen to go against the Phantom, the queen sent a small note. Beautiful, as were all things that came from the queen. The paper thick in Zara's hands, flowers pressed into the parchment, joining with the wood pulp. Zara lifted it to her nose, smelled the faint perfume. Not roses for this, nor lily either, but lavender.

And on that page, the swoop of the queen's hand. "The mare is with child."

THE FIRST CONTESTANT did not return. More boys applied.

Zara knew she was supposed to think of them as men, but none of them looked it—all limbs and pomp and ignorance.

At first they had sallied forth by ones. One for each month, the princess taking on new applicants for every boy who didn't return, never accepting a man who was older than twenty-five. For each rejected applicant, the princess gave a reason, though it was clear that the princess was not keen to have an older man win her hand, no matter how clever or skilled or brave he was. She needn't have worried, for none who went forth against the Phantom ever returned to claim anything.

And despite the stupidity and vanity and pride of the many applicants, Zara couldn't help but pity them. It was sad to see them wander through the western wall—the terror on their unbearded faces as they realized the thing they must do, as the howling took up from the edge of the wood, growing closer.

Most boys the Phantom did not kill outright, but dragged away into the woods.

Soon, instead of just the killings or kidnappings, they started to have batterings, and not only at Moonface, but other times when rebel shifters and sometimes even halflings would beat at the Western wall with the trunk of an enormous tree. These rebels came from the woods as wild men, hair grown so long it looked like the shifting had already taken place, faces and nails dirty, voices growls. Some women took part too, though it was no secret that the female shifters grew harder to find. Some said it was on account of their weaker constitutions, although the maids of the kitchen and gardens scoffed at such talk. "They hide," they said. "Because women hide better." And because without the women of the race, you have no race.

After several months the men started applying in twos or threes —willing to divide the spoils of the contract. This diversified the groups a bit. Several older men were now chosen as long as it was a younger who would take the hand of the princess, making it clear that her majesty had a bit of her mother's romanticism in her after all.

But not enough of her mother to stop the madness after thirty-one months (an unlucky number, the queen said) of killed or kidnapped hopefuls. After that, the groups of applicants thinned from the nearly-worthy to the old to the desperate to the insane, and then to nothing at all.

Rosebeth would be crowned queen in less than a year.

~

Zara had waited all this time, thinking—some might say plotting, though it wasn't a word Zara favored.

On the month that no applications came, Rosebeth boiled into a rage, tearing through court, ripping tapestries and tumbling chairs. Zara could feel the vibrations up in her room, the waves of language that poured from her princess's mouth. Then the queen's footsteps, a rhythm Zara knew better than any other, leaving the room.

Zara fingered the piece of paper she'd bribed a serving boy into bringing to her. Now was either the perfect time, or the worst. She gathered her courage, donned a blue cloak (the princess's favorite color), and made her way to the courts, empty except for a furious princess and the ever-calm head advisor.

Zara bowed. "M'lady," she said, knowing that the smudge of her words rang unfamiliar in the ears of any except the queen.

"And what are you doing here?" Rosebeth asked, slumping into the small throne her mother had commissioned for her. "Hopefully you're not waiting for some imbecile strong enough to go against the Howling Phantom, because apparently one of those doesn't exist."

"I do not wait," Zara replied, kneeling and holding out her application.

Rosebeth leaned forward, one ebony eyebrow arched in a perfect question mark, but before the princess could do anything, Councilman Rodolph snatched the paper from her hand and tore it neatly in two.

"Denied," he said, just as neatly, but Rosebeth had raised herself from the throne and was staring at the two halves of the paper.

"Grandfather," she said. "Retrieve it and reposition it. It is hardly your duty or your position to make this decision alone."

"I do not see what part of this application needs discussion," he blustered (Zara realized she had never seen him bluster before). "She is a female and a shifter, not to mention her infirmity." He tugged at his ear and Zara watched his lips very closely through her eyelashes.

"We set forth no such boundaries," the princess responded. "Not in writing at least, only in expectation."

"If another such as this had applied, she would have been promptly denied," Councilman Rodolph responded.

"Perhaps," Rosebeth said. "But none such as her has applied, and there are some who would argue that there is no one quite like Zara."

"Indeed," Rodolph answered, watching the princess very closely. Zara saw the moment when he realized what Zara understood deeply. If Zara died on this foolish mission, Rosebeth would be rid of her, and while Zara was never enough of a threat to give much heed, she did take quite a bit of her mother's time and she did have certain talents for which Rose had always been jealous—her skill with training the new horse, Lavender, being a prime example.

Indeed, Zara's elimination at the hands of the Phantom would be supremely convenient.

"It may set a precedent," Rodolph warned.

"I hardly think many women, especially of this fading race, will eagerly face the Phantom. Not when all the men have already dried up."

"Perhaps not," Rodolph conceded. "But it cannot be denied that she must not in any way take your hand in marriage."

It was clear that Rosebeth considered this a non-issue since she fully expected Zara to die, but decorum required she go along. "Of course not," she replied. "It would be unacceptable on so many levels, the least of which is that I must marry one who can give me an heir."

"Is that the only issue?" Zara asked.

"The largest that I can see," Rose replied.

"Then perhaps I could *be* the heir. For I do not wish your hand or any other privilege, only to be the true daughter of the queen; and your sister. Your *younger* sister."

"But you are not younger," Rosebeth replied.

"In contract, I will be so."

"My *heir*?" Rosebeth said.

It was clear that the word gave Rosebeth pause, as Zara had suspected it would. To hear your worst fear spoken always did.

After several moments, the princess replied, "I accept these terms. Grandfather will draw up the new contract."

"Sisters then," Zara said. "If I destroy the Beast, we shall be nearly as equals."

"Only if you succeed at destroying the Phantom. This creature—the murderer of my father—he must be utterly destroyed." The princess smiled then. "You will be suited up on the afternoon of the next Moonface, two weeks hence."

"I will require only my horse and riding clothes."

"Don't be stupid," Rosebeth said, but Zara did not move or respond. "Very well," the princess replied. "Have it however you wish, though every warrior gets a bit of Silver to use against the Phantom."

Zara wrinkled her brow. "My lady."

"I understand that it weakens you. I will have it encased in iron, but you must use it, *New Sister,* or your mission will surely fail. There is nothing else that can kill him."

"Have the others used it?" Zara asked.

"Most have failed to even remove it from their sheaths," Rosebeth replied. "If you are able to use it, you will only get one shot."

"I will only need one shot," Zara replied, smiling at her soon-to-be sister with teeth that glittered white like diamonds.

"Wʜᴀᴛ ɪs ᴛʜɪs?" the queen asked, waving the contract over her head and tossing the brushing basket at Zara's feet. "I never would have let this go forward."

"Would you have stopped it, my queen?" Zara said.

The queen sputtered. "Of course, girl. Such foolishness."

"I only wish to be your daughter."

"You will not live to become my daughter."

"You have no faith in me."

"I have no faith in anything."

"I own the Silver," Zara said.

The queen paused on hearing this thing that neither of them had spoken. "You are still a child."

"No longer," Zara replied, retrieving the queen's favorite brush.

The queen huffed. "You have no idea, foolish creature. You would leave me?" The queen turned to the mirror, so that they faced each other in the glass.

"I would be yours." Zara threaded a lock of soft black hair through the brush, the ritual she'd performed for her queen since her memory had begun.

"You would go beyond your station."

"I would," Zara said simply and the queen's anger burned into a deep brooding.

"I demanded the contract," the queen said after several minutes of quiet brushing. "If you do conquer, through some miracle of the moon, I wanted to have the agreement in writing."

"Thank you, M'lady,"

"Oh, do not call me that," the queen replied.

"What would you have me call you?" Zara asked, surprised at this response.

"Call me Aemalia," the queen replied.

Zara watched the lips, asked her queen to say it again. They were difficult sounds to read and the queen laughed at her attempts. "No, no child."

Zara worked with her lips and tongue, trying again. "Is that better?"

The queen looked into Zara's blue eyes. "You know, child, I believe it is. Use the name only in my presence."

"Of course, M'la... Of course, Amia." For that is the sound that had come from her mouth.

The queen smiled at the name, then sighed. "Too bad you'll be dead within the month."

"Have a little faith, M'lady. M'Amia," Zara corrected.

"Faith is a privilege of the young," the queen replied.

"Well, lucky for me," Zara replied, wrapping the queen's hair in a braided knot at the top of her head. "I still qualify."

"You're a naughty child," the queen laughed, though it was always a sad sound. "And I will truly miss you when you're gone."

ZARA SAW it through the eyeglass her lady had given her—the slightest movement of tree limbs, like a boy had climbed the branches and was resting there. But no boy ventured into the Western wood. It could have been anything—from hawk to bear, even a cat if you believed they still roamed the woods. Yet something in the movement reminded her of something from the time before her memory—the way the branches bent down from the weight then swung up when released.

She slipped from the room, wearing her riding clothes and carrying a sack. In minutes she was at the stables. "And where are you off to today?" the boy who had become a man asked her when she arrived.

"A little exploring," she answered. "To see what I can see."

"Good day for it," he replied. "Can I help you with the satchel?"

"No need," she answered. "It's quite light. Is Lavender ready?"

"As always, for you."

He opened the stall, then puttered around the animal, tightening straps. "They say you've agreed with the princess to fight the Phantom, that you have an eye for the throne, and are willing to do anything to get it."

"Not much of a truth," she replied.

"Which parts are true then?" he asked, tucking a few carrots into one of the saddlebags before turning back to her.

She was surprised at the perception. Perhaps he had grown up in more than just limb and beard. "Few," she replied. "Though I do go to fight the Phantom."

"A foolhardy venture," he answered, fidgeting with the stable key. "And to what end, if not the throne?"

To find a mother—that is what she had told herself—and with a mother, a place in the only world she could remember knowing. But there was something else in the venture, in the task that brought her to oppose one of her own—the Phantom shifter. "I seek my place in this world," she answered.

The stable man turned back to the horse, stroking her mane. "Many cheer for you, Zara. They say that if you succeed, both peasant and shifter will have won some ground again in court."

"I did not peg you for one that would give heed to the political murmurings of the people."

"I am one who has come to notice the comings and goings of some, most particularly you."

"And do you cheer for me?"

"I do," he answered, "though perhaps not in the way you mean. I don't care if you gain the throne or defeat the Phantom, only that you come back. Can you do that?"

She felt a small heat rise in her cheeks. She noticed now that the stable boy's hair was thick and the same color as the cherry nuts that grew in the fall, his eyes soft and darker than his hair. "I do not know what I can do. But you need not think much of my comings and goings. I will succeed or I will fail and the kingdom will roll on."

"I would very much like for you to roll on with it," he answered.

"Perhaps I will."

"See that you do." He took her hand then and slipped the stable key—warmed by his own palm—into her fingers. "Come back."

ONE COULD NOT SIMPLY RIDE through the western gates and into the woods. Not on a normal afternoon at any rate. She took the south-western passage, bribed the guard, and made her way into the woods and then followed the wolf paths toward the setting sun. She knew she had come to the correct place when she could see the flags of the western gate through the trees. The Howling Gates. Now called by many the Crying Gates. The place where their men and boys went to die.

She found the tree—it was not difficult—she knew it for the bark that peeled in curls from its trunk. The birch tree. But how did she know the name? The queen had not taught her. She walked her horse underneath it, closed her eyes—shutting off her second-best sense —and felt for the vibrations.

Almost as a breeze they came to her, the scent too. The Phantom was apparently not given to frequent bathing.

"It is difficult to avoid notice," she said loudly against the soft winds, trying to form her words as tightly as she could, "when one does not make good use of the clear streams the western wood provides you."

Almost a laugh—she was nearly sure of it from the vibration. Though almost a growl too.

"How would a girl child know what state the streams of the western wood are in?" He walked a limb with the grace of a bird, perched upon bare toes, just as such an animal would have, though without Moonface he was only a man. A filthy man. She looked up. His face was smeared in grime, which made it difficult to see among the trees, though it accented the flash of pink tongue and lips when he spoke—an advantage to one such as Zara.

"Perhaps the streams run with mud and muck," he said. "Perhaps they're stopped with the carcasses of beasts, poisoning the drink. Perhaps they stink with the blood of my victims."

"Perhaps they stink with the state of your poetry," she replied. He retreated back into the trees where she could not see his mouth, though she felt the slightest touch of a vibration. The man had replied.

"Are you he?" she asked. "He who takes the men who seek the hand of the princess. He who howls and pounds every month against the gates." Grasping the lower limb, she swung up onto it, then climbed the next. The man perched at the tip of a limb—how it could hold his weight, she could not imagine—with his back to her. She grunted in frustration, climbing higher up.

The man looked over his shoulder, shaggy hair brushing his neck and a look of annoyance across his features.

"I do not know of any men who have sought the hand of the princess. Only a lot of silly boys who cannot tell which end of their body is used for thinking." With that, he struck the limb on which she stood and she stumbled, swaying to the side, catching the trunk, and thunking down to her bottom.

The Phantom—the creature who had killed the king and his men, the beast who had fought and stolen every boy who had sought him in these last two years—he laughed.

"Would you kill me then, too? Add me to your stinking carcass stream?" she said.

"You are even sillier than the boys."

"Am I?" she asked.

"Well, perhaps not. But that is a very low limb, so don't let it go to your head."

He turned again, said something else.

"Face me," she demanded, doing her best to keep her hearing infirmity hidden.

He held up a hand in a gesture she could not understand, probably a rude one. Then he let the hand fall against the limb again, striking it with a fist. But this time she was ready for it. She held the limb above her head, lifting her legs and waiting for the shaking to stop.

As a reward, he turned to her. "I do not kill girls."

"I have noticed that you do not kill many." She sat, one limb dangling over either side of the branch.

"I kill men," he replied. "And with ease."

"You are not the first to do so."

"I would kill your simpleton of a queen if I had the chance."

That struck a little closer to home. "She is no more simple than the bud of a purple climbing vine—curling and tender until the days roll into months, and she hardens."

"The queen?" he asked. "With her lusts and vanities, her gems and metals."

"You do not know her," Zara replied.

"I know her better than you, peasant child."

"Those things you say—they are merely the shell that holds the real queen."

"The *real* queen," he muttered. "As though there is anything but fluff under her adornments."

Zara pinched her mouth shut and the dirty man gazed at her. "Very well," he said. "Suppose it is so. Suppose our lady has changed. Unfortunately for her, change in one does not keep many from remaining the same. Let's take the princess, for example. Boy after boy she sends to me. Victim after victim, you might say."

"You *might* say that," Zara replied.

The man stared at her. "At any rate, apparently the princess has now taken to sending girls after the Phantom, the Howler, the Haunter of the Crying Gates. Perhaps she sends those stronger and prettier than herself—those she has grown jealous of. A simple solution, isn't it?"

"I do not come to kill you."

"Then what is your mission?"

"It is one to destroy."

"Echoes of our ancient Lady Sadora. Unfortunately, I'm not sure destruction suits me well either."

Something about the lilt of the rhythms as he spoke struck Zara as familiar, though she couldn't place where she had known one such as this before.

"I do not know the word 'echo,'" the girl warrior replied.

He looked at her, cocked his head to the side, then released a scream. She felt the vibrations rock through her skin, her feet, the tree. And then the smaller ones that followed.

"There now," he said. "You hear it. This sound that comes again and again. Much like me."

"A sound that vibrates," she replied. "Like a heart."

He laughed, a hard, deep vibration. "Not at all, foolish child. An echo is the sound of an empty chamber of a heart shriveled to dust."

"I come again at Moonface, Old One."

"Then you come to your death."

"Like so many others?" she asked.

"And worse."

"If that is to be my fate at your hand, then I welcome it. A historic finish—dying at the hands of the mighty Phantom. He who cries to the moon for the stars gone old."

"He who has forgotten the heat of tears when everything fell cold."

The circle of the sounds at the end of each phrase. A rhyme like the cats were said to do. "Then perhaps it is time to bring some heat," she said.

"If you could do that, child, I would die singing your praises."

"Hum them, Old One, and I will hear."

She dropped to the ground, and stamped for her horse. It felt the vibration, whinnied to that call.

And the old, unbathed man who threatened the safety of their culture, who hunted anyone who came through the western gate, he narrowed his eyes.

SHE RODE. Almost the same pounding as all those years ago, though this time she knew the horse's rhythm as well as she did the beating of her own heart.

And beat it did. Each step of her horse pushing more blood to her veins, thrusting more air into her lungs.

The moon rose—fat as blossoms at the peak of spring. Lavender whinnied at Zara's wolken shift, the added weight, or perhaps the repositioning of it—the muscles of her legs taut and sinewy, the fur fanning in a spine along her back, the nails long, dense, unbreakable.

Under the moon it seemed impossible that she would need any weapon outside of herself, though she knew this was foolishness, for the Phantom also grew in the moon, easily double her size. And even if he did not, the moon tonight was traitorous—exposed, then hidden by drifting clouds. For a shifter it was difficult—their bodies aching and pulling with the strength and weakness of the moon's light—human and wolken features melting, then sharpening. A small torture for shifters under the best conditions, an especial danger under these.

Lavender frothed as she ran and Zara held the reins, leaning her body so that it nearly rested on the animal's neck. When Lavender reared to a stop, she knew they'd arrived.

Dismounting, she slapped the horse's hide, signaling permission to retreat. Lavender did slightly—whinnying and dancing, but she remained nearby.

"You loyal fool," she murmured. "Take your chance and run." The horse didn't obey, retreating only a few more paces into the shadow of the woods.

"Have it your own way," Zara grumbled.

From a branch above her, she heard the vibration of laughter and then the unmistakable thud as the Phantom landed beside her. He stood directly under the moon, its rays bathing his face, giving him its blessing. "Perhaps you should take the advice given to your steed."

Zara watched his lips.

"And run while the chance stands," he concluded.

"My chance is gone, Old One."

He squinted at the sound of her voice, as though reaching into the syllables. "A feeling I understand," he replied. "As mine thundered away years ago."

"You speak riddles," she replied.

"Ah, a girl of action, not words." He broke a thick branch of tree and hurled it toward her. She leapt away with ease.

"Already better than half the boys," he said, though she found it difficult to capture all the words, dodging the narrow, long switch that he now whipped in her direction.

From that moment on, she would have only motion, vibration, and what little sight the moon deigned to give her.

Which wasn't much. Within moments, a thick, lazy cloud drifted in front of the moon. She felt her body shrivel. Stumbling, she caught herself on her palms. Through her hands she felt the vibration of his roar. She rolled to the side as a fearsome, nearly naked man thrashed toward her, now wielding two whips instead of one. But a whip was easy to fix.

She reached for the sword at her back and swung. The whips shortened. Again, and again. With each chop, the man drew closer until only a step away. One step, a thrust of her sword, and it would be done.

She held her stance, steadied her breath, then the moon tore out of its hiding place. She felt the rippling nausea, the pain of the shift. And now, the creature stood just a step away—three heads higher and twice as broad, as though he had planned the timing himself.

She reached for her heavier sword and swung. He jumped, a graceful arc over her head, landing behind her.

The moon left again and she felt the weakness coupled with a double blindness—her adversary at her back, and dark night every-where else. It left her with no choice, but to do what she did best. Feel, and dance.

The shifting of his weight—she knew it from the tremble in her right leg. A quick turn, a swing of the sword, more for momentum than to strike. The Phantom now danced in his own rhythm around the trees. And why did it feel familiar—that movement, the way he climbed—the branches shifting from his weight, the breezes of the leaves grazing her face.

The sword felt a little too heavy in her human-ish hands. She looked to the skies—only clouds—and reached for her lighter sword. It was gone.

Impossible. She felt each vibration, the sway of a leaf, the breeze of breath during speech. How could he have taken it? Yet when she looked up, its metal glinted from the branches. "The shifting is a moment of weakness," he said, looking down at her from his spot on the trees. "You have not yet learned to work with its flow; instead you fight against it. This fighting weakens you further."

She did not understand each word, but caught several and with them the meaning. She abandoned her dance, ran toward the tree, striking it with a thin human shoulder.

He shot the sword toward her like an arrow. She hit the ground, feeling the wind from the blade, sensing the delicate hum of its vibration as it struck into the ground. An inch away.

An insult? To give her the weapon she needed. A show of his strength? It didn't matter. She grabbed for the blade, only to find that the hilt was missing.

And how?

He leapt to the ground. She watched him warily, a dull chunk of moon exposed, which gave a little brightness to his face. Her bruised shoulder ached for the moon's full exposure.

Nearby the Phantom said something she couldn't understand, his mouth barely visible through the dark trees. She looked around. He'd lured her deeper into the forest, all without her noticing. He walked toward her, one heavy step, then another. Again, something familiar to his gait, like a dream pecking at her brain.

She twisted away from him, from his face, and with it, his words. When she ran, she held out one hand, feeling through the air, running it along the bark of passing trees—each piece of vibration feeding her information. A habit from childhood.

The Phantom stopped.

She gathered herself, found her footing, drew the only useful weapon she had remaining—a small iron box.

He spoke, but she couldn't make out the words. She twirled

away, her weapon still in its iron case, the moon just beginning to peek from the clouds.

But he, he had turned from her, was using the hilt-less sword to scratch into the tree. More of the moon shone from its cover and she clicked open the case. He jumped—higher and higher into the branches.

She ran toward the tree, knees bent, ready to follow when the moon beamed fully, lighting up the trunk and illuminating the letters—symbols she'd written every day since childhood. *L-i-l-y-c-u-p.*

She staggered back as she shifted to her wolken form. Then she reached for the heavy sword, which she thrust into the tree, using it to climb to the lowest branch.

Until then, she had not thought of the Phantom as evil, only brutish. But if he knew such a thing as her name, who had he killed to know it? Her family, the queen had said, could not be found, not in all the kingdom. The queen had put out notices for an orphan who had arrived at the palace. Zara had seen them all around the city. And Zara, in her hope, she had waited months for someone to arrive, to claim her. No one had. Perhaps because the Phantom had taken her father. Murdered him, as he had done to the king and his men.

When she began to climb, he thudded to the ground again. Such a fall, such a vibration. The tree limbs shook.

"You say you have come to destroy me," he said, his face clear in the moonlight. "And it is clearly so."

From the branch, she could see him perfectly, could aim the Silver dagger.

And then the word again, formed perfectly on his wolken lips.

"No," she screamed, hurling the dagger at the spot between his eyes.

He reached up and snatched it from the air like it was a moth. "My Lilycup."

The word again, the name.

"You killed him," she screamed, leaping down and running.

"They let you live," he murmured, following her, catching her shoulders, then dragging her even deeper into the forest. In a rush of wind, the moon vanished behind a cloud, and she sank, kicking against the man.

"You killed him," she shrieked again, scratching and biting at him, no longer caring if she lived, no longer remembering her goal of destroying him.

"That could be said," he answered, staring like a ghost into her face. She struggled, but he held her face so that she was forced to look at him. She closed her eyes in defiance. He moved his face closer to hers so that she would feel the rhythms of his breath. "Though it is not entirely true."

Her eyes flashed open. "Where have you hidden him? My father?"

"Can you not now tell?" he asked, looking at her.

The tears bit into her eyes as a memory rushed at her—the rhythm of his steps, the strength of his climbing. She pinched them back. "No," she said, spinning away from him and kicking the back of his knee. He fell forward, kneeling, not even bothering to try to keep his balance.

The moon pierced the clouds and she jerked the heavy sword from the trunk of the tree as she shifted, swinging it toward him.

He moved slightly, avoiding the blow. She swung again, wilder, the steps of her dance forgotten, everything forgotten except the rage she now felt. She kicked at his side, then swung the sword around, cutting a sharp line across his chest, then his back, two more along either arm.

He rose to his feet, stepped back, holding up his hands.

Still she swung, moving in like he had with the whips, one step closer then another, until all she had left to do was thrust the sword into his heart. She waited for the clouds to cover the moon, to throw her into her human form. She waited for the Phantom to fight back, to stop her in her advance. She waited for a bugle call from the castle or a sliver of dawn.

But the moon hung bright and full, her arms trembling with strength. The shifter in front of her did not move to escape, did not even flinch. And the forest remained as still and dark as the new dungeon of her heart.

She tightened her grip on the sword. "If it's true, then tell me her name."

And without asking who, he answered. "Simone."

She froze at this final secret, this last thing she had remembered all these years. This torture to know of a mother who had died, but not be able to remember the father who had not.

She let the sword clatter to the ground, turned from him. "I hate you," she said.

"I can understand that," he answered. "For many years I have hated myself." He held the Silver dagger out for her to take. She continued to walk away.

"It will not hurt you," he said.

Feeling the rhythm of his voice, she turned back to him. He held the silver, repeated, "It will not hurt you."

"Those who could lord it are decades gone," she replied.

He fingered it, cleaned his nails.

"Well, almost," she said.

"But not you?" he asked.

"The princess gave it to me in an iron sheath so it would not weaken me."

"And this princess—she is your ally?"

Zara did not answer.

"For iron will only hold the power of the metal while it is contained. After that, there is little that will hold back the strength of the Shining Grey."

"The queen has renamed it Silver."

"Oh, I know what the queen has done." He gazed at her, then in a swift movement jumped toward her, wrapping a strong arm around her shoulders and forcing the metal to her cheek. She writhed and fought, feeling the cold press of the dagger against her skin. She bit his wrist and the Silver clattered to the ground. "You do not seem weaker to me," he said, nursing his arm.

"The queen told me never to tell," Zara hissed, staggering away from him.

"Better advice than the princess has given." He wrapped the wound with a ragged piece of cloth.

"The queen raised me, gave me speech. She waits in the palace, to see that you are ruined."

"Oh, she ruined me moons and moons ago. Kept you from me."

"You were a monster. Are a monster. Robbed her of her husband." The moon vanished, and her stomach lurched as she returned to her human form.

"Not until I was robbed. Do you not remember that night?"

"My head was struck. I have only fragments—the smell of the horse, its race to safety."

"Safety," he snorted. "For it, perhaps. For you, apparently."

"But not for you," she replied, trying to piece things together.

"I have known neither safety nor peace since then," he said.

The moon slipped into view and they both rippled to beast.

"Horrible, nights like these," he said. "Especially when you are young."

That voice, no longer animal, despite his wolken form.

"You took all those boys," she said, trying to reconcile all the information, to sort it into digestible categories. "Probably murdered them."

"Did I?" he asked.

"Dragged into the woods."

"Hmmm, yes. Good knocks to the head also."

"Abandoning them to the woods is nearly the same as killing them yourself."

"They were not abandoned. At least not to the woods."

"Where then?"

"A clearing. To heal."

"Anyone could say that."

"Led there by a gray-streaked cat. Perhaps you remember her."

At once she did. Cat, tea, flowers. She held her head.

He paced, occasionally shifting with the wiles of the moon. It did not seem to bother him as it did her. "So you've made an oath to kill me."

"Destroy," she corrected.

"Of course. That should be easily managed since I will no longer fight you. I only regret that it took these circumstances to find you. Surely you know that I have been looking."

She stared into the darkest shadows of the forest, but he waited for her answer. "The shifter children," she finally said.

"Yes," he replied. "I started taking them when I was looking for you. And then, when it seemed I would never find you, when it seemed that you were probably dead, I kept taking them, freeing them from the queen, sending them to the witch's wood."

"Their families..." she said.

"Were sent a message concerning their whereabouts," he answered. "Which is more kindness than your queen had shown them. Do you know where many of the shifter parents were?"

"Camps," she answered shortly.

"Most were in prisons," he said. "The dungeons of your queen."

"It was not the queen," she murmured.

"The queen's seal," he said, looking directly into her eyes. "And thus the queen's responsibility, no matter who wields the seal."

She did not have an answer for that.

"Quite the tragedy, isn't it? Having your heroes fall."

"The queen was not my hero."

"What was she then?" he asked.

And what? Part mother, teacher, child, friend. "The one who saved me," she answered. "When no one else would have."

"I would have," he growled.

"But you could not," she replied simply. "Say what you will about the queen, she did the thing you could not do."

"For her own selfish reasons," he snarled. "Her needs."

"Perhaps," Zara answered. "And then for more than that. You and she," she said. "You are not so different as you want to believe."

"Another tragedy," he murmured.

"Is it?" she answered. "She waits, even now, upon my return. Just as you wait, ensuring that return."

He nodded. "It is good to know you, my Lilycup, after all these years. To see the woman you have become. But the moon waxes pale and the time has come for you to finish what you came here to do."

"We both know I cannot now do it, even if I want to."

"Do you want to?"

She didn't answer.

"A simple thrust correctly through the heart. I will help you if you need it. When the moon comes, use your heavy sword."

"How many have you killed?" she pressed.

"The king and his men," he answered. "A few hunters. The twelve who came for me."

"But most live in this clearing?" she asked.

"Yes. The witch's wood. It is the place where you found life. A place that gives life."

"But not to all. My mother died there."

"She did. For all must die. As I will tonight."

Zara, again changing to Lilycup, bent over and picked up the forsaken dagger, the metal that this creature, her father, had called the Shining Grey. "No," she said. "You will be *destroyed*. It makes it easier, that clause."

"Clause?" he asked.

"Of course." If she'd learned anything at all from her years at court, she knew what a good clause looked like. She also knew that it really meant *loophole*. "But you're right, we must hurry. They cannot see us this deep in the woods, but it won't take long before the queen sends her spies. I am sure that even now she is watching with her viewing glass, trying to see, worried that I do not return."

"Is she so changed?" he muttered. "When I knew her, the queen thought only of one girl—herself."

"Her life has grown long since then," Zara-Lilycup replied. "Though her daughter's has not yet, and her daughter is soon to become queen. Once this business is complete I will become the princess's sister in all but blood—and her heir."

"Heir to the human princess?"

"Heir to the most powerful woman in the land."

He nodded. "The 'business' being my removal?"

"Destruction," she clarified.

"I see," he answered. "A sound agreement."

"Now listen," she said, speaking quickly. "For our timing must be perfect. When we are through with your destruction, you yourself will return to the clearing that gave me life."

"A difficult task," he said. "On all counts. First off, we've not fully discussed my destruction. In general, the term means that a person won't be returning anywhere. Secondly, on the off chance that one was to survive his own destruction, I'm not sure I can return to the clearing. I doubt the witch will have me back."

"Point one," Zara-Lilycup said. "My task was to destroy the Phantom Howler. Which I plan to do. After tonight, the creature that was will be no more. Destroyed. As for the clearing and the witch, I thought they had the purpose of reclaiming the lost."

"And forgotten," he murmured.

"Then it should suffice."

"And what is your plan?" he asked. "After all, they'll be watching, eager to see my death."

"Then perhaps you should put on a good show," she replied.

"I offered to put on a perfect show and actually die. You're the one with different plans."

"But of course you will die," she replied. "Just not in the usual way."

"You could die with me," he said slowly, his eyes so dark they were almost black. "Come back to the gardens."

"You wish for me to return?"

"Yes."

"And if I did?"

"I would grow old," he said. "And be happy."

She waited.

He paced. "While my race rots in dungeons and batters against walls they cannot break."

"So?" she replied.

"I will die," he said. "You will rise."

"But you will die as the phoenix," she said.

"I will die as the forest burned. Much more subtle the way it regrows."

She smiled at him. Such a strange thing, to smile at the Phantom. "You will fall to the realm of myths."

"And you?" he said.

"Perhaps I will too. Destroyer of Phantoms. Daughter to a Queen. Changer of Worlds, if not Suns."

"Quite the title, but to me," he replied. "Dancer Among Flowers. Rhythm Chaser."

"Yes," she said. "I would like to be remembered like that."

"Then make it so, Rhythm Chaser, Rhythm Knower," he replied.

She pulled out her sword—the heavy one, for the moon had come out full and clear—and swung it toward him. With a growl, he dodged away, running from the dark thicket, back into full view of the castle.

She chased him, clasping both the heavy sword and the Grey dagger, barely remembering to sheath it back in the iron, so the princess would not suspect. Her feet flowed in the dance she had practiced for so many years, the one she had started in childhood. Her father, on the other hand, lurched and leapt, crowed and growled, hopping into trees, then thudding down in front of her.

She rolled away from him, swinging the sword in the show of battle. He stamped his way to her, picking up the hilt-less sword, and bearing down against her, steel to steel. She held the heavy sword with both her thick wolken hands, though under his weight it threatened to break.

At that moment, a cloud slit the moon in two, one half darkened, so that they sank into their human forms. The heavy blade sliced through his shoulder; the hilt-less one cut along her hand. She screamed, scampering away. When she did, she saw the tears in his eyes.

She pressed her hand against her side to stop the blood—she would not have full use of that limb again tonight. Then she stood, watching the moon, unsheathing her final weapon—the small sliver of Silver, the Shining Grey.

He sprang into a tree. She watched the moon, felt the breeze that would blow the clouds away. Counted the moments. Three, two. *One shot.* The Phantom thudded behind her. She whirled around, saw his mouth open in a howl, released the final blade from her hand. It found its place just as the moon broke and his fur rippled. A direct hit. And then a burst of blazing light. Enough light to blind the moon, so that she fell again into her human form. The wound in her hand throbbed; her eyes burned; but somewhere behind her, she felt the breeze, the rush of his escape.

The Phantom was destroyed; a new man reborn. A scar of that old, howling creature all that remained—a deep burn in the forest floor. An empty space. One from which new things would grow. In time.

In the distance, trumpets sounded, though Zara—turned again to Lilycup—could only know because of the vibrations that traveled to her through the hard soil at her feet. When she turned, multi-colored flags were being hoisted onto all the towers, and there, at the West gate, the largest of all—the color of Silver, of Grey, flapping in the wind.

Phantom lost, father found, now lost again. When she returned she would demand they fly a black flag at the West gate as well. *In honor of all gone before me,* she would say when asked, *all those lost to these gates.* Though only she would know of the first who was lost here years ago, and of the Phantom of that man who was destroyed this night.

With a solid strike, she stamped her foot for her horse. And from every rooftop, the people sang. She could not hear the words at the time, though later, she would read them. "He who howled will wail no more. He that devoured is now consumed. He that haunted becomes a ghost. Hail, Zara, destroyer of Phantoms. Hail, Zara, savior of men. Hail. Hail. Hail."

For now, she felt only the thunder of their voices, the crush of vibration. What she did know: He who was tortured could now find rest.

Rest.

Her horse thundered through the gates.

Rest.

Flowers fell from the buildings in a rain of white and pink as the sun broke the horizon.

Rest.

She looked to the highest tower—the place upon which her new sister stood, holding the silver banner and looking like she wished to slit it into a thousand ribbons.

Rest.

Councilman Rodolph's face was dark in the shadows behind the princess—this man who had plotted his rise through two generations. He would not take joy in another heir.

Rest.

A thing Zara, once Lilycup, would not find for many years to come.

She dismounted the horse, letting the red blood flow from her injured hand, climbing the steps one by one as booming vibrations of shouting and song clattered against her bones.

Ascending—the Silver Sister—to her new place in this world.

ALSO BY JEAN KNIGHT PACE

If you enjoyed these stories and haven't read Grey Stone and Grey Lore, what are you waiting for?

Grey Stone

Grey Lore

You may also enjoy our newest series, starting with *The Determiner*

To sign up for my newsletter, click HERE!

Acknowledgments

Huge thank you to all our fans who have read and enjoyed Grey Stone and Grey Lore. This is for you!

And, as always, thank you to our families for giving us the time to do this wacky, time-consuming thing we love. Thank you for allowing us to keep creating stories.

ABOUT THE AUTHOR

Jean Knight Pace and Jacob Kennedy are the co-authors of the fantasy novels *Grey Stone* and *Grey Lore*, as well as The Determiner series.

Jean lives in southern Indiana with her husband, kids, cat, ducks, and chickens. When not writing, you can find her teaching yoga or singing show tunes.

Jacob, on the other hand, can be found enjoying basketball or other sports.

Both of us love to read (Jean more in print; Jake more with audio) and enjoy conjuring new worlds.

www.ingramcontent.com/pod-product-compliance
Lightning Source LLC
Chambersburg PA
CBHW060815190726
48285CB00002B/674